T0244885

GRAVE
TALK

Life . . . Series

Life . . . On a High

Life . . . With No Breaks

Cornerstone Series

The Cornerstone

Wordsmith (The Cornerstone Book 2)

GRAVE TALK

NICK SPALDING

LAKE UNION
PUBLISHING

Text copyright © 2024 by Nick Spalding
All rights reserved.

Published by Lake Union Publishing, Seattle

www.apub.com

Amazon, the Amazon logo, and Lake Union Publishing are trademarks of Amazon.com, Inc., or its affiliates.

ISBN-13: 9781662519987
ISBN-10: 9781662519994

Cover design by Emma Rogers
Cover images: ©Chipmunk131 ©Viktorija
Reuta ©chocolat-10 ©Francesko221 ©saepul_bahri ©hanaravecto
©NadzeyaShanchuk / Shutterstock

Printed in the United States of America

*I have close friends who have lost people they love
far too early in life. Their strength while coping
with this pain amazes me. This book is for them.*

Year One

The Lady And The Frog

Alice

I can do this.

I know I can. I wasn't sure when I woke up this morning, and my hand strayed to his side of the bed again. But after two cups of the strongest coffee I could manage, and a good, long cry in the shower, I felt like there was a chance I could come here, and not immediately feel my legs go out from under me.

They've done that a lot recently. So many times, in fact, that I've started to fear for their long-term stability. Maybe the gym membership that's been gathering dust in the corners of my brain should be put to better use.

I might ring the gym tomorrow, and see when the best time to go in would be.

Ah . . . *tomorrow.*

The day I keep hoping will eventually arrive.

It hasn't yet.

Every day is *today*, and has been for the past six months, since Joe left.

I prefer to say that *he left*, rather than anything else, as that sounds somewhat *temporary*. Like he just got up to go over to M&S and get a tub of chocolate mini rolls.

'Where's Joe?' someone might ask. And I would reply, 'He's just *left*. Getting me a tub of those chocolate mini rolls I love so much. And he pretends not to like them, but then three days later the tub is nearly empty, and I know I've only eaten two or three.'

I like to play out these little conversations in my head. Because in all of them he's still coming back. With chocolate mini rolls.

I should probably get out of the car.

I'm sure my legs will take my weight. I don't need a gym to tell me that. They'll be fine. *I'll* be fine.

I climb out of my Clio, and my legs do indeed take my weight. I won't need rescuing from the pavement by a kindly passer-by.

I feel a tremble in them as I go through the open wrought-iron gates, though.

Because this is the first time I've done this *alone*. Walked into the graveyard all on my lonesome. Like a big, strong girl, who isn't afraid of anything.

Anything – other than the *future*.

And going to sleep.

And waking up again.

And feeling my right hand stray to the other side of the bed . . .

My nails dig into my palms.

Nope.

You can do this.

I can do this.

On legs that still tremble, but hold me up quite alright, thank you very much, I walk through the graveyard to where Joe is, under the oak tree.

He's not actually there, of course. Whether he's actually *any-where* anymore is a matter for more philosophical and learned

2

people than me. But if he is, I guarantee you he won't be lying under an oak tree.

Not after what happened with the squirrel.

What happened with the squirrel kept him from ever going under a tree again.

Of course, he didn't even think to change the location of his burial plot after it happened, because . . . well, you wouldn't, would you? Nobody's thought process runs '*A squirrel dropped on to my head, so I'd better make sure I move my final resting place.*' And if it does, I don't particularly want to spend any time locked in a room with them.

Also, it really is a *very* pretty spot to spend the rest of eternity. The oak tree is broad and magnificent, with boughs that spread across the graveyard to such an extent that it would actually be quite difficult to stipulate you wanted one that *wasn't* underneath it.

I'd certainly be okay with being buried under it. Which is just as well, as there's a space right next to Joe's grave that has my name on it. His parents are buried over there, on the other side of the graveyard, so I'm the only family Joe has left.

Had.

He always planned ahead, did my husband. The plots were booked long before the squirrel. He probably thought the oak tree was a good idea back then.

It really is a *very lovely* oak tree – and I am entirely aware that I'm spending so much time looking at it because that means I'm not looking at his gravestone.

Trees are lovely. Gravestones, most assuredly, are not.

I close my eyes for a moment, take a deep breath, relax my nails from digging into my palms quite so much, and turn to where my heart is lying under six feet of fine English soil.

The tears, which were of course inevitable, don't start small and build up.

One second I'm dry of face and resolute, the next my cheeks are soaking wet and I can barely see. Grief tears work differently to other types, I've noticed. Normally, when something makes you cry, there's a build-up period, while your brain fixates on the bad thing that's happened, and your tear ducts dutifully well up in response to those thoughts.

Not with grief tears. They just instantly appear – like the world's worst magic trick. You don't get any time to prepare yourself. *Ever.*

I stand there sobbing for as long as it takes my body to get exhausted by it. This is not very long, given how little sleep I've been getting.

The sobs turn into sniffles, and the heat in my face calms down a bit. The waves of grief are also a little calmer now, though they most certainly haven't disappeared completely. I'm aware that I'm occasionally letting out a small whimper – which disgusts me, as much as it hurts my soul.

I want to be stronger than this. I want to be *braver.*

Touch the gravestone, my brain orders.

But I don't want to.

Do it. It might help you feel a little closer to him.

This is an idiotic suggestion, as far as my rational, thinking brain considers it. But rationality is something that really doesn't help that much when you're lost in grief. Thinking rationally is about as impossible when you're grieving as breathing is underwater.

I stumble past the grave itself, and place one shaking hand on the cold, grey stone.

'Happy birthday, sweetheart,' I say in a voice that sounds like I've aged a thousand years.

I thought about writing a birthday card and placing it on the grave, but that felt . . . *tacky.* Or the kind of thing someone in denial would do.

I am neither, I'd like to think. Not after six months.

The idea of putting a birthday card that no one will ever read on top of this gravestone filled me with no small measure of disgust, if I'm being honest.

It's a simple gravestone.

Of course it is, Joe couldn't do ostentatious if you put a gun to his head.

. . . and that just reminds me of the boxer shorts.

The red, plaid boxer shorts his aunt bought him for his birthday five years ago. He put them on to show me, and you've never seen a man looking more dejected in his life. Joe didn't do flashy, silly or weird. Anything like that made him feel *deeply* uncomfortable.

A gravestone that was anything other than a simple, grey slab, with sensible writing carved on to it, would have brought Joe out in a cold sweat.

That one standing close by, for instance. That would have *terrified* him.

It's much larger, a far darker shade of grey, and is emblazoned with golden writing, golden filigree and a golden rugby ball beneath the name of the deceased. It looks like someone fired an entire branch of H. Samuel at the stone, and a passing rugby ball got caught up in the chaos.

I then remember Joe taking off the boxer shorts, and what we did next.

And I'm crying all over again. Because after the sex we had, he told me that he was as happy as he'd ever felt in his life, as he caressed my arm, which sent tingles up it, as it always did.

Tears dry very quickly on granite when the sun is out, it appears.

Because the sun *is* out, and apparently it's a lovely day, according to the weather app on my phone. I can't believe that, though, because from where I'm standing, it's pitch black, cold, and empty of anything other than drying tears on granite.

My hand goes white as I grip Joe's headstone, and the rage joins the grief for the first time today. This always happens. They are like best friends who can't bear to be apart for too long.

The unfairness of it all slams into me once more.

How the hell does a man like that die of a heart attack in his mid-forties?

How did they manage not to save him?

How could all those doctors and nurses let him die?

What the hell am I supposed to do now?

How the hell do I go on??

Oh shit . . .

There go my legs.

I should have gone to the gym.

And I also should have brought Sonia from work. She's been making the pilgrimage to the churchyard with me, bless her. Up until today anyway, and her support has stopped me from becoming what I am now – an absolute mess.

But no . . . stubborn Alice Everley just had to come here all on her own, didn't she?

And where did it get her? Wracked with tears, and slumped against her husband's gravestone, like she's some sort of distressed heroine from a terrible black-and-white romance movie from the 1940s.

But I can't help it.

And I don't *care*.

My heart lies in that grave, and there's nothing left for me to do, other than bawl my eyes out, and think the darkest of thoughts about the people that failed to save him.

The tears return as heavy as they've ever been – heavier, in fact.

I take a great heaving sob, and bow my head, staring at the dry dusty earth.

He's down there . . .

Forever.

I wail again, and snot flies out of my nose.

Will this ever end? Will I ever be able to function like a normal human being?

I'm lost. I'm in a hole deeper than the one they threw my poor, dead, sensible husband into, and I have no idea how I'm going to climb my way out.

Everything is darkness . . .

. . . . . .

. . .

It's at this point I look up and see Kermit the Frog.

Ben

Oh, you bastard. You absolute *bastard.*

Kermit the sodding Frog?

I can just see the look of absolute glee on your face as you wrote that one down.

You could have chosen something a little less embarrassing. You could have chosen something a little less *silly.*

Like the Stormtrooper costume I wore for your thirtieth fancy dress birthday party – which while pretty damned uncomfortable was also pretty damned *cool*, if we're being honest about it. It's *Star Wars*, after all.

Something like that would have been fine, you absolute maniac. You could have taken pity on me, and let me start this ridiculous thing you're making me do in a way that wasn't so comprehensively embarrassing.

A Stormtrooper would have been fine. At least my face would have been hidden!

But this bloody itchy, nasty Kermit the Frog costume has my face fully on display for everyone to see. Poking out from between Kermit's big flappy lips, like he's just swallowed me whole, and I'm attempting to escape before I get digested.

Also, I'm inexplicably *fat*. The body section of the suit is extremely rotund. Even though Kermit is a skinny bastard, as far as I remember.

It's like you spent hours online trying to find the absolute *worst* version of this fancy dress costume that you could.

Oh yes, I can see you giggling your head off at this, you lunatic.

What made the whole thing worse was when Mr Sharp handed the stupid thing over to me in such a solemn manner. I don't know how long you've employed the poor man to do this on a yearly basis, but whatever you paid him, it wasn't enough. I doubt any of his other clients have tasked him with such a hare-brained scheme. The expression on his face when he handed Kermit over was a mixture of confusion and dismay.

Our mother and father got the Jaguar. Melanie got the house. I got . . . *this*.

You couldn't even let me do it in the middle of the night, could you? It had to be at midday. Slap bang in the middle of the summer holidays, for maximum exposure.

Urgh.

I can feel the green paint on my face starting to run.

Why the green face paint, Harry?

Why?

Wasn't the costume enough for you?

No. Clearly it wasn't.

What's next year got in store for me? A baboon costume, where I have to paint my arse red and go about on all fours?

Oh God.

I shouldn't make terrible assumptions like that. They are ones that could very well come true, because I have a maniac for an older brother.

Had.

Had a maniac for an older brother.

It's testament to how much I love you that I'm sat here in my car, dressed in a Kermit the Frog costume, with tears starting to make the green face paint run even more.

Best I get out of the car, and get this bloody silliness over with.

Looking around, it seems like things are quiet. Thank the Lord. At least it's a Monday, and not a Sunday, when the church grounds would no doubt be a lot busier.

The one saving grace I have in all of this ridiculousness is that I persuaded my mother, father and Mel not to tell anyone else in the world about this insane scheme of yours. That means I can do this with some degree of secrecy.

I sigh heavily. Whether this is with relief that I can do this in private or sadness at my ongoing loss, my brain can't quite decide.

I walk around to the car boot and open it up. Inside are the enormous foam Kermit the Frog feet I will have to wear up to the grave. They go on over the green tights without too much bother.

Yes.

Green tights.

Of course, *green tights.*

. . . oh, how he must have laughed.

Then I begin to waddle – for that is the only way you can walk in enormous green frog feet and a bulky green fat suit – across the car park and up the steps that lead to the back entrance of the cemetery. I'm smart enough to avoid the main entrance around the corner at the front. My mother and father didn't raise any fools – even if they did raise one absolute maniac, with the worst sense of humour on God's green earth.

They also raised another son who wet himself with panic before coming on stage as the archangel Gabriel in the nativity, when he was five. So walking through a quaint English village cemetery dressed as Kermit the Frog is about as nerve-wracking as it gets. But I guess that was the whole point, wasn't it, *Harry*?

But look! My luck is holding out. I see no one. The cemetery is completely empty.

My peripheral vision in this stupid foam Kermit helmet is dreadful, so I have to move my head around like I'm doing an impression of a malfunctioning lighthouse, to make sure I really am on my own. I can't hear a sodding thing under all this foam and rubber, either, so I wrench the mask away from the side of my face for a moment to listen properly . . . and hear *nothing*.

I might just get away with this.

I gird my froggy loins, and start to slap my feet a bit quicker on the ground as I walk down the path that runs through the cemetery, and around the side of the little church that both my mother and father, and Harry and Mel, got married in.

Still no one to be seen.

Excellent!

I round the corner, looking along the church, and still see no one.

Great!

I reach the fork where the path leads off to the row that Harry's grave is in, under the oak tree he loved so much, and slap down it, holding on to Kermit's head for dear life as it rocks back and forth on my greasy, sweaty head.

It briefly comes down over my eyes, restricting my field of vision even more, before I am able to push it back up, just as I reach the place where my older brother is buried.

Now all I have to do is spend exactly two minutes and fifty-nine seconds stood in front of the grave, and I can leave. That's what Harry wants, and I'll do it – because even though he was an utter, utter bastard, he was still the greatest brother any kid could have, and I miss him more than I can possibly express. His laughter. His bravery. His charm. His kindness.

I hate doing this. I absolutely *hate it*. But I will keep doing it for as long as he asks.

And if he is somewhere laughing his head off and watching me, then that sounds pretty damn wonderful, as far as I'm concer—

Oh, bloody hell and buckets, there's a woman here.

Alice

No, no. That really is a tall, fully grown man dressed as Kermit the Frog. Your blurry eyes do not deceive you, Alice.

You'd better get up from where you sit slumped against your husband's grave before he comes any closer. He could be a sex pervert!

Yes. I'd say that's a *distinct* possibility, actually. What other kind of person would be wandering around a graveyard dressed as Kermit the Frog?

Only a sex pervert, surely?

Or maybe a children's entertainer who's got very lost on their way to a party – but obviously they'd know they weren't performing in a graveyard on a Monday morning. Not unless the child who the party was for was very, *very* strange.

No. This is *clearly* a sex pervert, and you'd better get up, before he tries to rub that big green belly of his against your person.

I climb back to my feet as quickly as possible, thankful that a rush of adrenaline has suffused my entire body – no doubt in preparation to fight off Kermit the Sex Offender.

It's as I do this that I see the look on his face. It is not the look of a would-be sex pervert, to be honest. There's no dribbling going on, and that expression is definitely not one that could be described as a 'leer'.

If anything, he looks extremely panicked and embarrassed – which, given the circumstances, is the exact face you'd hope to see on someone dressed as Kermit the Frog, who's just stumbled upon you at your most vulnerable.

'Oh God! I'm so sorry! I . . . I didn't realise you were there!' Kermit cries.

I run two hands down the front of my shirt in the time-honoured gesture of 'sorting myself out', and then grab the bottom edges, pulling them down, as if that's going to pull the creases out. I then run my hands through my hair in an attempt to calm it down from the ridiculous hornet's nest it has no doubt become in my distressed state.

Still, at least I'm back on my feet and not crying anymore.

It's a little hard to engage in a display of overwhelming grief when there's a man stood in front of you dressed as Kermit the Frog. The two things are largely incompatible – unless you were married to Jim Henson.

'What are you up to?' I snap at the frog. 'You scared me!'

'Sorry! Sorry! I didn't mean to!' Kermit says, holding up both hands.

Or are they flippers?

Do frogs have hands or flippers?

And for that matter, does Kermit? Is he an anatomically correct frog?

Would I want to know this fact, if he was?

'Well, you did!'

'I'm so sorry,' he repeats, 'I was just . . .'

Oh God, now he's going to tell me what he was doing here, and if the sentence ends with the words 'with my green frog rod' I'm going to scream the graveyard down and run for my life.

'I was just here to visit my brother,' he replies, and points with one hand/flipper down at the large, ostentatious gravestone next to Joe's.

I look down at where he's pointing. 'Harry Fielding,' I read out, rather unnecessarily. I'm sure Kermit knows the name of his own brother. I cringe a little inside. Not least because of my rather waspish reaction to him. He's clearly not a sex pervert.

He's here to see a loved one. I know exactly how that feels.

That doesn't really explain the stupid costume, though . . .

'Yes, that's right,' he says, and nods. This causes the giant Kermit head atop his own to wobble about a bit – and if I wasn't wracked with grief and loneliness, I'd probably find it quite funny.

Oh hell. It is quite funny, anyway.

Joe would have probably laughed. I seem to remember him enjoying *The Muppet Christmas Carol* a great deal when we babysat Sonia's kids a couple of Christmases ago.

And then I'm reminded that I'm never having another Christmas with Joe again, so I'd better say something else to Kermit here, before I can't hold it together anymore.

'I'm here to see . . . see my husband, Joe,' I tell Kermit, pointing at my husband's grave.

'Joe Everley,' Kermit reads, and makes much the same expression of instant regret that I probably did when I read his brother's name out. Such a silly thing to say to the person visiting them.

'Yes. That's him,' I confirm.

'I'm sorry for your loss,' the man in the costume says.

'Thank you, Kermit,' I reply, not really knowing what else to say.

The man – who seems to be somewhere in his mid-twenties – looks extremely embarrassed.

I almost apologise for calling him Kermit, but then this is a fully grown man wandering around a graveyard, scaring innocent grieving widows, so I'm not really sure it's all that necessary.

'Ah. Yes. I'm . . . sorry about this,' he says, gesturing up and down himself.

And thus, we come to the question that my brain has been screaming at me to ask for a while now. 'Why are you dressed as Kermit the Frog?'

The look of absolute dejection on his face is a sight to behold. 'My brother made me do it.'

I look down at the grave, and then back up at him. 'This brother?' I say, pointing at the gravestone.

'Yes,' he says, nodding that stupid Kermit head back and forth again.

'Your brother, who is . . . *in there* . . . told you to wear a Kermit the Frog costume?'

'Yes, he did.'

Oh, fabulous. He's a nutter.

He thinks his dead brother is telling him to dress as Kermit the Frog.

Why did I not buy that personal alarm when I had the chance?

The young man sees the look of extreme concern on my face, realises what he must sound like and once again puts his hands up. 'No! I mean . . . he didn't *tell me* to wear the costume, because he's . . . not here anymore. What I mean is, he asked me to do it in his will.' His face contorts a bit. '*Told* me to do it actually, for reasons I have yet to fully fathom.'

'He told you to come here today dressed as Kermit the Frog . . . in his will?'

14

'Yes. It sounds bizarre, but if you knew my brother, you'd understand it's actually pretty much par for the course. He once covered his best mate's house entirely in tin foil. Cost a fortune, and they're still finding the damn stuff in nooks and crannies to this day.'

'And you were . . . happy to do this?'

The man shakes his head. 'No. Absolutely not. He's a complete *bastard*. But . . . I loved him and . . . well . . .'

'Doing it kind of keeps him close?' I blurt out, before really understanding what I'm saying.

The young man's face contorts for a moment with obvious pain, before he clears his throat. 'Yeah. Something like that.'

My hand unconsciously strays back to Joe's gravestone. 'I get that,' I tell the young man. 'I mean . . . I *understand* that. I doubt that if Joe had asked me to do the same thing, I'd have been able to say no, either.'

Not that Joe ever would ask me to do something like that.

He'd be *aghast* at the expense of that much tin foil. He'd also have to work out exactly how much money it would cost, and the logistics of wrapping that much stuff in it . . . because Joe always needed to know how things worked. How they came about.

Kermit nods thoughtfully, making that ridiculous headpiece wobble about again. His eyes then dart down to Joe's grave. 'I really am very sorry for your loss,' he says in a quiet tone. 'And sorry I'm in this stupid costume . . . ruining your day.'

I swallow hard. 'Thank you. And you. Losing a brother must be so difficult. And trust me, you haven't ruined my day. They've all been ruined, since . . .' I trail off.

He nods, fully understanding where I'm coming from. 'I'm Ben, by the way. Not Kermit,' he tells me.

This actually makes me laugh a little. It feels nice.

I'm now very sure this isn't a sex offender. This Ben person may be a little weird (though the enforced Kermit costume accounts for most of this) but he also seems harmless enough.

Besides, I know that look in his eyes. I know it very well.

You can't fake that.

You can't fake *loss*.

'I'm Alice,' I reply, and move towards him to shake his hand.

Thankfully, he pulls off Kermit's, and takes my hand in his own.

'I really am very sorry to interrupt you like this,' he repeats. 'This always seems to happen to me when Harry plays one of his silly jokes.'

'Always?' I reply, incredulous.

'Yes. It was his favourite hobby . . . after the rugby anyway. And I was always his favourite victim. It was the look of horror on my face, you see. He said it was better than on anyone else's.'

I think about the young man's expression when he first discovered me flopped against Joe's gravestone, and can see where his brother was coming from. The poor guy does do 'horrified' extremely well.

My brow creases. 'How many times did your brother tell you that you had to . . . do *this*?'

He looks distraught. 'I don't know! All I do know is that I have to turn up on this day every bloody year, dressed in a different costume of his choosing each time, until the will tells me I can stop.'

'Bloody hell,' I breathe. 'That's . . . quite something. How many times have you done it so far?'

'This is the first. Harry died three months ago. Of . . . Of leukaemia.' There's that look in his eyes again. The same one I see staring out at me from the mirror every day. 'How long has it been for you? If you don't mind me asking?'

I shake my head. 'No. It's fine. Just under six' – the words catch in my throat – 'just under *six months*,' I force out, like I'm

16

lancing an auditory boil. 'Joe died of a heart attack.' I swallow hard. '*Somehow.* He was very healthy, you see. And sensible. I still don't understand how . . . or why . . .' My fists twitch, as if they want to clench.

Calm down.

Breathe.

I almost can't stand the look of pity this young man called Ben now gives me. I think it's because it's so damned incongruous with that stupid costume he's wearing.

'I'm so sorry,' he almost whispers. 'You know exactly how I feel. And I don't know if I could cope with an idiot walking up to me dressed as Kermit the Frog.'

I laugh again, but this time it feels heavy. 'It's quite alright. I was having . . . a bit of a moment before you arrived, so you probably shook me out of making a spectacle of myself.'

He looks down at his costume. 'Yeah. Bit hard to maintain a spectacle when there's a man dressed as Kermit the Frog standing next to you.'

The laugh that escapes my lips this time is lighter again, but there's a dose of exhaustion in it too. 'I might go and sit down under the oak tree for a moment,' I tell him. There's no seat there, but it looks dry, as well as being nice and shady.

'Oh, okay,' he replies. 'I just have to . . . stand here in front of Harry's grave for a few minutes, then I'll leave you to . . . you know.'

Wail and gnash my teeth, slumped against my dead husband's grave again?

Why thank you, Mr Kermit the Ben. I may just do that.

On legs that are still pretty damned shaky, I walk over to the oak tree, and sit myself down under it. Shortly – once Ben Kermit has left – I will muster up the courage to touch Joe's gravestone again, before leaving this place. This will be the last time I attempt to come here on my own for a while. Sonia will just have to come with me, until I'm better prepared. Maybe in about twenty years or so.

I sigh, and watch my fellow griever stand in front of his brother's grave.

He starts to glance at his watch every few seconds or so.

This goes on for a minute or two, with Ben continuing to look at his watch every few seconds, like he's timing something down.

Curiosity eventually gets the better of my manners. 'May I ask, Ben? Why do you keep looking at your watch?' I call over to him, perplexed. 'Is everything okay?'

Ben

I am ten years old. Harry is nineteen.

It is the annual sports day at my summer school.

I *hate* summer school, but it is something my mother and father have forced on me, so I must do it. I must also win the father-and-son relay race, because that's what Harry did with our father ten years previously.

I *must* win.

And I know I *can* win, because I am *fast*. Nearly as fast as Harry was when he was my age.

And the day is here! At last!

My father and I will win the relay race, and I will make him and my mother *proud*.

Only, my father is not there . . . because he's stuck in a fourteen-hour emergency surgery.

I am distraught.

But then my big brother, Harry – tall, animated, wild of hair and wild of nature – is home from Imperial College for the summer. And he comes to my rescue, volunteering to fill in for our father.

'Don't worry, bro!' he says, that big broad grin on his permanently amused face. 'I'm here now, and I'll do it with you.'

I am delighted.

Mostly.

And we win!

Of course we do. Harry is a lightning bolt. He leaves all the dads standing.

And the pride that swells in my heart as we take to the wooden winners' rostrum is only slightly dampened by the fact that our father is not there to see Harry and me take the top step, while 'We Are the Champions' by Queen plays loudly in the background on an aging tannoy system.

'Don't worry about it, little bro,' Harry says to me, noticing the brief but clear look of sadness that passes across my face. 'He won't always be like this . . . and you've always got me. I'll always be around for you.'

'Yeah, I know,' I reply, shaking off the feeling of childhood regret – for now.

This is the best thing I've ever done with my big brother, Harry, and I'll remember it for the rest of my life.

'We Are the Champions' lasts two minutes and fifty-nine seconds.

I glance back at the lady, who I still feel like I should be apologising to, and tell her that yes, everything is okay.

I just have to stand here for another thirty-two seconds, and then I'll be done.

At least I'm not crying. A Kermit the Frog head is uncomfortable enough without having a flushed hot face, and tears running down your cheeks.

I'll probably have to explain what I'm doing, because otherwise I'll look like a lunatic.

More like a lunatic, I should say. I'm sure this Alice probably thinks I've taken leave of my senses anyway, given what I'm wearing. But then again, she looked like she understood when I told her what Harry was making me do.

Grief makes you do mad things, sometimes.

I've learned that.

And I did disturb her from what looked a lot like a proper, full-scale breakdown when I got here. Poor woman.

I really should apologise again.

Three minutes pass on my watch, and I breathe a sigh of relief.

When I turn, I see a look of extreme puzzlement on Alice's face.

I probably should just say my goodbyes and let her get on with what is clearly a difficult period of mourning. But then again, I hate the idea that someone doesn't understand what I'm up to. I don't want anybody on this earth thinking I'm some sort of madman who's taken leave of his senses. I'll have to explain things a little before I go.

'I . . . I have to stand at Harry's grave for two minutes and fifty-nine seconds,' I tell her. And then go on to detail the exact reasons why.

'The summer sports day was held on this date seventeen years ago,' I say, finishing my explanation.

'Oh, I see,' Alice replies. 'That's . . . very sweet, I guess?'

I laugh abruptly. 'Yes, it should be, shouldn't it? But Harry always has to make a joke out of everything – even our greatest shared memory. It would have made him laugh his arse off, thinking of me standing here dressed like this – with "We Are the Champions" going around and around in my head.'

'But you did it,' Alice says. 'And I think it's very sweet that you did. You must have loved him very much. And he must have loved you very much too. To step in for your dad like that.'

The tears are in my eyes again before I know it.

They are tears of grief, of course. But they are also tears of *frustration*.

Frustration with a father who always seemed to have something more important to do.

'Yeah. Er . . . I guess he did,' I agree. 'It was . . . a special moment,' I then say, a bit lamely.

It was more than a special moment. It was the moment that cemented my relationship with both my brother . . . and my father.

Until Harry went and got cancer and died – and I was left with the man who always has something more important to do.

'But I really should get out of your way,' I say, clearing my throat and blinking back the tears. 'I've taken up far too much of your time with your husband.'

Alice's eyes flick back to his grave.

'It must be very difficult for you,' I continue, stating the obvious.

'It is, yes,' she says, sounding completely lost.

Oh God.

'I'll be getting out of your way, then,' I say, turning to go.

'No! Please . . . it's okay. You're welcome to stay . . . if you'd like. I'm sure all of this is very difficult for you too.' She looks down at the ground. 'I . . . probably shouldn't have come here on my own,' she confesses. 'This is the first time I've tried, and it's . . . proving to be a bit too difficult for me. I usually bring my friend along, but . . .'

'Oh,' I say, a bit dismayed. To be quite honest, I'd rather back out of this supremely awkward situation, and get the hell out of here. Not least because this Kermit head is extremely itchy. And things aren't much better in my groinular area – which isn't enjoying the thick, uncomfortable green material any more than the rest of me.

But this woman is clearly in need of some moral support. She must be, to ask it of a complete stranger dressed as a frog.

I know it would be my last resort.

'It's no problem if you have somewhere you need to be,' Alice says, reading the look on my face quite accurately.

I shake my head. 'No. No. It's fine. I'm in no rush. If you'd like a little company while you are . . . with your husband, then I'm happy to stay.'

I am incredibly sympathetic to how Alice is feeling, and I'd feel like a right bastard if I left her at a time like this.

With an undignified struggle, I plonk myself down under the oak tree as well, a little way apart from her.

We both sit there for a few moments in silence.

Alice eventually breaks it by saying, 'Funny how they are next to each other like that, even though they died three months apart.'

'It's a fairly small village,' I reply.

'Fair point,' she agrees. 'I'm surprised we've never bumped into each other.'

I then pull at the Velcro under my chin that holds the Kermit head in place, and pull the stupid thing off.

'Are you . . . allowed to take it off?' Alice asks me. 'Is that okay with your brother?'

I flap a hand. 'Yeah, it's fine. Once I've done my bit, I can do whatever I like. Though he did stipulate that the costume should be donated to charity after I'm done with it.'

She smiles. 'That's nice.'

I nod. 'That's Harry.'

We both lapse into silence again for a few moments, looking around the cemetery. 'Lovely day,' I eventually say, and instantly regret it, for obvious reasons.

But Alice smiles again. 'It is. Joe loved days like these. Not too hot, but clear blue skies. He'd want two things on a day like today – time to tidy the garden and a pub lunch. Preferably in that order.'

'I can certainly agree with the second one,' I reply, trying to ignore the fact that my stomach is rumbling, as it's now gone midday.

'It's his birthday today,' she then blurts out, staring at the grave as she does so. 'That's why I had to come here, even if it was on my own. I couldn't let him . . . let him . . .'

'I know what you mean,' I say quickly, to stop her having to say it. 'My family came here on Harry's birthday too, just after he . . . *passed*. All of us. First time I worked up the courage after the funeral.'

God, I hate the term 'passed'.

And the only reason we all use it is because it's a handy euphemism for the word that none of us want to say.

'We had a picnic right here,' I add.

'That's nice,' she replies. 'I've been coming with my friend Sonia from work. She usually brings a Thermos of coffee, and we sip it while we . . . stand here. And then we take a little walk around the graveyard.'

From the way Alice says this, you can tell it's a ritual that brings her some comfort. That's something else I understand entirely as well. Grief blows your life out of the water. It renders your normal day-to-day existence obsolete. Everything becomes about the loss you feel, and anything you can do to give yourself some structure against the maelstrom is welcomed.

I clean my flat every Thursday between 7 p.m. and 9 p.m. Every Thursday without fail. I look forward to it, because it's something *normal.* An island of boring normality in a sea of confusion, pain and overwhelming sadness.

'We could have a little walk, if you like?' I say to Alice.

She looks at me for a moment, before nodding. 'That would be . . . helpful,' she tells me, and gets to her feet.

She then has to help me to mine, as this idiotic costume is so bloody cumbersome.

After about seven or eight hours, though, I am back on my feet, and I hold out a hand to indicate the path. 'After you,' I say, which earns me a smile and a nod.

I'm glad to see her mood has lifted a little. I am ill-prepared to deal with someone as distraught as Alice obviously was when I first got here. I don't know how long I could keep it together myself, being around someone that upset.

'Thank you for staying,' Alice says as we walk away from the graves of her husband and my brother. This act, in and of itself, probably helps her. It certainly helps me. Gravestones have an inertia about them when it comes to grief. Like gravity, it increases the closer you get.

'No problem,' I reply. 'I know how hard all of this is. Especially if you're on your own.' I hesitate to say the next part, as I don't know whether I'm constitutionally prepared to lend this level of support. 'Would you . . . Would you like to talk about him? People tell me it helps. I think it helps me.'

Alice nods, but remains silent for a moment, as we turn left on the path and start to walk towards the main gate.

'He wouldn't have liked being under that oak tree,' she eventually says.

I look at her. 'Why not?'

'The last time he sat under an oak tree, a squirrel fell on him.'

I stop dead in my tracks. 'Pardon me?'

It happens just as I am raising a toast to Joe's success at scoring the BP contract. It's something he's very proud of, and so am I. The work he's put in at Bremer Marketing has been long and tiring – but entirely worth it.

'Well done, sweetheart,' I tell him, my eyes a little misty.

'Thank you, honey,' he replies. He's got that little awkward look on his face he has when he's worried about showing too much emotion in public. He had it all those years ago, when he came back into the salon after I'd cut his hair to ask for my phone number, and he has it now.

Not that this forest glade is exactly what you'd call *public*.

'Couldn't have done it without you,' he says – and I know that's the truth, because Joe *always* tells the truth. It's why I trust him so much. 'And better days are ahead now,' he adds.

'They are,' I agree.

I smile at him. He smiles at me.

It's a lovely moment.

Then a squirrel falls on him.

Right out of the tree above our heads.

It's a fat squirrel, which doesn't help matters.

Both squirrel and Joe let out squawks of surprise and alarm, as the one bounces off the top of the other's head.

The fat squirrel then describes an arc outwards and downwards, landing headfirst in the Camembert.

I am scarcely able to comprehend any of this. It's not easy to segue from misty-eyed celebration over a marketing contract to unbridled panic over a ballistic squirrel.

'Good God!' Joe wails, thrusting himself backwards.

I do much the same, as if we're both worried the fat squirrel is about to explode.

It does not explode.

But it does climb rather unsteadily to its feet, shakes its little grey body free of at least some of the Camembert, gets its bearings, sees me looking down at it, lets out another squawk of horror, and bounds off towards the edge of the forest glade.

Joe climbs to his feet, his face red with fury. 'That cheese cost me thirty quid, you little bastard!' he shouts at it, waving a fist.

My mouth hangs agape. I've never seen Joe so riled up. All over a ballistic squirrel.

It's a side to my husband that rather amazes me. He's always so level-headed. In comparison I feel like a permanently capsizing boat. It's testament to how important this picnic obviously was to him that the squirrel has riled him up to the extent that he actually shouts at it. I am truly gobsmacked by this change in his demeanour.

It also *delights* me somewhat as well, if I'm being honest. Still being surprised by the person you've spent fifteen years of your life with is worth its weight in gold.

As is the knowledge that even your placid, held-together husband can join you capsizing momentarily, if the right problem comes along.

In Joe's case, it's evidently The Way of the Interrupting Squirrel.

Ben

The loud snort of laughter that escapes me is wholly inappropriate in a cemetery. But I simply have no choice in the matter. I don't know if it's the story itself or the way Alice tells it – but the vision of a squirrel with a head covered in runny cheese, bounding off into the forest, while this woman's dead husband soundly berates it, is enough to send me off into gales of laughter.

Maybe it's also because I'm dressed as Kermit the Frog. The ridiculousness of my present situation only makes the ridiculousness of Alice's story all the more hilarious.

'Gets its bearings?' I say to her between guffaws.

'Yes,' she replies, also smiling broadly. 'You'd probably have to do the same if your head was covered in cheese.'

Oh, thanks very much. Now I'm picturing myself dressed as Kermit the Frog, with my froggy head dripping with runny French Camembert. This makes me laugh even harder. Thankfully, it makes Alice laugh too.

So we both stand there, just to the left-hand side of the church entrance, in fits of laughter, to the point where my stomach starts to hurt.

'Thirty-quid Camembert?' I gasp at her.

She nods. 'The champagne cost him fifty. He was most put out. We had . . . We had to pack the picnic in . . . and go for a pub lunch.'

This sends me off into another gale of laughter, which Alice merrily joins in with.

None of this is actually all *that* funny, of course. I'm well aware of that. But human emotions have a habit of rubber-banding back and forth at times like this, and this is the best – and only – laugh I've had since Harry died, so I'm not going to look a gift horse in the mouth.

Or should I say, a gift squirrel.

And now I have the vision of a Camembert-covered squirrel offering me a neatly wrapped present with a bow on top, and that sends me off once more into a fit of the giggles that I might never recover from.

Alice

I never thought I'd laugh again.

Truly I didn't.

And yet, here I am, babbling laughter like a loon, with a complete stranger dressed as a frog. What an extremely strange turn of events.

But I'll *take it*.

I really will.

I'll take laughing like I'm going insane, over actually *going insane*, any day of the week. If Ben hadn't turned up, I might still be slumped against Joe's gravestone, unable to function. Someone would have found me eventually, I'm sure. But it wouldn't have been a young man dressed as a frog, who knows exactly what it's like to lose someone you love.

Our combined laughing fit (which I would honestly have paid good money for) finally dries up, just as Ben's green face paint has virtually run off his face completely.

'I'm . . . I'm exhausted,' he chuckles, taking a deep breath, and giggling softly one more time.

'Me too,' I agree.

Now the laughing fit has passed, I realise just how bone-weary I am.

I need my couch.

I look at my watch. 'I guess I'd better get going.'

Ben nods. 'Yeah, me too. If nothing else, because I really need to get out of this costume,' he says, wriggling around a little bit in discomfort. 'I'm sweatier than a sumo wrestler in a sauna.'

'It was very nice to meet you,' I tell him, which earns me a doubtful look.

'Was it?' he replies. 'I didn't intrude on your time here . . . wearing a frog costume?'

'I wouldn't have had it any other way,' I chuckle, before growing serious again. 'Thank you for hanging around with me for a little while. It . . . means a lot.'

'No problem. I know what you're going through. At least, partly,' he tells me.

A question hangs on my lips that I do not want to ask, but have to.

'Do you think it gets any easier?' I ask him.

He looks at me for a moment, and then his eyes stray back up the path towards the graves for the briefest of moments. When he looks at me again, his face is solemn. 'No. No, I don't think it does.' His brow furrows. 'But it might get . . . more *familiar*? Like . . . you can learn to live with it? You can learn to cope.'

The tears are in my eyes again. 'That would be . . . nice,' I tell him.

I don't think I could have handled it if he said he thought it does get easier, because *I know it won't*.

But familiar?

Yes, I can believe that.

I can *cope* with that.

Ben clears his throat. 'I'm parked up the back,' he tells me, jerking one of Kermit's thumbs over his shoulder, 'so I'll be headed that way.'

'I'm down there,' I reply, indicating the main car park.

He nods.

And I nod too.

It's time to part company.

. . . that's what a nod like that means.

But I'm strangely reluctant to do so. Because I haven't laughed like I just did in so long – and this young man seems to know exactly what I'm going through.

It might get more familiar.

I bet it does.

'It was very nice to meet you,' Ben then says, and I get the impression he's a little reluctant to go our separate ways too. I won't ask him how long it's been since he laughed like that himself, but I'd be willing to bet it's a long time.

'And you too, Ben,' I reply, offering him my hand again. When he takes it, the handshake is warmer and longer than the first.

'I hope . . .' He pauses, face contorting a little. 'I hope it gets a little better for you very soon.'

'Thank you. I hope so too. The same to you.'

He thinks for a moment. 'What was it the Queen once said? Grief is the price we pay for love?'

I nod, unable to answer.

'Goodbye,' he then says.

'Yes, goodbye,' I repeat back, not trusting myself to say more.

I turn away from Mr Kermit the Ben, and hurry off towards the main entrance of the graveyard. I don't look back, because the poor lad doesn't need to see me crying again.

Grief is indeed the price we pay for love, and I feel like it's a price I am completely unprepared and unable to pay.

In the nights to come, when my sleep is haunted by dreams of Joe, and in the mornings that follow, when my hand strays across the sheets to his side, I will cling to the idea that it will become more *familiar*, over time.

That it won't be so sharp. So angry. So *immediate*.

As I get back into my car, wipe my face and start the engine, I decide that I have been very fortunate to bump into somebody like Ben.

Because he gave me some hope. Some hope that things *will* get better.

More *familiar*.

And I think that will have to do, for now.

I think that will keep me going.

I *hope*.

Year Two

SCREAMS AND OLD WALLS

Ben

3 a.m.

It's always 3 a.m.

Even when it's daylight, and the middle of the day, it's also pitch black and 3 a.m.

Because I feel like it's 3 a.m. *all of the time now.*

And all I want to do is sleep.

But there's the chest infection in bed eight. And the blood test results for twelve. And the exam in bed seventeen. And I still haven't done any of my dozen or so write-ups. Karen the Karen from admin will be after me. Karen the Karen is *always* after me when I haven't done my write-ups! But there's a leak in the doctors' lounge so I can't use it. And Didi still needs my help with that recast. And Alexa still needs my help with the dog bite.

And I'm walking along this hallway not really knowing where I am supposed to be going . . .

Where the hell am I going?

What floor am I on?

The walls are piss yellow, so I must be near radiology on level C. But why am I near radiology? Or is it piss yellow for obstetrics? Is it the baby-sick yellow for radiology?

What am I doing here?

Am I even *supposed* to be here?

Oh God. What if I'm not? What if I'm supposed to be helping Alexa with the dog bite, and the bite starts to bleed out, and I'm not there to stop it?

'Fieldinggggggg . . .' The rasping hiss of the monster comes from behind my shoulder.

I spin around. It's Karen the Karen from admin! Only she's not five foot three and wearing a crisp shirt and slacks anymore. She is now horrifically bloated, and fills the entire hallway. Her arms are long and distended, both of them clutching ragged, torn and unwritten procedure write-up forms.

'Fieldinggggggg . . .' it rasps again. 'You're three weeks late, Fieldinggggg . . .'

Its mouth opens impossibly wide, and the creature starts shuddering down the corridor towards me at a startling rate.

She's going to eat me! Karen the Karen is going to eat me!

But I need to help Alexa! I need to help Didi!

Please don't eat me, Karen the Karen!

I promise I'll have those procedure write-ups done by Thursday! I promise!

'FIELDINGGGGG!'

The monster's maw opens even wider!

Aaaargh!

Run, bro, run!

NOOOO!

Run before it gets—

I start awake and bash my arm on the steering wheel.

'Ow!' I exclaim, rubbing it.

It takes my addled brain a few moments to remember where I actually am this morning.

The church. That's where I am. Of course. Not at work (for once). I'm at the church. Karen the Karen is several miles way – and probably hasn't turned into a corridor-filling monstrosity.

Probably.

I'm not anywhere near her today, thank heavens.

I'm where Harry is.

That's it. That's where I am.

. . . oh God.

Karen the Karen might actually be a preferable alternative.

I'm too tired for this . . .

Hell, I'm too tired for *anything*.

But I'm especially too tired to stand in front of a bloody grave, dressed as Robin.

. . . he couldn't even let me be Batman.

At least the grim expression on my face, and the fact I live in a perpetual 3 a.m., would fit better if I was Batman. Maybe the Robert Pattinson version, given how exhausted and fed up he looks throughout that movie.

But no – here I am, dressed once again in tights. Though these are flesh coloured, instead of green.

Don't worry, though. The little pants I'm also wearing *are* green. They go very well with the yellow satin cape, the red waistcoat and the black domino mask that makes sure my identity remains a secret to the good people of Popping Village.

Christ on a bike. Even if I'd had nine hours' sleep every night for a month, I still wouldn't want to be doing this, but Harry's timescale doesn't account for the things going on in my life.

Hell, he'd probably find it funny that his younger brother is now the one who spends his nights and days on a hospital ward, rather than him. Harry never looked as tired as I feel, though. At least I never saw him like it. My twenties are being a lot harder on me than his were on him.

I climb wearily out of the car, and drift my way slowly over to Harry's grave.

All I have to do is get the two minutes and fifty-nine seconds of 'We Are the bloody Champions' out of the way, and I can get out of here.

I have the rest of the afternoon off, before going back in at 7 p.m. I intend to drive home as quickly as possible, and spend the rest of the time unconscious on my bed – probably still dressed as Robin.

I start the timer on my watch, and sway a little back and forth, as I look down at Harry's grave and blink a couple of times.

I've never fallen asleep on my feet before, but there's every chance I'm going to do so now.

It should be completely impossible, but I guess nothing is impossible when you're dressed as the Boy Wonder. If he can easily scale the side of a building with a tiny bit of rope holding him up, he can surely catch forty winks on his feet while Batman is explaining what the Penguin's dastardly plan is for the twelfth time.

The three minutes of Queen passes, and still I stand there, continuing to sway, with my eyes closed. It's very peaceful here in Popping Church cemetery. The birds are singing. The air is fresh. There's a gentle summer breeze, and the smell of freshly cut grass is rather lovely.

Maybe . . . just maybe, instead of driving the three-quarters of an hour back to my flat, I'll go and lie down over there under the oak tree, and have a little daytime snooze right here.

Mmmm.

That sounds lovely . . .

I may be dribbling slightly at this point.

'Ben?' a voice says from a thousand miles away.

Oh no. My black domino mask has failed me! The Penguin knows my identity now, and everyone in Popping will find it out. I must run!

. . . right after I sway and dribble a little bit more.

'Ben?' the voice repeats, now far closer to me. 'Ben? Are you alright?'

I reluctantly open my eyes and blurrily look around to see a woman who looks vaguely familiar.

Not someone I've seen recently, though. Maybe someone I met in the times before.

The times before *the hospital* . . . with its never-ending nights, its never-ending patients, its never-ending admin, and its never-ending destruction of my physical and mental well-being.

The woman's name is . . . I want to say . . . Peggy?

Is her name Peggy?

No. No. That's not right. Peggy was the eighty-three-year-old with pneumonia, wasn't she? Yes. That's right. She said I looked just like her brother. Which was nice. And then she told me she was pleased she had a doctor she could finally understand. Which probably wasn't.

Peggy was last night. Peggy was at *the hospital*.

This is today, and I'm in *the cemetery*.

A place Peggy has managed to avoid for a little while longer, thanks to the ministrations of my good self, and all the other staff at St Mary's.

The woman standing and looking at me right now with a perplexed and slightly haunted look on her face is definitely not called Peggy. Peggy was *old*. This lady is in her late thirties at most, with a kind face and searching eyes. And her long hair is dark brown. Peggy's hair is grey and short.

Also, Peggy didn't look *haunted*. Peggy looked happy to just be alive, God bless her.

It's the haunted look on this woman's face that finally lets my fractured memory slip a few cogs together and come up with the right answer.

Alice.

This is *Alice*.

She was here last year . . . back before I started my foundation training.

'Hello, Alice,' I say to her, trying desperately to bring myself back from the brink of sleep. 'How are you?'

'I was going to say pretty bad,' she tells me. 'But from the looks of you, I'd say you're probably a fair bit worse.'

I nod and give her a thumbs up. 'I could certainly do with a lie down,' I confirm.

'The Joker been giving you and Bruce the runaround again, has he?' she replies, a wry smile appearing on her face.

Bruce? Who's Bruce?

Does she mean Bryce? The small American girl who works down in maternity? Only how would she know her? Even *I* don't know her that well. Which is a shame, because she really is rather pretty.

'Seriously, are you alright, Ben?' Alice asks again when I don't respond to her line about Batman's most famous villain.

The more concerned tone in her voice brings me out of my exhausted stupor a bit. I don't want her thinking I'm actually not okay. That's the last thing I want anyone to think. Whether they are on the ward, here in the cemetery or back home.

I'm fine.

Honestly, I am.

Everything is *fine.*   !

'Sorry, Alice. I'm just a little tired.' I give her a wan smile. 'It's very nice to see you again. How have you been?'

The haunted look deepens. 'You were right about it not getting any easier,' she says.

Alice

'*Go*, Alice,' Lauren says to me, reaching out to take the scissors from my hand.

I shake my head. 'I can't, Lauren! We're way too busy today!'

'Yes, we are, but we're way too busy every day, and this is a *special* day for you, so please go.'

My face twitches slightly when Lauren says this.

Yes, it is a *special* day. A *special* day for all of the wrong reasons . . . and I wish Lauren didn't know anything about it *at all.*

I look around the salon to see how many clients we've got to get through. God damn that automated booking system for screwing up so badly again!

'All these people need seeing to!' I point out to my boss, who rolls her eyes.

'They're *fine*, Alice. They'll happily wait. You saw to that with all the coffee and biscuits you sorted out earlier. Stop worrying about them.'

'But Mrs Allen will be in soon for her refresh. And the GHD stocktake still needs doing, and I've got two dyes booked in at three and four!' I can hear the irrational panic in my voice. Of course I can. But I've worked myself up into a right state that I can't seem to get myself out of.

Because work is extremely busy.

And because it's Joe's birthday.

I *should* be at his grave to see him today (of all days!) . . . but how can I do that with all of *this* going on here? I just can't leave work now – not with Briony quitting last week, and Sonia out for the count with her problems . . .

They need me *here*, where I can manage things. Where I can make some sort of difference. Where I can *help*. Where I don't feel completely out of control – the way I do virtually everywhere else.

Oh God! I can't go!

'Alice,' Lauren says in a very matter-of-fact voice. 'You have more annual leave to take than I can shake a stick at, and you've been working yourself far too hard recently. You're frankly making the rest of us look bad, girl. Take a couple of hours, and go . . . do what you need to do.'

I give her a stricken look for a moment, feeling like I should continue to argue, but then Joe's face swims into view in my head, banishing everything else.

'Alright,' I tell her, and carefully relinquish the scissors. 'I'll be back a bit later, then.'

Lauren nods. 'Good. We'll be fine while you're gone.'

And they will.

I'm being silly. I know I am.

But it's Joe's birthday, you see.

And that is so very, very *hard*.

'Alice?' Lauren asks in a soft voice. 'Are *you* fine? Are you okay?'

I stare at her for a second before answering with a sharp nod of the head. 'Yes! Yes, I'm fine. Of course I am. Absolutely. No problem. See you later, Lauren!'

I spin around and head for the salon's front doors before Lauren has a chance to say anything else to me.

It's best that way. Always is.

So here I am again, then. At the graveyard . . .

A little flustered, and more than a little stressed, but I'm here. Thanks to Lauren's insistence.

And at least I can hold it together these days when I visit my husband's final resting place. I don't have to worry about a crying fit, or my legs going out from under me.

This is because it really has become *familiar*. The weight of it sits across my shoulders more evenly now, metaphorically speaking. I am used to the emptiness. I am used to the absence.

Also, my hand no longer strays across to his side of the bed in the mornings, but this is only because I moved to it about eight months ago. That felt like the right thing to do.

Sleeping on the right side of the bed has now become familiar to me, just as much as the pain has.

My thoughts stray back to the conversation I had with Ben Fielding right here in this graveyard a year ago. It often does. Because it really did help.

As I ponder this, I walk around the side of the church, and Joe's grave comes into view.

As does a man dressed as Robin.

Oh, my *God*. He's here again.

Of course he is. Didn't he say something about having to come here every year on this day, dressed in a ridiculous costume?

In the year that's passed I think I forgot just how determined Ben Fielding seemed to be about honouring his brother's wishes. But now I remember.

The thing is, do I go up and talk to him? Or leave him be?

For a moment, part of me wants to stop in my tracks and back up behind the church again, where I can hide. That part of me would rather just go and see Joe for a few minutes, tell him how I am and then leave again. That's easier. That's *cleaner*. That's probably better for my sanity.

And the GHD stocktake really does have to get done, and Mrs Allen only likes it when I'm the one cutting her bangs.

Also, Ben might not want to be harassed by me again. I doubt he wants to stick around for long, either, given what he's wearing.

No. It's probably best that I just hide for the few minutes it'll take him to get through his strange ritual, and let him be on his way. I don't need to speak to him. I don't need to . . . pour my heart out again.

But then he did help me last year – when I was in a very, very dark place. It'd be nice to thank him. And see how he's doing.

Maybe he'll tell you it does get better this time around. Maybe another year down the track has changed his mind, and he can give you more hope.

I start walking towards Ben again, my heart hammering a little. This man is still pretty much a stranger to me. Hell, I can barely remember what his face looks like, thanks to that green face paint he was wearing.

But I *do* want to speak to him. To thank him . . . and see what other pearls of wisdom he might have to help me on my way.

I walk right up to him, expecting him to notice me and turn. But he doesn't.

Oh God. Is he ignoring me? Does he want to avoid the mad woman, who was such a mess of crying, wailing grief the last time he saw her?

But then I notice him swaying a little, and that his eyes are closed behind that silly mask.

'Ben?' I say, a little tentatively.

'Ben? Ben . . . are you alright?' I try again.

This seems to wake him up.

Because I'm pretty sure that's what I've just done: wake him up. Which should be impossible. But there you have it.

He looks *awful.*

Even the mask doesn't disguise that fact.

He's definitely thinner than the last time I saw him, and his face looks a little sunken.

He finally seems to recognise me, and asks me how I am.

Which is a harder question to answer than I thought.

On the one hand, my days are full with work, which is no bad thing. But on the other, my nights are filled with . . . not very much at all, actually. I tend to sit alone at home watching TV, until I feel tired enough to go up to bed . . . where I lie awake for another couple of hours, before sleep finally decides to grace me with its presence.

I elect to be truthful and tell Ben I'm pretty bad – but probably not as bad as he's doing, by everything I can deduce from the state he appears to be in.

He says he could do with a lie down, and I reply with what I feel is an excellent joke about his costume, which he fails to understand completely.

Something is not right here, clearly.

He was quite the animated chap the last time we spoke. This is not the same person.

He apologises for not paying attention, straightens himself up a bit, looks me in the eye properly for the first time, and asks me how I've been.

The last twelve months crash in on me all at once.

Whatever defences I've erected against the way I feel just so I can function as a normal human being are blown away by the way Ben looks at me.

'You were right about it not getting any easier,' I say to him, my voice dull and heavy.

He sighs, and nods, blinking a couple of times as he does so.

'Do you . . . Do you want to sit down?' I ask him, indicating under the oak tree.

'Yes. I think that would be a good idea,' he agrees, and immediately starts to walk . . . or more accurately *stumble* . . . over to where we sat briefly twelve months ago.

When he gets there, Ben plonks himself down, takes off the Robin mask and leans gratefully against the tree trunk with another sigh.

'If I fall asleep, just poke me, will you?' he says, rubbing his eyes as he does.

'Is that likely to happen?'

He nods. 'It's a common occurrence these days.'

'Why is that?'

'My job. I'm a doctor. Currently doing my foundation programme on a hospital ward.'

Oh . . .

That explains everything.

For the briefest of moments, there's an irrational part of me that wants to get up and run away as fast as I possibly can. I don't like doctors. I don't like medical *things*. Not after what happened to Joe.

But then I quash that irrational voice, because it's incredibly stupid and unfair to be angry at someone who's a doctor, just because your last run-in with one was him telling you your husband was dead.

It wasn't Ben's fault.

Hell, it wasn't the other doctor's fault, either – who looked less tired than Ben, but no less grim of expression, thanks to having to break the worst possible news to a distraught wife.

'I'm due back in a few hours, but had to come and do this,' Ben says, and lifts up one corner of his satin yellow cape, 'because of course it would have to fall right in the middle of my shift pattern.'

I look a bit dubious. 'You didn't have to come, though. I'm sure Harry would have understood.'

He lets out a long breath. 'Eh. I'm not so sure about that. He never seemed to suffer from this kind of fatigue when he was training.'

'He was a doctor too?' Oh great. More of them.

'A surgeon, eventually. Cardiothoracic. Just like our father.'

'Good God. Are all your family in medicine? What does your mum do?'

'Take a guess,' he says with a wry smile.

'Surgeon?'

'Bingo! OBGYN.'

'Christ,' I reply, a little taken aback. That's a hell of a family, right there. 'And you're following in everyone's footsteps, then?'

'I am, indeed. Whether I like it or not!' He says this in a bright and cheery tone, but I can tell there's a darker undercurrent there, which feels a lot closer to the truth.

'You sure?' I hazard.

He sees the look on my face and waves my concern away. 'Oh, I'm just joking. You've caught me at a bad time. Had about three hours' sleep every night for the past week. I enjoy my job right enough . . . when I'm a little more awake, and not dressed like a sidekick.'

'It's better than Kermit,' I tell him, truthfully. Though not by much.

'I suppose it is,' he says with a smile.

'Do your mum and dad know you come here and do this?'

Ben nods. 'Oh yes. Most definitely. In fact, it was my mother who impressed upon me yesterday the importance of honouring Harry's wishes.' His face darkens. 'Which is a bit rich, to be honest, because she certainly didn't support his shenanigans while he was still with us. He once filled her car entirely with bananas. She was . . . not impressed.'

'Why did he do that?'

43

'She mispronounced the word "banana" once at Christmas. Said *nanana* instead. She was a bit tiddly at the time.'

'That's it?'

Ben laughs. 'Oh, something like that was more than enough for Harry.'

'Sounds like your brother could be . . . quite hard work?' I say in a tentative voice.

Ben notices the expression on my face. 'Oh, he could be, indeed. But nothing was ever *that* serious, don't worry. He knew what he could get away with. Had a real knack for it.'

'I see.' I think. 'So here you are, then, at your mother and your brother's behest.'

'And father's. He looked down his glasses at me while my mother was telling me to come.'

'Right . . .'

I'm not entirely sure that this is a particularly healthy family dynamic. But I daren't say that to Ben. I just don't know him well enough.

Besides, at least he *has* a family dynamic. My own mum has been gone seventeen years now, and my waste of space of a father is somewhere up north, with whatever poor woman he's shackled himself to this time.

There isn't anyone else. Not now, anyway.

Joe and I are only children. I guess that was one of the things that drew us together. And we had friends, of course – but many of them moved away or had kids in the last decade or so, so it was more and more just the two of us. Which was more than fine. We loved each other's company too much to need anybody else's. That was never a problem, or a source of regret for me – until Joe was gone, that is.

These days, I think I'd probably be very happy to have a family like Ben's. Even if they were all doctors.

44

Although I can almost feel the pressure he's under coming off him in waves. That look in his eyes while he joked about being a doctor whether he liked it or not spoke volumes.

'It's nice that you've taken the time,' I tell him. 'Have you visited Harry much other than this?'

I almost know the answer before it leaves his mouth. If he'd have been coming on a more regular basis, I would surely have seen him, as – up until the last month anyway – I've been a regular here, whatever the weather.

I talk to Joe, you see.

I stand there and I talk to him, and it makes me feel a little better when I am talking, but a little worse when I know I won't get an answer.

I like to think I'd know what he'd say in reply if he could . . . but you can never be 100 per cent sure, can you? Joe was a solid, sensible man who never raised his voice. But then a squirrel once dropped on to his head, which he then proceeded to berate at the top of his lungs, so you never really know.

But it's still nice to talk to him. Nice to imagine him listening.

'No. I don't really get down here enough,' Ben says, and for a moment I have no idea what he's talking about. Then I remember the question I asked him, and nod in understanding. 'This is home, but it's . . . not really *home* anymore, if you get my meaning.'

I kind of do. Joe was the one born in this neck of the woods, whereas I'm a south London girl – but I understand what it's like to move away from the place you were born.

'And your parents? Are they still local?'

'Oh yes,' Ben says. 'Popping's proudest son and daughter. They're very well known in the community.'

'I bet. I'd imagine they get a lot of people asking them medical questions.'

'They do. But they never answer. They just tell people to go to their doctor.'

'Seems a bit weird.'

'Not if you know what surgeons are like,' Ben replies ruefully. 'The worst thing about being a surgeon is having to deal with *people*, as far as the vast majority of them are concerned.'

I make a face. 'And this is what you want to be?'

For a moment, Ben's face is frozen solid. Then it slowly thaws, as what feels like a well-practised response comes from his tight lips. 'Yes. It's a very worthwhile job that will make me a success.'

'Aah,' I say, and nod slowly. A very strong picture is starting to form in my head of Ben's relationship with his family. Including his deceased brother. It doesn't necessarily feel like a particularly good one.

He regards me rather solemnly for a moment, his eyes blinking slowly as the tiredness tries to take over again. 'Honestly, don't be concerned about me,' he eventually says. 'I'm fine. Like I say, you've just caught me at a bad moment. I'm not in the fairest frame of mind. My parents are *good* people. They just have some . . . *quirks* that are hard to deal with sometimes. Don't think too badly of them, just because of the state I'm in. If you saw me in a couple of weeks when I've had a break, I'm sure I'd be much better company. Much more Harry-like.'

Everything seems to come back to Harry with this boy. I flick my eyes over at the brother's grave and bite my lip.

There are things I would say to Ben Fielding, if I knew him better. Things that he probably wouldn't want to hear, but would do him a great deal of good, I'd bet.

There you go, butting into someone else's life again, Joe's voice says with mild reproval. *You shouldn't do that, you know. You don't like it when other people do it to you.*

Well, there you have it, woman. Maybe Joe does answer back now and again, after all.

Or at least, my subconscious does, doing a very good impression of my late husband.

I don't know Ben Fielding enough to butt my head into his life, but I do feel like I know him enough from our two brief meetings to at least say the following.

'I'm sure you don't need to be like your brother to be good company, Ben.'

He smiles back at me in a way that tells me he doesn't agree in the slightest.

And then he changes the subject.

Which would be absolutely fine, if the subject he changed to wasn't one that caused my heart to freeze in my chest.

'You said I was right to tell you it doesn't get any better?' he says, genuine concern on his face.

No. This is not a man best suited to being an aloof surgeon. I can say that with some certainty.

'The grief?' he continues. 'Has it been hard? The last year?'

God bless you for remembering, Ben Fielding. And God damn you for asking.

I can't look at Joe's grave for the moment. It's too much.

'Yeah,' I say, head bowing a little under the weight of it. 'It's been very hard.'

Ben

It's none of my business, really.

I shouldn't be prying into this woman's life.

But I had to change the subject. Get away from talking about my family. Because those conversations never end well.

They don't when I'm talking to the other doctors, they don't when I'm talking to ex-girlfriends, and they don't when I'm talking to myself. *Especially* when I'm talking to myself.

So, I take the coward's way out, and steer the conversation around to how Alice is feeling. I already know the answer, but it's easier for me to deal with someone else's problems than it is my own. That's what doctors are good at, after all. And I am a doctor. One who will no doubt be starting his surgical training the minute he completes his foundation course. That will last eight years.

And then I'll be done. I'll have made my parents proud. I will have honoured Harry's memory.

I will be able to get a decent night's sleep.

Sleep . . .

Those little slices of death. How I loathe them.

That's what Edgar Allan Poe wrote. At least I think it was.

Obviously a man who never had to do a night shift on a hospital ward.

But I *think* I know what he means about those little slices of death. The tiny moments when it sits on your shoulder, reminding you that it's *always* there. When you're suturing the gaping head wound in the drunk idiot's scalp – thinking about how he could have easily died if his face had hit the kerb just a little harder. Or when you hear the hideous rattling sound in Peggy's chest down the stethoscope – knowing that you'll probably see her again soon . . . if she's lucky.

Or when you have to come and stare down at your poor dead brother's grave – trying your hardest not to think of the skeleton he became, because all those little slices take their toll, until the body just gives up, and—

'I miss him so much,' I hear Alice say from ten thousand miles away, and immediately snap back to the present.

Congratulations. You've made her cry.

I thought it was 'first do no harm' *not* 'do a little harm, if it stops you feeling terrible'?

'I'm sorry,' I bluster. 'I shouldn't have asked.'

Alice shakes her head. 'No. It's fine, Ben. Honestly.' She pulls a packet of tissues from her pocket. 'I always come prepared,' she says, holding out the packet for a moment, before extricating a tissue and dabbing her eyes with it.

'Do you . . . Do you want to talk about it?' I ask her.

All I want to do is sleep. All I want to do is listen to nothing other than the sound of my own breathing.

But first I have to help Alice.

Because that's what doctors do.

I am a doctor.

And one day I will be a surgeon, and I'll be telling people to go see their doctor, just like my mother and father do. I wonder if I'll be able to do it in the same cold voice they always use?

'I don't know,' she replies, her brow creasing. 'I don't really know if I can put it into words, without sounding . . . *weird*.'

'What could possibly sound weird?'

She looks up to the sky for a moment, the tears still glistening in her eyes, but no more than that, for the minute. 'I see him,' she says in a flat voice. 'Just for a fleeting moment, every now and again. Sat on the couch, standing in front of the bathroom mirror, or out on the patio with his morning cup of tea. I *see him*, Ben. And it feels as real as looking at you now. My brain sees the hole, and tries to *fill it in*. And it does such a good job that I'm slightly terrified by it.'

'That's not weird,' I tell her, trying to smile, but feeling it fall off my face almost instantly. 'That happened to me as well.'

And it did. I'm not just trying to humour her.

The same way someone who has an amputation feels the limb that's gone, when you lose someone you love, your traitorous mind

49

does its best to bring them back. I used to see Harry – healthy and happy – just about everywhere I went that was familiar to us. One of the reasons I barely visit home these days is because he's there too – a phantom image of him, anyway.

No wonder people believe in ghosts.

'Did it?' Alice replies, and there's a look of relief in her eyes that I don't know I like all that much. I want to be kind to this poor woman, but I also don't want to have to poke at my grief just to make her feel a little better about hers. I'm just too damned tired.

And sad.

. . . but mostly tired.

'Yeah,' I tell her, but offer no more.

She nods into the silence, and then plucks a blade of grass from the ground. 'Good to know I'm not cracking up.'

I shake my head. 'No, you're definitely not cracking up – even though sometimes it does feel that way.'

'Thank you. And thank you for talking to me . . . again. I find it hard to speak to anyone about Joe, because . . . because they don't really understand.'

'And you hate them for it,' I find myself saying, before I even realise it.

Where the hell did that come from?

'Yes!' Alice replies fiercely, before looking instantly ashamed of herself. 'Oh God, that's a horrible thing to say, isn't it?'

It certainly is, especially when you had no idea you were thinking it yourself. Not anymore, anyway. I thought I was . . . over that part.

Maybe it's just the exhaustion talking.

But if so, why do I feel the tears pricking my eyes as I remember all those times I looked at my friends with frustrated jealousy, because they hadn't been through what I went through? Every one of them with siblings who were still alive and kicking.

I *hated* them.

And I hated myself for feeling that way.

And I hate the fact even more that it's still with me.

'It's not horrible,' I begin, then realise what I'm saying. 'No . . . it *is* horrible, but not for the reasons you think.'

'How so?'

'You don't really hate other people. You just hate the situation *you're* in. But there's nothing you can do to get out of it, so you . . . I don't know . . . lash out at other people, I guess?'

Bloody hell. For someone who didn't want to get too deeply into his own grief, you're sure as hell doing a good job of it.

Alice nods. 'Yeah. I can see that.' Her hand, which had just been brushing the tips of the grass, now grips it. 'Because it's just so *unfair!*'

'It is,' I reply, knowing that I'm very probably lying.

You don't spend the amount of time I have around sickness and still think there's any real fairness in the world. I've seen bastards walk out smiling, and saints rolled down to the mortuary.

Was it unfair that Harry Fielding was cut down so quickly in the prime of his life, by a disease that refused to loosen its grasp, even for the briefest moment?

I don't know.

I look at Alice, and for a second I feel like I want to share her anger. But I know what would happen if I did.

Grief doesn't keep that anger focused in one place. It likes to leap around. One minute you're angry that other people don't know how you feel, then you're angry at the hospital because they couldn't save him, then you're angry at yourself for not being able to do more.

And then – the worst.

You're angry at *him* for leaving you.

I can see it in her eyes, as she stares down at the grass clenched in her fist. They twitch as the anger *jumps*.

'The one thing I learned,' I say – very carefully, because this is a tense moment, and if I say the wrong thing, that anger will be turned on me – 'is that the anger isn't something to feel ashamed about.'

'It isn't?' Alice replies sharply, and I can hear the self-loathing in her voice.

'No. It's . . . part of how you process. How you cope.'

'I don't feel like I'm coping much,' Alice says with a bitter roll of the eyes. 'I don't talk to anyone. I see my dead husband around the house, and I feel like screaming 90 per cent of the time.'

I look around at the empty graveyard. 'Go on, then.'

'What?'

'Scream.'

She blinks a couple of times. 'What?'

'You should scream. Right now. There's no one around, other than me.'

'You want me to scream into an empty graveyard?'

I nod. 'Yes. I do. God knows I wish someone had just told me I could scream out loud after Harry died. But everyone expects you to cry when someone you love dies, not scream.'

'I can't.'

'You can, you know.'

'It'd be embarrassing.'

I give Alice a look that's probably more withering than I'd like, thanks to the exhaustion I feel. 'Do you really care?'

She thinks about it for a moment, and then shakes her head slowly. I gesture to her to carry on.

Alice takes a breath and attempts to scream.

'That's not a scream, Alice,' I tell her. 'That sounds like you have trapped wind.'

The laugh that escapes her lips is nice to hear.

I'm being a *good doctor*.

'Try again,' I tell her. 'And like you really mean it . . . which I know you do.'

The smile drops off her face as her eyes flick over to her husband's grave.

She's going to get it right this time.

And indeed, that's exactly what happens. The loud, drawn-out scream that she draws up from somewhere unreachable to anyone else echoes around the cemetery, bouncing off the fourteenth-century walls of Popping Church.

I nod in approval. 'That's more like it. Maybe you should try t—'

Alice screams again. This time even louder. 'Okay, that's very good and you sh—'

And again.

'Maybe just—'

One more time.

Good lord. There's every chance someone is going to call the police. Maybe this wasn't such a great suggestion on my part. I could do with ending the day without me being under arrest.

Although that would mean I could probably get some sleep . . .

Thankfully, Alice appears to be done screaming. For the moment, anyway. She looks more exhausted than I feel.

'Better?' I ask her.

She stares at the ground and nods. 'A little. I don't feel it crawling around inside me quite so much.'

Some people would wonder what the hell she means by that, but I don't. I know exactly what that feels like. 'Good,' I tell her approvingly.

Alice looks up at me. 'Now you.'

'What?'

'It's your turn.'

'To do what?'

'Scream, Ben. You should scream too.'

I shake my head and smile ruefully. 'I don't need to.'

The look Alice gives me pins me against the tree trunk I'm slumped against. 'You sure about that? You said it would have helped you before. Maybe it still can.'

I shake my head again. No smile on my lips this time. 'Honestly . . . it's not something I need to do.'

Alice nods. 'Okay. So do it for me. So I don't feel so embarrassed.'

A third shake. 'I'm too tired.'

'Please? It'd make me feel better?'

What is she trying to do here?

'Alright, alright,' I say, holding my hands up. 'If it'd make you feel better.'

She smiles. 'It would.'

I heave a long sigh and sit a little more upright. As I do this, I catch a look at Harry's grave, the same way Alice did with her husband's.

And it's all back.

Of course it is.

The thing crawling around inside me has woken up again, and I shouldn't be surprised about that.

A year and a bit is *nothing*.

The blink of an eye.

The scream is loud enough to bounce off the church walls again, though, and come back over me like a wave. One that I still feel like I could drown in at any moment.

The sob that follows the scream comes from a place of extreme tiredness, as much as it does grief.

Still, Alice shouldn't feel all that embarrassed anymore, should she? I'm a *good doctor*.

Alice

I shouldn't have pushed him like that.

It was grossly unfair of me.

But he needed it.

I could see it in his face.

That exhaustion isn't all from being a doctor. I know that because I see the same look of abject tiredness in my eyes most mornings.

The edges of grief get rounded off, but the *weight of it* never stops. And Ben's suggestion that I scream really did help. I felt a little lighter after it.

And I knew he would too.

But now he's crying, and I'm an absolute bitch for forcing it out of him.

'Oh, I'm so sorry, Ben!' I exclaim, and move towards him reflexively.

He waves a hand and closes the other over his eyes for a moment, wiping the tears away. 'Don't worry. I'm okay,' he insists. 'I'm just . . . tired. Very tired.'

'Should I go?'

I probably should go, whether he tells me to or not.

What was I thinking?

'You don't have to go anywhere,' Ben says, leaning back against the tree, and staring up into the branches. 'That was . . . unexpected. I'm sorry.'

'I'm the one who should be apologising.'

'Don't. Sometimes I need to be reminded that . . . that it's all still there.' He rubs both hands down his face. 'Maybe I'm not just tired because of all the long shifts,' he says, echoing the very same thought I had.

'Maybe, but I still feel bad.'

He lets out a sharp report of laughter. 'You'll feel even worse when the coppers turn up to arrest us in a minute. We sound like we've been trying to murder each other.'

I point at his costume. 'Robin wouldn't murder anybody.'

Ben looks down at himself. 'He should kill Batman for making him wear this shit.'

I grimace. 'The tights, certainly.'

He plucks at one leg, lifting it off his knee for a moment, before letting the material snap back into place. 'I think Harry's instructions wouldn't be so bad if he didn't make me wear tights so much.' It's his turn to grimace. 'I don't have the legs for tights. They look like someone's tried to strangle a Twiglet.'

It is quite incredible how you can move from the deep-flowing waters of extreme grief into a lagoon of sudden hilarity in what feels like a split second.

'Twi— *Twiglets*?' I say, looking at him and barely able to contain my mirth.

'Yes,' he says with a nod. 'My legs are knobblier than a supermarket shelf of the buggers.'

'Mine look like sausages,' I say, in a mock-serious tone. 'Chipolatas to be precise.'

'Surely not,' he says in a reproving tone.

I nod. 'Oh yes. Smooth . . . but a bit chubby. That's my legs.'

Ben nods slowly. 'I understand. I bet they still look better than mine do in tights.'

I look at him gravely. 'On that, I'm sorry to say, I wholeheartedly agree.'

This sends us both off into another wave of laughter.

What is it about talking to this young man that means I can be crying one second, and laughing the next? I don't do it with anybody else I know. Not least because I'm not close enough to anyone these days to be that open and vulnerable with them.

So why is it different here, with what amounts to a stranger?

My chuckles diminish somewhat as I ponder this. 'Are we weird?' I ask Ben.

'How do you mean?'

'We're both sat here giggling like idiots. In a graveyard . . . with the people that we love . . . *over there*. Surely there's nothing funny about it.'

Ben shakes his head. 'Oh, Harry would think this is *hilarious*. That's why he's making me do it.'

'I don't laugh much these days,' I say, feeling the humour drain out of me. 'In fact, I think the last time I did laugh was here with you a year ago.'

Ben thinks for a moment. 'You know what, I think it might be the same for me. At least . . . I haven't laughed this *hard* since we were here last time.'

'Why do you think that is?'

He looks down at himself again. 'Well, the stupid costumes must have something to do with it, but I don't know. I guess we don't know each other well, so . . .' He trails off in thought.

'So it's . . . *easier*?' I hazard.

He nods. 'Yeah, maybe. Because we don't have to worry so much about the other person?'

My turn to nod. 'I hate upsetting people with it.'

Ben chews on his lower lip for a moment. 'Yeah. I get that. It's hard to . . . bring it up. Even when you really want to.'

'Because you don't want to put it on them. Don't want to upset them, by letting them see *you* upset.'

He lets out a long, slow breath. 'Christ. You're right. I think I keep it all to myself so much just so I don't . . . ruin their day too. You keep it all hidden.'

We both sit in silence for a while, letting this sink in.

The thing they never tell you, or show you in the movies, is how grief becomes so . . . *fundamental.* To everything you do. It changes the world around you in ways you never expect – including your relationships with other people.

They're kind to you because you've lost someone, but they also . . . *move away* from you. Because deep down, nobody wants to be around grief for too long. It's a reminder of their own fragility. You become a walking, talking symbol of something that will happen to all of us eventually.

So you get a hug, and a kind word. And then they're gone.

And you can't blame them for it. Any more than you can blame them for not being the one with the dead husband, and for not having a life in tatters.

So Ben's right. You do hide it. You do put up walls that make you seem okay.

It's easier that way. Keeping people in the dark is better than watching them move away from you.

'Of course, the problem you and I now have,' Ben says, 'is that we might become friends . . . which would ruin it, wouldn't it?'

I smile ruefully. 'That's a fair point. You'll just be another person I don't want to talk to.'

He laughs in an exasperated tone. 'It's all a lot harder than you'd ever imagine it would be, isn't it?'

'Immeasurably,' I agree, and I look over at Joe's grave.

Then my eyes turn to Harry's.

And then I look back at Ben.

'So, how about we *don't* become friends, then?'

He blinks. 'I'm sorry? Are you about to punch me in the face or something?'

I chuckle. 'No. What I mean is, we shouldn't be friends with one another. We shouldn't get too *familiar.* I like talking to you, and laughing with you when it feels right, and I'd like to continue with that. With no . . . *pressure*.'

'Okay . . . so what are you proposing?'

I think for a moment. 'We meet here. Same day, same time next year. Midday on 8 July. You can fill me in on what's happening with your life, and I'll do the same.'

'And we won't have to worry about how the other person feels so much, because we won't see them again for ages,' Ben says, nodding along.

It sounds on the surface like a crazy idea, but it also feels like a very *good one*.

I'd love to be able to turn up here in a year and tell Ben I'm doing so much better, and I'd equally like to hear the same from him. But if we don't – then that's okay too. Having someone there to vent at, without fear of repercussions on our social lives, is as good a reason for doing this as any other.

And it means you don't have to worry about actually getting close to anyone, doesn't it, Alice?

'That's right.' I smile, ignoring myself. 'And it means I get to see whatever hideous costume your brother has made you dress up in.'

Ben rolls his eyes. 'Yes, thank you very much for that. I'm glad to know my attire will keep you on tenterhooks all year.'

'I know!' I reply with mock excitement. 'What will it be? Maybe a pirate? Or a banana? I can hardly wait!'

Ben rolls his eyes harder. 'I'm not sure I like this idea anymore.'

'Think of it as a challenge, if you like,' I say to him. 'For us both to come back here and talk again. Openly and honestly with one another.' I cock my head. 'And come on . . . aren't you excited to see what state I'm in too? I may not be the one wearing the silly costume, but I look like a horror when I've been crying. Will my hair look like a bird's nest? Will my face be super blotchy? Or will I be as white as a ghost? Will I – in short – look like I've been dragged through a hedge backwards?'

Ben smiles. 'You don't look like any of those things.'

'Oh yes I do, young man. I don't need you to pretend otherwise. I am an ugly crier, and I'm comfortable with that.'

'Probably more comfortable than I am sat against this tree,' he replies. 'Shall we have a little walk, just to get the blood going again? I'll have to leave soon, but the fresh air is doing me good.'

'Yes, that sounds like a lovely idea,' I reply, rising to my feet.

Having decided upon the framework of this strange relationship, I feel like I've actually accomplished something constructive.

I've met someone who knows exactly what it's like to feel the way I do, and I know that whatever else happens in my life, I'll be able to see him again – and ugly cry as much as I want to, if I need to.

Without having to get too close . . . which is the painful part, isn't it? Because fathers leave and husbands die, and friends move away if you make them feel uncomfortable . . .

Ben and I continue today's chat for about half an hour more, as we once again stroll around the graveyard, until he yawns so widely I'm afraid the top of his head is going to fall off.

'Right, you, that's enough for today,' I tell him. 'Home time.' Ben smiles, nods slowly and gestures at me to lead us out of the graveyard.

This time we are both parked in the church's main car park, so I get to see Ben off in his BMW. At least it's black, so it kind of resembles the Batmobile.

The last thing he says to me is that he hopes things go well for me in the next year. I wish him the same.

Neither of us go through the pantomime of hoping we both feel better about our losses.

Will I actually see Ben again, this time next year? I do hope so.

But twelve months is a very long time. You never know what might happen.

My world ended in the space of less than twelve hours, so God knows what another twelve months could do to me.

Ben

I doubt she'll be there next year.

The whole thing sounds like a lovely idea . . . but that's probably how it'll stay. Just an idea.

Because sometimes the idea of something is far more powerful than the reality.

And a year is a long time. A lifetime for some.

I'm sure Alice's life will change in the interim. Hell, mine probably will too.

I'll be back here in twelve months because my brother wants me to be.

But Alice has no such demands placed on her.

In a way, I hope I never see her again. If I don't, it means she will have moved on.

I hope that next year, when I'm stood in front of Harry's grave again, wearing whatever idiotic thing he's demanded I dress in, I am doing it completely alone.

Because she deserves that, I think.

It seems strange to hope you never see someone nice again.

But I hope I don't.

I truly do.

But now I really should go home and get some sleep.

I *should*, but instead I will find the nearest Costa and buy an Americano with a triple shot of espresso, and then I will go back to work. Because people need me there.

And I am a good doctor.

Year Three

HAEMORRHOIDS AND KANGAROO HATS

Ben

I am a terrible doctor.

The medical profession and Ben Fielding do not get on. No matter how hard he tries to convince himself that they do.

Therefore, it is with no small degree of chagrin that I put on the sexy nurse's outfit Harry has stipulated for me this year.

I should not describe it as a *sexy* nurse's outfit, because on me, it is about as sexy as a full bedpan. In fact, I'm rather afraid that if I refer to it as a 'sexy nurse's outfit' one more time, some sort of hole in existence will appear, due to the catastrophic misuse of the word 'sexy' – and I will be transported to a parallel universe where I don't have a dead older brother who hates me enough to demand I dress up in a sexy nurse's outfit.

Dodging the newly created rip in the space–time continuum, I stumble across the asphalt of the small rear church car park, and make my way into the cemetery.

I snapped the heels off the cheap white knee-length go-go boots before I got here, so at least I'm not afraid of breaking an ankle as I climb the steps to the back entrance.

Oh Christ. I suppose I'd better describe the whole damn outfit, and just get it out of the way . . .

Yes, those are white fishnet stockings, and yes, I *am* wearing my boxer shorts underneath them. Otherwise the holes between the material could be large enough for things to . . . *fall out.* The white uPVC dress with the red trim is as uncomfortable as it looks, the stethoscope clearly isn't functional, and I had to rip the side of the little nurse's hat with the red cross on it to get it to fit on my head.

If you saw me stumbling towards you in a moment of emergency, you'd probably take your chances with the compound fracture in your leg and attempt to run away.

Ninety-six per cent of me is pure, unadulterated and finely extracted embarrassment.

I'm grateful that the cemetery is as empty as it tends to be on these annual occasions. All the time the day I have to come here is a weekday, I can probably get away with this stupidity with very few people seeing me. Popping is not a big village, and the church only really gets visitors at the weekend.

Needless to say, I am dreading it when we reach Saturday and Sunday in a few years. With any luck an asteroid will have hit planet Earth by then and I won't have to come here at all.

I would be at full 100 per cent embarrassment, but there's a small part of me that is incredibly curious as to whether the one person I wouldn't mind actually seeing will be here or not.

I'm pretty convinced Alice won't be, but I can't be absolutely sure.

And would I be happy if she was?

Yes and no.

No, because it means she will still be having trouble with her grief about . . . Joe, was it? Yes. That's right. Joe. She will still need to talk about how she feels, and that would be very sad. I really hope she has managed to move on.

On the other hand, I would really like to see her – and God knows I could do with talking to her about the absolute mess my life is in.

Several times in the past couple of months I've hoped I would see Alice again, because I can't think of anyone I can express my true feelings to better than her

I certainly couldn't talk to Mr Sharp about anything, as he handed over the sexy nurse's outfit. I doubt Mr Sharp ever wants to talk about anything to do with me, with the possible exception of an eyewitness statement to the police.

He must think I'm an absolute lunatic – and possibly a pervert – for going through with this idiocy.

How would I explain to him that what he sees as sheer idiocy, I now see as *penance*? Punishment for the colossal wrongs I have wrought upon this earth in the last twelve months?

Or at least on my family and career, if not the entire planet itself.

. . . which has resolutely not been hit by an asteroid – so here I am, in a massively unsexy nurse's outfit, hoping to turn the corner of the church and see Alice stood there waiting for me.

The wave of sadness that overcomes me when I see that she is not hits harder than I thought it would.

It would have been nice.

It would have been so nice for her to be here – to laugh at my costume and lend me some moral support.

Maybe I could have laughed too, like we did before. That would have been nice as well. That would have made a refreshing change.

Alright, dickhead, let's just get this over with, then, eh? I want to get these fishnets off before the undercarriage goes into traumatic shock.

I stumble (because even with the heels snapped off, these go-go boots are awful) down the path back to Harry's grave, feeling slightly dismayed as I reach it to see that the grass hasn't been cut yet. The whole area looks a little untidy because of it.

Maybe I should ask in the church about how often the groundsman works.

Oh yes. That'd be a good idea. The vicar can sit next to Mr Sharp while he gives his witness statement.

My watch tells me it's nearly midday, so I find the stopwatch on my phone and get ready to get the ritual over with again for another year.

I look behind me down the main path to see if Alice is walking up it, but there's still no sign of her.

Dammit.

And so it's time for the worst two minutes and fifty-nine seconds of my life again.

All on my lonesome.

And this year, I also get to feel absolutely ashamed of what I've done. I get to stand here and stare at Harry's gravestone, knowing how deeply embarrassed he'd be at being my brother now, given what happened on Ward C12 on 19 May.

My mother and father certainly were. To the extent that I can't help thinking they'd be perfectly happy if I sank to my knees right now, and started digging myself a grave on top of my brother's.

But thankfully 'We Are the Champions' has now finished, and I can get the hell out of here. I've called in sick (again) and I have a couch at home with my name on it. Where I can sit and worry over what the hell to do about my life.

And even that is better than spending one more minute in this painful get-up, so I start to make my way back up the path towards the car park.

But if I want to get out of this churchyard, and this awful costume, as quickly as I possibly can, why do I smile with relief when I hear my name being called from the other end of the cemetery?

Alice

I almost let him go.

In that moment, as I saw him start to walk away, I considered just letting him do that.

The fear, which has been with me now for most of this year, rises in my throat again.

I don't really know if 'fear' is the right word, though.

But then again, neither is 'excitement'.

There's got to be something in between that I could use to describe this feeling.

I could ask Ben. He might know. He's a doctor.

But only if I call out to him. Only if I make him turn around and stay in this graveyard for longer than he wants to.

Because even though I'm a good thirty yards away, I can see what he's wearing.

Just let him go, then. Don't make him stand around here in that get-up. You don't need his advice. You should be able to make your mind up without it. You're just being—

'Ben!' I cry, waving a hand over my head.

He starts to turn, and for a millisecond I regret my decision thoroughly. What if the last thing he wants to do is go through another afternoon of conversations with Alice?

But then he sees me, and a smile appears on his face. It then falters a little, before returning as he starts to walk back towards me.

Yep. Well done, you damned fool. He's covering it up to be nice, but it's obvious he doesn't want to do this again.

'Hey, Alice!' Ben says to me as we meet more or less right at where Joe and Harry's graves lie together, forever.

'Hey,' I reply, trying not to look at what he's wearing too much.

Ben looks down at himself. 'Yeah, I know. It's bad, isn't it?'

'It's not great, Ben,' I tell him. 'Do you want to . . . go somewhere else? Maybe go and sit in your car, or something?'

He waves a hand. 'No. I'll be fine. Under the tree feels . . . I don't know . . . *right*, somehow?'

I nod. He *is* right.

This is the third time we've met like this, and it's already starting to feel like there's some sort of weird *ceremony* to the whole thing. And part of that ceremony is sitting under that enormous old oak tree, in front of the graves.

I don't know why.

I doubt Ben does, either. And he's the one who has to remain in public dressed like that.

He holds out a hand, and gestures for me to take the lead over to the tree. 'Would you . . . Would you like a little time on your own with your husband first?' he asks.

I think about it for second. 'No. That's okay. I can . . . be with Joe after we're done. I'm in no rush today.'

'Neither am I,' Ben says as we both sit down on the grass under the tree's wide and leafy boughs.

'Oh . . . You're not working today, then?' I ask.

'Um. No. No, I'm not,' he replies, looking quite distraught.

'What's happened?'

Ben takes a deep breath. 'I . . . I'm . . . kind of dodging work at the moment, because something pretty catastrophic happened. So bad that all I want to do is quit my stupid job.'

'Oh no!'

Well, that's torn it, hasn't it? There's absolutely no way I'm going to be able to ask Ben's advice about what's going on with me now. It'd be rubbing salt into a very obviously open wound.

I should have just let the poor guy go . . .

'What's happened?' I ask.

Ben's lips purse together as he tries to think of the best way to tell me.

Ben

I've *tried*. I honestly have.

I've tried my very hardest to enjoy being a doctor, despite the long hours and stress. And there were moments . . . times when I did feel good about myself and the position I was in. This usually happened when I knew I'd done a good job of helping someone.

There's nothing like the thrill of watching a sick person recover from injury or illness with your help. It's extremely good for the soul.

Sadly, those moments are fleeting. Unlike on TV, hospital doctors rarely get to see their patients improve. The poor buggers usually get turfed out long before they're back to their old selves. And people who are still suffering (but not suffering *enough* for a hospital bed) aren't usually feeling in a particularly good mood, so it's rare for any of them to show much gratitude for everything you and your colleagues have done.

That's absolutely fine, though. Totally understandable.

But every now and again, you do get thanked. And sometimes there are even chocolates.

And those are the moments that keep me on my feet.

But overall, the strains and the stresses have got worse and worse. I've become more and more miserable as the days and weeks have passed. I've even started to dread going into work after a good ten hours' sleep.

And then, a Saturday arrived.

A Saturday when three of the nurses were off with the flu, and my already understaffed ward became virtually unmanageable.

Saturdays are the days you dread most when you work in a hospital with an A&E department. On top of the usual influx of people that happens on a daily basis, whatever the day of the week is, you get the drunks on Saturdays, and the idiots – and the drunk idiots.

This means that both doctors and nurses get pulled off ward care, because the A&E starts to overflow.

Which means that I get to be on the ward with one nurse to help me – and a whole shitload of patients needing care.

Mistakes are bound to happen.

And I made one.

I got two patients mixed up. Both of them men in their eighties. Both called George. George Winters and George Willoughby. Which are very similar names, you'd have to agree, right? And they had very similar descriptions too. Both of them had degrees of cognitive impairment.

The odds that both of these men would be in on the same day are vanishingly small. I know. I worked it out afterwards on a calculator.

And what happened would make anybody laugh. Up to and definitely including a grieving widow in a church cemetery. But I can't blame her for that.·

Any more than I could blame many of my patients for not buying me a box of Roses on their way out of the door.

Neither George Winters nor George Willoughby was going to buy me chocolates or thank me for what I did to them, that was for certain.

George Winters was in for a broken right wrist, and George Willoughby was in for grade four haemorrhoids.

Anyone with half a brain can at this point see exactly where this tale of horror is going.

Yes, that's right. I got the two of them mixed up. I gave a rectal exam to a man with a broken wrist, and spent thirty minutes applying a cast to the right hand of a bloke who couldn't poo without screaming.

The worst thing was that I managed to convince both of them that what I was doing was worthwhile. Because you trust your doctors, don't you?

Yes, of course you do. And I can be very convincing.

I have something of a reputation for putting people at their ease in the hospital. All I do is talk to them, though. Nothing earth-shattering. But it's amazing what you can get people to do if they trust you, just because you've asked them how their day has been.

And bless him, poor old George Winters didn't complain when I rolled him over and looked up his arse. God knows what he thought I was doing up there that would help him with a broken wrist.

And George Willoughby sat in stunned silence while I wrapped his perfectly healthy hand in a cast. It was only when I'd completely finished that he asked me why I'd done it.

I told him his wrist wouldn't heal without a cast on it. He then asked me if the wrist had something to do with his bottom. Was I doing some sort of new-fangled reflexology stuff on him, he asked me. Only, he saw a documentary about it on the BBC once, and didn't think it looked all that good.

You'd have thought that this would be when I'd realised I'd made a cock-up, wouldn't you?

Only it was gone one in the morning, and I was extremely tired *again*, and both of them had degrees of cognitive impairment, so . . . *I sent them both home.*

We needed the beds! And George Winters had no sign of grade four prolapsed haemorrhoids, and I thought I'd done a great job with George Willoughby's broken wrist!

Good God in heaven.

They brought George Winters back in four hours later, white-faced with pain, and ranting about the doctor that poked him up the bum.

'Well, that's fair enough,' Alice says with a straight face, having digested my extreme tale of woe thus far with a degree of self-restraint that could be considered almost superhuman. 'Having a broken wrist must've been a right pain in the arse.'

There is a moment of silence while my brain attempts to digest this terrible, terrible pun. Then I look at Alice in no uncertain terms.

This is when the dam breaks, and she starts to laugh like several drunk hyenas.

Sigh.

It's to be expected.

Let's see if I can make her laugh any harder . . .

'George Willoughby was a lot better off,' I say to her, 'and didn't come back for a couple of days. Seems like he thought the cast on his wrist was my way of preventing him from wiping his bum so much and making the 'roids worse.'

Yep. That did it.

I should have brought an oxygen tank and a mask with me. Alice is going to need if it she continues to laugh that hard.

I let her do so, though. I can see the comedy in my mistake, after all.

Hell, even I had to chuckle about a week later when I found that the nurses had stuffed my locker with haemorrhoid cushions.

There were no real repercussions on me for my error. Both men had their issues sorted out by other, more competent doctors, and the mix-up was put down to the extreme circumstances on the ward. Everybody got over the incident in a short period of time.

Everyone except yours truly – who hasn't really recovered from both the embarrassment and the crippling doubt.

I'm not in the right job, am I? That's obvious to anyone with half a brain!

My heart had known it this entire time, but now my head has caught up as well. And I don't know what the hell I'm going to do about it.

Oh look. Alice is calming down a bit. That's good. The next part of the story isn't all that funny, and I didn't want to ruin her mirth before it had time to run its course.

'Did you get into trouble?' she asks me, wiping tears away from her eyes.

'Not really. That's the NHS for you these days. Everyone knows it's knackered, so these kinds of things barely register.'

Alice sobers up immediately when I say this. 'That's good to hear,' she says in a level voice. Any trace of mirth left her completely the second I mentioned the problems with the health service.

'But I don't think I can go on,' I tell her.

'What do you mean?'

'With the job. The mistake has knocked what was left of my confidence, and it's made me realise that being a doctor is something I actively *hate*.'

'Oh no.'

'Yeah. Not great, huh?'

'So have you . . . you know?'

72

'Nope. I have my letter of notice sat on the arm of the couch at home . . . but I just don't think I can go through with it.'

'Why not?'

I give her what I know is a hangdog expression. 'My parents. I can't disappoint them like that. With Harry gone, I'm the only one left who's in the profession. They'd be devastated if I left my job. If I quit.' I point at my brother's grave. 'Harry would too, I know it.'

'Oh no. I'm so sorry, Ben,' Alice says. 'All that time spent doing something you don't like. It must be awful.'

'It absolutely is. Even when I broached the fact that I'm not enjoying it, and was thinking of handing my notice in, my mother and father were at great pains to tell me to just suffer through until it gets better. They think this is all just temporary . . . but I know it isn't. They don't understand at all.'

Alice's face crumples in sympathy. 'Oh. Yes. I bet. After what you told me last year about them.'

'My mother said Harry would be devastated if I quit.' A lump forms in my throat. 'And that he'd be ashamed of me.'

'Bloody hell!'

'She apologised for saying it afterwards, but I know she meant it.'

'I'm sure she didn't really, Ben,' Alice assures me. 'And I'm sure if you talked to them again, they'd understand. I doubt they'd want you to carry on in a job you hate that much.'

I raise an eyebrow to this. 'You haven't met my mother.'

Alice doesn't know how to respond to that. Can't say I blame her. My parents are something that has to be properly experienced first-hand before you can understand them. Like art house cinema, or warfare.

'So, what are you going to do?' Alice then asks, which for me is the million-dollar question right now.

'I have no idea. Carry on, I guess? I don't really have much of a choice in the matter.'

'You can't, Ben, no matter what anyone else thinks.'

I shrug. 'What choice do I have?'

We both lapse into an uncomfortable silence. Me because I've said everything I can or want to, and Alice because she's obviously pondering all that I've just told her.

'Is there any part of being a doctor you *do* like?' Alice asks. Which is a very good question.

'Yeah, of course. I do like helping people,' I tell her. 'It makes you feel good to make someone else's day a bit better.'

Alice nods. 'Well, you certainly do a good job of making me feel better when we sit here like this.'

'Do I?'

'Absolutely! And like you said yourself, you're good at talking to people.'

I nod. 'Yes. And I really like doing it.'

'Well . . . then maybe you should be in a job that lets you do that instead? You need to find one where you can do all that, but without all the other doctory stuff you don't like.'

'But what about my parents?'

'They can't run your life for you, Ben,' Alice says, a bit of sharpness to her voice. 'I know you don't want to let them down, but it's *your* life. *Your* job. I couldn't imagine doing something I *hate*. I love my job. The salon has kept me going these past couple of years. You need to find a job you love as well. It really helps.' She pauses for a moment. 'And besides . . . if you do quit, and find something else that you actually like doing, won't that make any unpleasantness with your parents a bit easier to bear?'

'A lot easier,' I confess.

I've never really thought of it like that. I've been so concerned about disappointing them, and Harry's memory, that it never occurred to me I could bear the brunt of all of that – if I was happier in the job I'm doing.

And do you know what? I *could* bear it. I absolutely *could*.

For the last two months all I've done is wallow in self-pity and fear, wandering aimlessly about, and fretting over ending my career as a doctor because of the effect it would have on my relationship with my mother and father. This is the first time it's occurred to me that whatever their reaction, it can't be worse than carrying on in a job I so obviously hate.

There are aspects of being a doctor I *do* actually like, and I *could* have those in a different job.

I always thought the only role for me was in healthcare, thanks to my family. My brain couldn't really comprehend the idea of doing anything else.

But here is my annual friend, Alice, helping me to do just that.

Christ, I'm glad she turned up here today . . .

'But what job is that?' I ask her, hoping that she'll just tell me what I should be doing. It would solve a lot of problems, and save me the trouble.

I'm fairly disappointed when she just shrugs and says, 'No idea. That's something you'll have to figure out on your own.' She pauses and swallows. 'But I'll tell you what Joe told me when I was trying to decide whether to train as a stylist . . .'

'What did he say?'

'He told me that I should always follow my own path. Do whatever feels right for me. Not for anybody else. Not even him. And he was *right*.'

I nod slowly. 'Sensible chap, your husband.'

Alice smiles, but it's a smile wreathed with tears. 'Yes, he was. I never had to worry about making the wrong decisions around Joe. He had a way of looking at everything from all angles. And he could be a lot more objective than me.' Her lip trembles a little. 'I haven't . . . haven't been able to make decisions anywhere near as easily since he's been gone. He was my rock, you know?'

I nod in understanding – though that's not the kind of relationship I had with Harry.

Would he agree with my decision to potentially quit medicine? Or would he be as ashamed as my mother thinks he would? I honestly don't know. He was as in love with the field of medicine as my mother and father are. I'm not sure I would get his approval to move on, any more than I'd get theirs.

But he would *understand*, I think. After a while. And I'm *fairly* sure he would say something to set me on a different path, the same way Alice has. But I'm only *fairly* sure about that, to be honest. Not 100 per cent.

'And I miss his opinions so much,' Alice continues. 'I could really do with his help right now.'

This piques my interest. 'Why's that? Do you have something you need to decide on? And can . . . can I help with it at all?'

Alice takes a deep breath and looks me in the eyes. Her expression tells me that she would like nothing more than for her husband to be in front of her, rather than me. But that's fine. I would still want Harry here instead as well. Though I really don't know for certain what he'd tell me to do . . .

But.

Neither of them is here, so we'll just have to muddle through together as best we can.

'Maybe,' Alice tells me. 'At least I can fill you in, and you can tell me what you think.'

Alice

I can't really sympathise that much with Ben's problems at work, because mine has been going from strength to strength in the past year.

I'm not totally sure why, but it must have something to do with the fact that when I'm at work I'm not thinking about Joe. Not so much, anyway. It's a little hard for even me to cry my eyes out when I'm trimming bangs or putting in foils.

I've been coming in early and staying late, because being at the salon is so, so much better than sitting in that house on my own. It's constantly busy and noisy at work – and that's good, because it drowns everything else out.

And all the girls have stopped trying to talk to me about Joe . . . which I'm very grateful for. It took a while for them to read my body language whenever one of them brought him up, but eventually it happened, and they stopped, so I don't have to cope with it anymore.

I've always considered myself to be a good stylist, but in this past year it feels like I've stepped my game up to another level. There's an urgency, and an obsessive quality to the way I work now. I've never been this intensely concerned with getting a cut just right before. To the point that if I'm not 100 per cent happy with the way I've finished someone, I'll fret about it for days, until the next challenging request walks through the door.

Look – I recognise this is possibly not the *healthiest* thing in the world, but I don't have another choice. At least my focus on anything *but* my grief is having some positive effects. Much better than sitting at home and wallowing.

Besides, Joe would be proud of me.

He'd also be very concerned about the bags under my eyes and the weight I've lost. He'd be demanding I get a good night's sleep and eat a large meal. But he's not here to do that, and I certainly wouldn't listen to anybody else's advice right now.

My grief, my choices.

. . . only here I am, sat with the one person I think I *would* listen to about things like my diet and my general well-being, but he hasn't mentioned either as yet. He really doesn't want to be a doctor, I guess.

'I've been offered a new job,' I tell Ben, fiddling with a strand of my hair as I do so. Joe pointed out that nervous tic of mine many years ago. I managed to stop doing it for a long time, but it's come back now.

'That's great!' Ben says, and God bless him, he doesn't for one moment look jealous. Given what's happening to him, I could understand it completely if he did. But no. This really is a very decent young man.

I shake my head. 'I'm not so sure that it is,' I tell him, and proceed to fill him in on the details.

'That's not what Taylor Swift looks like!' I hear screeched from across the salon floor.

Oh *God.* I knew this was going to happen.

The second she walked in I knew she was going to be trouble.

I should have taken over from Stacey. Right at the point the seat creaked ominously when the woman sat in it.

We get a lot of people in who want to look like a celebrity. And Taylor is a popular one, for that ever so cute long bob with the swept fringe.

But Taylor is also stick thin. This woman is . . . um . . . unfortunately *not.*

Stacey's actually done a relatively good job of trying to recreate Miss Swift's hairstyle on this person, but the considerable size difference between them is a mountain that's quite impossible to climb, I'm afraid.

Best I go over there and smooth things over, I think.

'Stacey! Could you go and check that I've booked Mrs Kelsey in properly on the computer? You know what she's like if we don't get everything exactly the way she likes it. I'll take over here.'

Stacey gives me a look of supreme gratitude, and is gone in a nano-second.

'Good morning!' I say to the customer's disgruntled face as I look at her in the mirror.

'I want to look like Taylor Swift,' she says in a disgusted voice.

And I want world peace, boobs that stayed where they were when I was twenty, and my husband back.

'And you will!' I reply, with a bright smile. 'I just need to spend a little more time on a couple of areas that Stacey has started, and you'll be done!'

She harrumphs at this – but allows me to get to work, with a surly expression stuck on her face.

The 'work' consists of slightly trimming a few bits here and there that probably didn't need it, along with some outrageous flattery. It's amazing what throwing some compliments a person's way will do for their mood and general demeanour.

By the time I'm done about half an hour later, the woman is beaming at me, thinking that I've now transformed her into Taylor's twin sister. Which I'm very pleased about.

I get the impression that this lady has had quite enough in her life of people telling her what she can't be. Maybe even looking just a little bit more like her hero will set her on a better path.

I've tried my hardest to help her with that, and I think it's worked out quite well.

I *love* this job. I really do.

When she gets up and leaves, both I and the chair she's been sitting on breathe a sigh of relief.

'Nicely done,' a voice says from behind me.

I spin around to see that my boss, Paul, is standing there with a smile on his face.

'Hi Paul. I didn't see you come in,' I tell him.

'No. You were clearly very busy making that woman feel better about herself.'

My face flushes red. 'Just getting Stacey out of a sticky spot. What brings you into the salon today?' I ask, by way of changing the subject.

'Well, Alice, I have a proposition for you,' Paul says, in that gentle Australian accent of his, as I set about tidying up the station I've been working at.

Paul DiMarco and his wife, Stephanie, have four salons across the UK, all dotted around the south-east.

Paul moved from Sydney to London twenty-five years ago to work for Vidal Sassoon, and met Stephanie on the job. From there, the two of them struck out on their own, buying their first boutique in Fulham, and watching their business grow slowly into the four-salon concern they have now.

. . . or should I say *five* salons, because they are about to open another one, and this is where my life gets very complicated very fast.

'I want you to work in the new salon in Sydney,' he says to me, excitement in his eyes. 'Word has got back about your work, and what you've been doing here has been incredibly impressive, Alice. I want that kind of dedication in the new place.'

'You want me to go to *Australia*?' I say, completely incredulous.

'Yes! As the deputy manager at DiMarco's in Sydney. Beata is a wonderful manager, but she's new to the job and needs a strong second-in-command. I think that's *you*. You'd be a huge asset to us out there. And it'd be no problem getting you a sponsorship visa.'

'You want me to go to *Sydney*. In *Australia*?' I repeat, still scarcely able to believe what I'm hearing.

'Absolutely! You're the ideal candidate for the job. You're dedicated, you're smart, you don't have—I mean, you'd make the transition well, I'm sure . . .'

Aah.

There it is . . .

There's another part to the equation in this job offer that isn't quite so positive. It's not one that he's voicing openly, but I know it's there . . .

I can move to Sydney because I have *no ties back here*. No husband or children to worry about.

All of this is quite literally only happening because my Joe is dead.

'Oh God.' Ben breathes hard as I say this.

'You're not going to tell me I'm wrong, are you?' I ask him.

'No. I'm not. You're probably right.' He thinks for a second. 'But you should take the job, Alice.'

'Should I? Should I really?'

Don't misunderstand – I'm not asking for Ben's permission here, but he knows what it's like to have your whole life warped through the lens of loss. It forces you to double-check every decision you make, because they all come from a negative place. How do I know what's right for me?

'You think you shouldn't?' Ben asks, a little surprised.

I shake my head. 'I don't know. It's such an upheaval. And it's such a long way away. And—'

I swallow hard.

Just say it. Just bloody say it, *and get to the bottom of what's really going on here.*

81

'Joe always wanted to go to Australia.' I can taste the bitterness in my mouth. 'He bought the Lonely Planet guide, spent hours online looking up the best places to visit. He even bought . . . a hat.'

'A hat?'

'Yeah. A big bushman's hat. Made from kangaroo. He used to wear it on sunny days here. Looked ridiculous.' I let out a short gasp of laughter. 'But he loved it.'

'He never got the chance to go, I guess?'

'No. We were both too busy all the time. And I . . . I never really had the same enthusiasm for it, like he did. It seems like a nice place, but I don't do long plane journeys very well.'

Ben puffs his cheeks out and blows out the air. 'So it must've been pretty strange to get offered a job there?'

I nod quickly. 'Yes. Especially when it's a very good one.'

I should be happy and excited. But I'm not. I'm sad and confused.

. . . and crying, of course. I'm doing that now too.

'It feels so *wrong*,' I say, blinking away the salty water. 'I can't . . . can't . . .'

'Go without him?'

'Yes!' I wail, and pull out the legendary packet of tissues from my jeans pocket, dabbing my eyes.

'Bloody hell. That *is* a tough one.'

'It is, isn't it?' I reply, with some force.

Every other person I've spoken to about this has told me what an excellent opportunity it is for me, and that I should, of course, take it. Triple the salary, way more responsibility, a chance to live in one of the best cities on the planet . . .

What also goes as unspoken with them, as it did when Paul offered me the job, is that I've got nothing holding me back, have I? Why would I want to stay here, when a new life and a fresh start awaits me on the other side of the world?

Like all of that's a *good thing*.

Like I wouldn't much rather work a dead-end job and barely make ends meet, if I *only still had my husband next to me when I fall asleep at night*.

'What would you do?' I ask Ben.

'I don't know,' he replies, apologetically. 'It's not easy. I can see the benefits of it, but at the same time . . .'

'Leaving him feels like the worst decision in the world,' I reply, in a voice that's tinged with some relief.

Ben nods, and gives me a sympathetic look.

I knew he'd understand. I *knew* he'd get it. I knew he wouldn't just sit there and tell me what a wonderful opportunity it is.

I'm looking for a way to back out of this whole stupid idea, and Ben Fielding just might be the man to give me one.

But then Ben Fielding says the absolute worst thing possible. 'You said you always valued Joe's opinion, so what would he tell you to do?'

No one else has asked me that. No one else has brought Joe up.

Because he's *dead*, isn't he? And why would anyone want to talk about the dead?

It's unpleasant.

Another tissue is most definitely needed.

'I don't think he'd tell me to do anything,' I reply. 'He wasn't that kind of man.'

Ben gives me a slightly withering look. 'You know what I mean, Alice. What would he suggest you do?'

'I don't know,' I snap.

'I think you do,' he presses. 'I think you knew your husband more than well enough to know what his advice would be.'

God damn it.

'I think you could actually play a lengthy conversation with him about it in your head, if you wanted to,' Ben continues. 'In fact, that's exactly what you've done, isn't it?'

'No.'

Yes.

Yes, yes, yes. *Absolutely.*

And every time, Joe gives me the same damned answer.

But he's dead. And it's not really him I'm talking to, or a real conversation I'm having, so I don't have to listen to him, do I?

Do I?

'Yes, you have. Because I do the exact same thing with Harry,' Ben tells me. 'With nearly every bloody decision I make.'

'Did he tell you to quit your job?'

Oh, for God's sake, Alice. None of this is Ben's fault. Just because you don't like the way this conversation is going . . .

I'd be happier if Ben's face flashed with irritation at this point. The fact he just looks a bit forlorn in response to my barbed comment makes me feel ten times worse.

'Sorry, that wasn't very nice of me,' I say.

'No . . . but I understand. You're trying to make a difficult decision, and you know what Joe would tell you to do. You don't like it, but you know it.'

I sigh. He's right, of course.

Joe would 100 per cent tell me to go to Australia. He'd look at me with one of those sensible expressions on his face, and tell me that I'd be passing up the opportunity of a lifetime if I didn't go, and that it might be good for my mental health to go and live somewhere far away from the place where I lost him.

I look at Joe's grave, and can picture him standing on top of it, looking at me ever so sensibly, knowing he's right. 'He'd tell me to go,' I say quietly.

'Then I guess you have your answer,' Ben says.

I look at him. 'But what about you? What do *you* think?'

'I'd go. I'd definitely go. Because you have a *direction*, Alice. Don't underestimate how important that is . . . especially to a person who's lost someone they love. You should be proud of the fact you've been offered the job, and you should take it.'

'But . . . But . . .'

'But what?'

My lip trembles. 'I can't leave him, Ben! I can't go across to the other side of the world and leave him' – I stab a finger at the grave – '*here* all on his own. He doesn't have any family left, apart from me! His parents are gone, he doesn't have any siblings. It's just me!'

Ben looks at me for a second, and then leans forward, covering my hand in his. He looks into my eyes. 'He's not there, Alice. Wherever he is now, I know it's not *over there*. And you will carry him with you. Trust me on that.' His face goes a little ashen. 'Sometimes you won't want to, but he'll be with you anyway, you can count on it.'

I take a moment to let this sink in. 'I don't want any of this,' I then say in a half-whisper, my head bowed.

Ben sits back again. 'No. Neither do I. But you should go anyway, Alice. You really should.' He looks at me gravely. 'Take it as a challenge.'

'A challenge?'

'Yes. From me to you. Like last year, when you suggested we meet up like this again. And this year I challenge *you* to go to Sydney, Alice! I challenge you to go, and have the best time you possibly can in Australia.'

I smirk. 'Sounds like you're *telling* me to go, Ben.'

He nods. 'Yes, I am. Because it really will be the best thing for you.'

I know he's right. I know Joe's right. I know every other bugger is right.

But it's still *wrong*.

Because he *is* over there.

And I'm not sure if I can let go.

Or even if I *want* to.

Challenge or not.

Ben

She's still not convinced.

But I understand how she feels. Could I say I'd be any different if I was offered a job on the other side of the world? I doubt I'd be able to make my stupid annual pilgrimage here if I took it.

But Alice is going to have to make the decision for herself. I can't do it for her. I've challenged her to take the plunge, but I can't throw her in.

I'm quite envious, to be honest. Her ship is pointed straight at an island full of kangaroos and Vegemite.

Sadly, mine is floundering around in deep water.

I think maybe I want to go home now. This conversation feels like it's run its course.

And I'm *angry*.

I can feel it bubbling up inside me.

I'm angry at *Alice* – for reasons which I have trouble understanding, or accepting.

It's part envy, I think. When someone tells you how well their job is going, when you're desperate to quit yours, it's bound to have some sort of an effect.

But there's something else going on too.

If Alice does bugger off to Sydney, I doubt I'll ever see her again.

Crazy, huh?

I've met this woman three times in my life, but I feel a deep sense of loss at the idea of not meeting up with her again in twelve months.

Another person gone.

. . . stop it. Just get up and get out of here. Get on with your life. Get on with looking for a different job.

Something where I can help people – but not on a hospital ward.

Does such a thing even exist?

Alice looks a little surprised as I rise to my feet.

'Are you okay?' she asks.

'Yes,' I lie. 'I'm just very uncomfortable in this costume, and could do with getting out of it.'

Her look of surprise grows larger for a moment, before I see something in her eyes that tells me she knows the real reason why I've climbed to my feet. 'Oh, I see,' she says, in a rather dispirited voice. 'Time to leave, then?'

'Yeah. Sorry. I really am uncomfortable, and I – need to get back.'

She knows that's not true, because I've already told her that I'm not going to work today. The only thing I have to get back for is my Nintendo. Link won't find Zelda all on his own, will he?

Alice also stands up.

'Are you going to stay for a little while longer?' I ask.

She nods. 'Yes. I think I need a little time on my own with – with my thoughts.'

She was going to say 'Joe'. The fact she stopped herself might be a good sign.

'Well, it was lovely to see you again,' I tell her. 'And I hope that you can reach a decision for yourself as soon as possible.'

She smiles at this, but it's a distant one. 'And I hope you can find a job that you love, Ben,' she tells me.

I roll my eyes in a dejected fashion. 'Got to pluck up the courage to quit the one I have first.' I force a smile on to my face. 'It was very nice to meet you,' I tell Alice. 'And I hope that you'll be very happy in Sydney – if you do decide to go.'

'Thank you.' She cocks her head to one side. 'And who knows? Maybe we see each other again here next year?'

'Maybe,' I reply, not really believing it.

I awkwardly raise my arms to give Alice a hug, and she does much the same with an equally awkward chuckle.

We embrace for the briefest of moments. Like work colleagues who will never see each other again, after the company has laid them both off.

'Bye, bye,' I say, and immediately begin to walk off towards the car park.

'Wait!' Alice says loudly, forcing me to turn back.

She looks at me for a second. 'If you're challenging me to go to Australia, then I'm challenging you too, Ben Fielding.'

'To do what?'

'Quit that bloody job. To hell with what your parents want or think! Quit that job, and find one you *do* want. One that you love! If I'm going to accept your challenge and go to the other side of the world, then you can accept mine back, okay?'

I stare at her, a little dumbfounded at the passion in her voice.

I nod. 'Okay . . . I'll . . . I'll think about it,' I eventually say, a little lamely.

Because it would be the hardest challenge in the world to complete, wouldn't it? Even though it really shouldn't be.

'Do more than *think*, Ben,' Alice replies. 'That's something we both have to do.'

I nod again, now feeling more desperate to get out of here and take these stockings off than ever.

When I turn again to go to the car park, I don't look back, because it's painful to do so.

It always is, but this time it's not just because I'm leaving my brother behind.

Alice

I watch Ben Fielding disappear through the church gates at the rear of the graveyard, before turning my attention back to the only other man in my life.

Maybe I *will* go to Australia.

Because I'm not a fool.

And because Ben's right – Joe *is* always with me. From the moment I wake up to the moment I fall into a fitful sleep.

But he's also *here*, isn't he? Under the ground.

As if there are *two* Joes in this world.

Which is quite an achievement, given that he's been dead for nearly three years.

I go and stand at the end of my husband's grave and take a deep breath.

'Would it be okay?' I ask him. 'I don't think you'd ever tell me not to follow the path that's laid out in front of me, if it's the right one. But then I don't know how you'd feel about me going so far away?'

I sound crazy. I know I do.

'Only, I don't think I'd be able to visit you,' I continue. 'It's a long way away, after all . . . But then, you'd still tell me to go, wouldn't you?' I sigh heavily. 'But it'd be *hard*, Joe. Hard to go there without you.'

I wipe a tear off my cheek.

'If I do go, I'll come back before I leave, I promise.'

Good grief.

Is it the right decision to make?

Joe would say it is, and Ben Fielding has agreed. He challenged me to do it, after all.

And maybe you can give yourself permission, now you've talked it out with your friend?

Yes. Maybe.

I can't tell if the abstract pain I feel in my chest at that moment is because I might not stand here at my husband's grave many more times – or if it's because I might never see that kind young man again.

Can I do this?

Can I leave?

Can I start another life, when all I really want is the old one back?

Year Four

SPAM AND FEATHERS

Ben

One of the worst things about Harry Fielding was that you could never really tell if his tomfoolery would end with you embarrassed and humiliated . . . or laughing and delighted. His practical jokes ran the whole gamut. This is because he never had a filter, or a part of his brain that would tell him he was going too far. It was always gag first, apologies later.

It's testament to the man's charm that he managed to get away with some truly horrendous things, without seeming to lose any friends over it. Of course, as family, I had no real chance of getting away from him, even if I could.

Which is something he knew damn well . . . hence all of these stupid costumes, and a ritual that's become part annual pilgrimage of shame, and part opportunity to celebrate my brother's very unique sense of humour.

It's also a chance for me to remember him. Really, really, *remember* him.

As the years go by, I find it harder and harder to picture his face. Usually I'm most successful at this whenever I recall the practical jokes he would pull on me. Like the time he systematically dismantled my mountain bike, and hung every one of its constituent parts from the beech tree in our garden. It looked like someone had violently dragged the poor tree through the bicycle aisle in Halfords.

I can see his face in my mind very clearly, as he capered around the bottom of the beech, delighting in the look of absolute red-hot fury on my face.

I loved that bloody bike.

The fact that Harry then spent the whole of the weekend putting the bike back together himself in the garage probably says a lot about him. He would put himself out as much as you for the sake of the gag.

The super-annoying thing was that when he handed it back to me, it no longer had the irritating squeaking sound that constantly came from under the saddle when I rode it.

And that was Harry Fielding's superpower. No matter how bad something was, he could fix it. Even if he was the one responsible for the damage, he could always repair it.

It's what made him such a good surgeon.

It was also what made it so incredibly hard to watch him fade. The frustration and pain writ large across his face because he just couldn't find a way to fix *himself*.

That face isn't one I want to see in my mind's eye. That pale, drawn face. It didn't really look like my brother at all.

No. My brother was the nineteen-year-old kid, dancing around the beech tree singing 'I Wish It Could Be Bike-mas Every Day', while I stood trembling with apoplectic boyhood rage.

I think one of the reasons I continue to put myself through this ghastly annual ritual is that I know exactly what he'd look like if he saw me dressed in one of these hideous fancy dress costumes. I can see it as plain as day, and that feels like a *gift* – especially as the years grow longer, and my face ages further and further away from the way it looked when he was alive.

And this year, my brother has taken some pity on me. The costume is nowhere near as horrendous as the sexy nurse outfit from twelve months ago.

Okay, walking around dressed as Mario isn't exactly what you'd call being *sensibly dressed*, but at least it's an easy costume to get on and walk around in.

A set of red dungarees, a blue long-sleeved shirt and a red cap is not the worst thing ever, is it?

Yes, yes. I'll put the bloody moustache on too. Calm yourself.

Harry and I used to love playing *Mario Kart* together on the Nintendo when we were kids. He was always Mario, naturally. I tried to play as Luigi as much as I could, but he'd make me play as Princess Peach every now and again, for his own vast amusement.

But all in all, I could be a lot less happy about Harry's costume choice for this year.

Which means I can park in the main car park of the church and amble my way up to his grave without feeling quite the same level of misery I did last year.

I'm also forced to reflect that my mood is probably a lot better this time around, because I am very definitely out of the hole I'd dug myself into twelve months ago.

I don't know whether Harry intended these annual visits to be a way for me to reflect on my life at the same time every year, but it's certainly become an aspect of the whole thing for me.

When I think back to how miserable I was, it makes me shudder.

I hated my job, I was lonely, feeling like I'd let everybody down, and utterly aimless.

Probably the worst I'd ever felt.

. . .

. . . *second* worst. Right behind watching Harry fade, and seeing that cheeky smile disappear.

Yeah, okay, bro. Let's not do that, eh? Remember the bike tree, not the hospital bed in the lounge.

I nod once to myself, and walk through the cemetery gates.

As I do, I start to whistle the *Super Mario* theme – which somewhat disconcerts the two people stood in front of a grave off to my right. This kills the whistling straight away. It's bad enough I'm dressed like this in a cemetery, I don't think I need to make it even worse by whistling a jaunty theme tune to myself.

I try to ignore the looks of disgust the couple are no doubt giving me, and hurry up the path to the enormous oak tree that Harry's grave lies under.

And friends and neighbours, would you look at that!

The good and kindly people here at Popping Church have only gone and put a bench in right under the tree! No more sitting on the ground for me while I talk with—

Alice.

There's no sign of Alice.

But why would there be?

She went to Australia, didn't she?

Good.

Good for her.

I start whistling 'Waltzing Matilda' as I turn to Harry's grave.

The time on my watch slowly ticks towards midday, and I spend those few minutes continuing to whistle under my breath and standing in front of my brother, fiddling with the moustache.

'Thanks awfully for not making me dress up like a sexy witch or something, Harry,' I tell him. 'Given that there are actually people in the cemetery today, I don't think it would have been a good idea for me to turn up in a witch's hat and a thong.'

Harry doesn't reply. He's probably upset that I'm not feeling anywhere near as embarrassed as I normally do.

'Well, I'm only wearing the costume you picked out for me,' I say to him out loud. 'It's not my fault I'm in a good enough mood for it not to have much of an effect on me this year.'

I look at my watch again. 'Oh, would you look at that, it's time for "We Are the Champions".'

I adjust my red dungarees and start the now time-honoured tradition of standing like a berk for nearly three minutes. Only this time around I hum the song under my breath, and bob about a bit on my heels.

. . . which I'm sure Harry would be happy to see.

In my mind's eye, I can picture him up on a cloud somewhere, staring down at me and taking stock of where his little brother is this year.

I wonder if the same fanciful notion entered his head when he was stipulating what I had to do on this day each year in his will?

Again, I have to stop myself from thinking about that. Because it's much easier for me to picture my brother wasting away in that bed and writing his will than it is to picture him up there on some cloud, looking down at me with a thoughtful expression on his face.

When we are done with the song, I take the hat off and tip it towards my brother's gravestone. 'Okay, big brother, that's me just about finished for another year of this craziness,' I tell him. 'I'll see you sometime soon no doubt, though – in my regular street clothes. I can come and see you more now because of the new job, you see. I'm closer to home.'

Harry doesn't comment on this, either, which I'm not surprised about. I think he'd approve of the changes that have happened in my life this year – but there might also be a small part of him that is disappointed in my career change.

Like my mother and father are.

Nope.

Not going down that road today. I have things to do, places to be and people to meet.

'See you, Harry,' I say to my brother, and start to walk back down the path to the car park, making my way out of the cemetery, as I once again whistle 'Waltzing Matilda' – quite loudly this time, because the grieving couple I noticed before are now nowhere to be seen.

In fact, I even start singing the actual song, as I stride back to my car.

'Waltzing Matilda, waltzing Matilda, won't you come waltzing Matilda with me . . .'

I reach the crescendo of the song's jaunty verse as I throw open the door to my car, and rip the moustache off my top lip. *'And he sang as he sat, right down by a billabong, won't you come waltzing Matilda with me!'*

'Those aren't the actual lyrics, Ben, but nice try.'

My entire body swivels around to see Alice Everley, stood by what is clearly a hire car, with her arms folded, and a big smile on her face.

Alice

There was no real chance of me *not* coming.

Because the gravity was far too much, you see.

The *weight* was far too heavy.

I tried to resist it for the longest time.

96

For a while, it was okay. The first few months anyway. It's a little hard to feel *the pull* when you're working hard at establishing yourself in a new country.

My feet didn't really hit the ground for weeks when I got to Australia. What with getting up to speed in the new salon, and finding a more permanent apartment to rent, and . . . getting to know everyone.

I was determined to think *positive* about my new future – which is easier when you've moved to a country where the sun doesn't hide 90 per cent of the time, and people look happy just to be alive.

And a brand-new *shiny* salon to work in could mean a brand-new *shiny* Alice Everley, couldn't it? Of course it could!

Or at least, that's the way I tried to think initially . . .

But *the pull* is always there. Inexorably sat somewhere in the back of your mind, just biding its time before it starts to put more pressure on.

And that pressure really began to build about two months ago. On our anniversary.

I started to feel him in the apartment for the first time.

An apartment he never stepped anywhere near. And I had no frame of reference for his presence in – but he was there, nonetheless.

I began to picture what he'd say and do, if he could see where I now lived.

He'd surely have commented favourably on the view of Sydney Harbour. And commented equally unfavourably on the price I was paying for it a month.

Then I would have told him about how much my monthly salary is, and that might have quelled his doubts somewhat. He'd still have a nosebleed about the price, though. I think Joe could have been a multimillionaire and he still wouldn't have lost his careful ways with money. It was one of the things that made me feel most secure when I was with him.

And once I'd started seeing Joe again around my apartment, I started to think more about the *other* Joe. The one I'd left behind in the UK. And I'd start looking at the calendar more and more, realising how close it was getting to the anniversary of the last time I'd been to see him.

And that was that.

I was on Flight Centre and looking for the cheapest way back here before I knew it.

Because I really do need to see the *other* Joe. For reasons I still cannot fully comprehend, no matter how many hours I spend thinking about it.

And it's not only him I have to see.

If I time things right, I'll get to see Ben Fielding as well.

I'm only here for a week, though.

I'll visit the few people I left behind, and the husband I wish I never had to, and then I'll get back on the plane and return to Sydney, because I now have responsibilities there. Paul was kind enough to let me take the time off to come here. I don't want to let him down by being away for too long. He is, after all, the person that helped me get that view of the harbour.

Besides, spending too long in this country wouldn't be good for me. I can recognise that now I'm back again. Because it's *raw* here, isn't it? The closer I am to where my old life died, the more the memories weigh on me.

I even had to drive past the hospital where the old Alice ceased to exist. And for a moment, I wanted to turn into the car park, get out of this rental car and storm into the hospital, demanding to speak to someone who can give some actual answers about what happened to my Joe. How could he die like that? How could it happen to a man that young and healthy?

It's not the first time I've had that morbid fantasy, but it is the closest I've been to turning it into a reality.

But what would it accomplish? Absolutely nothing. Nothing at all. No one has answers for me in there, because there are *none to be had*. These things happen. People die.

Sad, sad story . . . but do try to move on, won't you? Way past time you come to terms with it properly, woman.

Shiny new salon, shiny new Alice, remember?

The cold, hard reality of what happened doesn't stop the dreams, though.

They never leave me. Because in dreams things can be different, can't they? For better or for worse.

Speaking of leaving, I should be leaving this rental car, and getting on with my ten-thousand-mile pilgrimage. Given that I've paid out several thousand dollars, and spent twenty-four hours of discomfort flying here, you'd think I'd be able to just get out and go up there, wouldn't you?

But I couldn't.

Not for quite some time.

No.

For a good ten minutes, I sat in the driver's seat, my hands white as they clenched the steering wheel.

Because the old Alice isn't really dead. She's right here inside me – and I'm not sure she can cope with another visit to Joe's grave. That's where the gravity is at its strongest. And where I'm at my weakest.

I don't have to do it.

I could just fire up the engine, drive out of here, go past that hospital without looking at it and get on with my life. My *shiny new* life.

My new life where I don't have to worry about people asking me about my poor dead husband. The girls at the new salon know nothing about it, and I have to confess, almost every day the feeling of relief is palpable that I don't have to engage with them about it.

I don't need to do this. Nobody will call me out for it. Nobody's going to criticise me for not going up there. Nobody's going to make me feel guilty for coming all this way and bottling it at the last minute.

Get out of the car.

Get out of the car and go and see him, because everything else is background. *Everything else is for a person that's moved on from her sad, sad story. And we both know you bloody* haven't.

I look up past the roof of the car, to somewhere I can neither see nor feel.

I could do with a sign, if you're up there, mate.

An angel or two, to swoop down and bear me up to the church on wings of heavenly support.

'*Waltzing Matilda, waltzing Matilda, won't you come waltzing Matilda with me . . .*'

Or, you know, Super Mario singing the unofficial theme tune of Australia.

Either is fine.

I climb out of the car just as Super Mario opens his, mangling the words of that most famous of bush ditties. My new Australian acquaintances probably wouldn't approve.

'Those aren't the actual lyrics, Ben, but nice try,' I say, a smile breaking out on my face for the first time since I touched down at Heathrow.

Super Mario Ben swings back around, and when he sees me an equally broad grin spreads across his face, and he punches the air. 'Wa-hoo!' he exclaims, and starts to make his way over.

The hug I give him feels absolutely and completely natural. I've only ever met this lad four times in my entire life, but I feel like I know him better than some others I've known for many years. I doubt there's another person on this planet who I'd hug like this.

From the way he hugs me back, it feels like he thinks exactly the same.

'It's so good to see you!' Ben exclaims, and I'm shocked by the change in him since the last time we spoke. Shocked and delighted.

'You too!' I reply, surprised by how animated I am as well. I'm actually excited to see Ben. We have a lot to catch up on, after all.

'It was lucky you saw me, I was almost on my way home,' he says.

'Yeah. I was . . . kinda stuck there in the car for a few moments, trying to decide what to do. It's a good job you're here, otherwise I might have . . . left without, you know . . .'

Ben nods. 'Yeah, I get that. Without this silly bloody ritual, I might struggle with it a bit too.'

'Super Mario this year, then?' I say, by way of deliberately changing the subject.

Ben looks down at himself. 'I actually don't mind it. I don't mind it at all.'

I laugh at this. 'No. I can see that. You're in a much better frame of mind than you were last year, it appears.'

'Oh yes. I most definitely am.'

'What's the reason?'

He thinks for a moment. 'Spam, Alice. A tin of Spam. The best tin of Spam in the whole wide world.'

Ben

It's late.

About eight o'clock at night, and I'm *starving*.

I haven't eaten a damn thing since lunchtime, and even that was a hastily demolished chicken Caesar wrap, which I wolfed

101

down before the start of the meeting with the council about the new shelter in the city centre – the first project I've been given lead on since I started in the job.

'What job?' Alice asks me, interrupting my flow for a second.

'Ahh . . . I'll get to that, don't worry,' I tell her. 'But this is more important.'

'There's something more important than you changing jobs?'

'Yes, unbelievably. There is.'

So I'm starving hungry, and in desperate need of something to eat – only I'm also having to very carefully watch the pennies at the moment, given how junior my new role is, so fast food is out.

I'll have to pop to Tesco Express to pick up a few things.

I don't know what yet – but they always have a load of stuff on a shelf with knocked-down prices, so I should be able to pick something up there.

God is clearly with me that evening, because there are three things on that shelf that go together incredibly well: white bread, Branston pickle and Spam. You need butter as well obviously, but I've got some Clover at home, so we're good on that front.

There is a Spam and pickle sandwich in my very near future. And that is a future that we should all be able to look forward to and relish!

'Spam is *awful*, Ben,' Alice cuts in.

I am aghast. 'How can you say such a thing?'

'I have tastebuds. Carry on with the story, though.'

I gather up the glorious Spam, pickle and white bread with no small degree of eagerness. I also gather up a big fat packet of porridge because I need some of that too, for my breakfast.

Over at the till, I start to drool a little thinking about my Spam, as the girl behind the till pops everything through the checkout.

With my eagerness at fever pitch, I throw my shopping into a carrier bag and leave Tesco Express with the taste of the processed meat and pickle already in my mouth.

'Yuck.'

Ignoring the disembodied voice coming from somewhere in my future, I hurry across the road, swinging my bag merrily as I do so – and this is where disaster strikes!

Unbeknownst to me, my Tesco shopping bag has a rip in it, and it's just as I'm crossing the road that my glorious, wonderful, much needed tin of Spam flies out!

'Argh!' I wail, as I watch it describe an arc away from me, back into the centre of the road, before it rolls even further away.

'Hang on a bloody minute,' Alice says. 'Spam comes in a square tin, I know that much. How did it roll?'

I am aghast to see the tin of Spam do this . . . in apparent contravention of the laws of physics, but I truly feel there might have been a higher power behind it that night – pushing it into just the right position for what happens next.

Not thinking, I stumble back towards the tin of Spam, desperate to retrieve it.

And that is when it happens.

That is when I nearly get run over by a Honda Jazz.

'I'd rather get run over by a Honda Jazz than eat Spam.'

Once again ignoring the strange, Spam-intolerant voice from my future, I throw my arms up and screech in horror as the car squeals to a halt in front of me, squashing my tin of Spam utterly, completely and beyond redemption.

'Oh no. What a *disaster*,' future voice says.

And initially, I agree!

'My Spam!' I wail, completely inconsolable.

'Are you bloody mad?' I hear the voice of an angel call out to me. I look up, and there, standing with her car door cracked and an expression of the utmost rage upon her face, is the reason I am in such a jaunty mood today.

'You met a girl.'

'I did!'

'Who ran over your Spam.'

'She did!'

'Who nearly killed you with a Honda Jazz.'

'Yes!'

'I'm not seeing how an irate stranger who destroys processed food products turns into a love interest, I have to say,' she admits.

'No. Neither did I to start with.'

But then it becomes quite apparent that the destruction of the poor, defenceless tin of Spam has also led to the tyre that hit it being punctured.

Therefore, full of apologies, I help the woman pull her car over to the side of the road, and promise to sit with her while she calls the AA. I did offer to try and change the tyre myself, but the car didn't come with the jack when she bought it a mere four weeks earlier. I'm not sure she's all that grateful for my offer to stay with her, but I insist anyway, because it's now pitch black and who knows what kind of ne'er-do-wells might be out and about at this time of night.

I have to admit my chivalry is somewhat tainted by the fact that I've pretty much fallen head over heels in love with my would-be accidental assassin, and want to maximise the time I can spend with her.

Her name is Katie, and she has blonde hair. And a mole on the side of her neck. And when she's upset or anxious (like she was the night she nearly ran me over), she blinks a lot.

In the forty minutes it takes for the AA man to arrive, she calms down a fair bit, though, and we get to talking.

'To tell you the truth, this delay isn't such a bad thing,' Katie tells me. 'I could have done without the puncture, but you've given me a good excuse not to get to my friend's house too early.'

'You'd rather not go?'

Katie makes a see-sawing gesture with one hand. 'Maxine's lovely, but the drama with André is getting a bit much. I can honestly do without another three hours straight of her complaining about him.'

Katie talks like we've known each other for ages, instead of just a few minutes. I have no idea who Maxine or André are, but the fact Katie chats about them with me so informally makes me feel incredibly good, for some reason.

She also offers me Haribo from the packet she has discovered in her wildly overstuffed glove compartment. I take a few, even though they've never really been a sweet I've enjoyed all that much. I think Katie could offer me just about anything right now and I'd take it.

'I honestly think Maxine only likes me going round there at times like this so I can show her how being single isn't the end of the world,' she tells me.

'It isn't?' I reply, my voice strangely high-pitched.

'Not for me. Not at the moment, anyway.' She stares at the punctured tyre. 'Although I could have done with having someone here for this.'

'Yeah, I'm sure,' I say, trying desperately to lower my voice an octave or two.

A short spell of silence follows as I awkwardly try to think of something to say. It's Katie who breaks it, though.

'Sorry about your Spam,' she says.

'No worries,' I reply. 'I'm sure I can make something when I get home.'

'On your way home from work?'

'Yep.'

'What do you do?'

'I'm a doc—' I start to say, before remembering that I am not one anymore. 'I work for a homelessness charity.' The feeling of pride and happiness that swells my chest as I say this is almost a physical sensation.

Katie smiles broadly. 'That's lovely,' she tells me. 'Have you been doing it long?'

'No. Not long at all. But I'm loving it so far. It feels like I'm in the right place finally.'

Katie beams at this. 'Good for you.'

It *is* good for me, Katie. Thank you. If only the pleased expression currently on your face was the one my mother had when I told her about the new job.

If only . . .

'What do you do?' I ask Katie.

'I'm a teacher. Infant school.'

'Enjoy it?'

'For the most part – when I'm working with the kids, anyway. There's a lot of stuff around the job that gets me down sometimes. Especially when I'm at loggerheads with the head teacher, Simon, over supplies. Which happens more frequently than I'd like. I don't have the kind of personality that likes conflict, you know?'

I nod. 'Indeed I do.'

The way she's willing to offer up this kind of information about herself without being asked is amazing. The first thing I ever got to know about Katie is how open and honest she is as a person, and I doubt there's anything better you could learn about someone when you first meet them. I hope I've made a half-decent first impression too.

We continue chatting like this, and by the time Brian from the AA has arrived, I know Katie's full name (her surname is English), where she lives (agreeably local), what school she works in (a local infants), how much she worries about her friends (a great deal in Maxine's case) and perhaps more telling, how much she worries about what her friends think of her.

And Katie knows a fair amount about me as well. My surname, where I live and how hungry I am for Spam after a long day in my new job. If she's going to be so open with me, the least I can do is reciprocate.

My entire body is shaking as I watch Katie thank Brian the AA man, and open her car door. Because I'm going to ask for her phone number now, and I'm not sure I can survive if she rejects me.

Happily for all concerned she does not.

She does tell me she'd wished we met under different, non-Spam-related circumstances, but I assure her that I will do everything I can to make up for it on our first date.

Which happens a week and a half later, when we meet at a local pub for an after-work drink, which then turns into dinner.

I do not order Spam.

I feel like that's the perfect way to end my happy little story of the way I met my girlfriend, Katie, and look at Alice with a smile on my face.

'Well, I guess you were right,' Alice says, sitting back a little into the new bench under the tree. 'That was more important than a new job.'

'Yep. Although, don't get me wrong, the job is great as well. Your advice was absolutely right. Changing to a job that got me out of the hospital, but still helping people, was the best move I've ever made – other than trying to make a Spam sandwich.'

'Sounds like it's a job more suited to you, definitely.'

'It really is. I work in a team of people who are all a lot more like me, and there's a lot less pressure to perform. Doctors can be . . . pretty competitive. But everyone in our team just wants to help get people off the streets. There's no ego involved. The hours are easier too. And I get to see the outcomes of the help we give to people a lot more, which makes a real difference. I come away from work feeling positive most days, which is something of a miracle for me.'

'A lot has changed for you in the last year,' Alice remarks.

'Absolutely! Although it happened even quicker than that, really. Between quitting the job at the hospital, finding the job with Shelter and meeting Katie, it was only about three and a half months. Katie and I have been together for over six months now, and things have just gone from strength to strength. We moved in together last week.'

'Life comes at you fast, except when it doesn't,' Alice says, staring off into the middle distance.

'That's a strange phrase.'

She looks at me. 'Joe made it up. Back when he got his job with Bremer Marketing, and we moved into our house, all in the space of two weeks. Both things had taken months to get sorted out, and then they all happened at once. A really strange time.'

My mood at this point deflates somewhat. Because what I'm saying is obviously hard for Alice to hear. I know I've felt similar emotions when someone starts talking about the lovely time they had out with their brother last week, or about how wonderful Christmas was with everyone there in the house.

Katie has a brother.

I've yet to meet him.

I don't know how I'll feel when I do.

'Changing jobs would have been more than enough for me to contend with,' I say, trying to swim us into slightly shallower and easier waters. 'It all happened so fast, my feet barely touched the ground.'

Alice sits up a bit straighter again when I say this.

Good.

'What did your parents say?' she asks me, more than a little trepidation in her voice.

I heave a loud sigh. 'About as well as I was expecting, to be honest. My mother teared up a bit, and my father didn't speak to me for a few weeks.'

'Jesus Christ.'

'I was prepared for it. I'm from a family of doctors and surgeons going back generations. As their only son now, they were hoping I'd carry on the family tradition. They were never going to think well of me for making such a change. Being a junior caseworker for a homelessness charity isn't what they wanted for me.'

'For *them*, you mean.' Alice's hand flies to her mouth. 'I'm sorry, Ben. That was out of line.'

I think for a second. 'No. No, it wasn't. It was perfectly *in* line. I've had to accept that my happiness comes in a lowly second place for them, far underneath the importance of *The Fielding Legacy*.'

'I'm sorry to hear that.'

'Me too,' I confess. 'But I know it's worth it. I don't wake up every morning with a feeling of dread in my chest anymore. I only feel that now on the days I'm going to visit them . . .' – I look over at Harry – '. . . or when I'm coming here.'

Because I do still dread it.

Even when I get to dress in a silly costume that isn't all that silly, have a new job and a new girlfriend in my life, and I get to sit and chat with an old friend.

Would I rather have none of it, and my brother back?

Please don't make me answer that.

Please don't ever.

Alice reaches out a hand, and closes it over the one I've got resting on my knee. The level of understanding in the small squeeze she delivers is far greater than it should physically be possible to translate with so simple a gesture.

'He'd be happy for you, Ben,' she tells me. 'I certainly am.'

'Thanks, Alice. And I think you're right. I think he would be . . . even if my parents see my change of career as some sort of sign of weakness, which I know they do.' I think for a moment. 'And he'd definitely be happy I've fallen in love with someone. I remember when I got my first girlfriend. He seemed happier about it than I did.' I slide my hand out from under Alice's, and place it on top. 'Enough about me for the minute. How about you? I accepted your challenge, and it's turned out pretty well for me. I hope the same has happened for you?'

I'm dismayed that instead of answering me straight away, Alice sits in thought for a moment. 'I don't know, Ben, if I'm honest. I'm very conflicted about the whole thing. On the one hand, Sydney is a vibrant, wonderful city that has so much going for it. But on the other hand, Joe isn't there to enjoy it with me. Or help me chase off Jobbers.'

I blink a couple of times. I hope I haven't had some sort of mini stroke, because I didn't understand a word of the last sentence Alice just spoke. 'Help you do what?'

Alice rolls her eyes. 'It's not a squirrel this time, but Joe would have shouted at it anyway.'

Alice

He is Jobbers.

And in many ways, Jobbers represents everything wrong with what I've done.

110

I do not know why he is called Jobbers, and none of the people in the same building as me know, either. But Jobbers he is, and Jobbers he will always be. For some reason that is now completely lost in the mists of time.

Jobbers first entered my life a mere two weeks after I had moved into the small but exquisitely formed second-floor flat I now live in, with a view of Sydney Harbour that really is to die for. Within walking distance of the salon on Military Road, and a plethora of boutique shops and cafés that I could easily spend my entire pay packet in, the flat is a sanctuary of peace, nestled in a quiet suburb of Australia's largest city, which most people would give their right arm to live in.

A sanctuary, that is, until Jobbers turns up for a visit.

'You're going to have to clarify who Jobbers is at this point,' Ben says. 'I've got visions of some sort of Australian version of Gollum, wearing a hat with corks hanging off it.'

Nothing so large or disconcerting, I promise you.

Jobbers is a bird.

More accurately Jobbers is a kookaburra.

And Jobbers is a *nightmare*.

The first time I saw him was when he was peering in through the kitchen window at me, from where he was perched on a nearby tree. Kookaburras are big, fluffy birds with long beaks and big black eyes, so when they stare at you, you well and truly know you've been stared at. Jobbers makes things even worse by having a very visible scar running down the left-hand side of that beak.

I did what any self-respecting human being would do at that point. I banged on the window to scare him into flying away.

Only, Jobbers couldn't give a shit. He just sat there and stared at me for a bit longer, until I was the one who had to fly away. I'd terrified myself with a bit of doomscrolling on Google about all the incredibly dangerous creatures there are that live in Australia, but nobody ever mentioned the sodding kookaburras. I wasn't taking any chances, though.

The next time I saw Jobbers, it was three days later, and he was nicking my morning croissant.

I'd only gone into the flat to get a bit of kitchen towel to mop up the coffee I'd spilt on the patio table, and when I turned back around I saw the little fluffy shit steal the croissant directly off my plate.

He was long gone by the time I'd run back out on to the balcony.

Jobbers' third interruption to my daily schedule came a mere day after that, when he scared the living shit out of me as I was walking down the path leading to my apartment block's main door, after a hard day's work.

Kookaburras usually get louder and louder as they build up to that distinctive laughing call they are so famous for.

Not bloody Jobbers, though. He launches straight into the incredibly loud part instantaneously.

'Jesus Christ!' I screamed as Jobbers assaulted me from the fig tree off to the right of the path.

Then Jobbers, knowing his work here was done, flew off high into the sky, continuing to laugh his stupid birdy head off.

'See you've met Jobbers!' says a voice with a comedically strong Australian accent, from the now opened apartment block door. With my heart hammering in my chest, I look around to see the man at number 4. I think his name is Clive.

'Jobbers?' I repeat, not knowing what the hell he's on about.

'Yeah, Jobbers. He's an odd one, alright. Never seen a kook like 'im before. Little bastard.'

'He stole my croissant yesterday,' I remark, nodding in full agreement as I do.

'Yep. He'll do that. Fella who lived in that apartment before you got his wig snatched off his head.'

'Did he?'

'Yep. Jobbers came down. Divebombed the poor bugger, and nicked the five-hundred-buck toupee off his head. For the next couple of weeks or so, Jobbers would appear at his window with the wig in 'is beak.'

'He didn't.'

'Oh yeah. Bloody oath, love. He's a right one, no mistaking.'

He is indeed a *right one*.

And for the first few months of my new life in Sydney, Jobbers became my nemesis. I have no wig to steal off the top of my head. But I do have (or rather had) in order: a bottle of sun cream, a pair of expensive sunglasses, a pair of *cheap* sunglasses, another croissant, my copy of *Where the Crawdads Sing*, a third croissant – *which I'd placed a plate over* – and the skin off my index finger when I actually saw him coming for once.

'He stole an entire book?' Ben asks, incredulous.

'Oh yes. And he did more than that. He dropped the book back on to my balcony a few days later, with the back thirty or so pages chewed up and ripped – like he'd *read the bloody thing and was returning it with his review*. I thought the book had quite a good ending myself, once I'd bought a new copy and actually got to it.'

'Nothing you could do would scare him off?'

I shake my head. 'Not a damn thing.'

No amount of effort would stop Jobbers from his larceny-ridden interventions. Not shouting, screaming, threatening with a rolling pin, cajoling, pleading, feeding or singing to.

'Singing to?'

'Yeah. Clive at number 4 suggested I sing to Jobbers. Though I think he may have been winding me up. It didn't work, needless to say. Not even a rousing chorus of Taylor Swift shaking things up could get rid of him.'

It finally became so bad that I'd avoid going out on to the balcony completely. That didn't stop Jobbers peering in at me, though, through just about every window.

It was like being stalked by an angry chicken.

Eventually he broke me down so much that one morning I flung the sliding doors to my balcony open, and stumbled outside with the tears flowing down my cheeks at the frustration of not being able to get rid of him. There he sat, on the railing of my balcony, looking as impassive and unbothered by my presence as ever.

Only he wasn't the real reason I was crying, of course. No matter how expensive the sunglasses were, nor how much I love a croissant, none of this was cause for me to have a full-blown emotional breakdown in front of a kookaburra.

'Joe?' Ben says gently.

'Yes. Definitely Joe.'

Because I'm pretty sure Joe would have been able to chase Jobbers off.

He would have been systematic about it, you see. He would have googled kookaburras, and spent several days learning all about their behaviours, before coming up with a three-stage plan to ensure Jobbers never came back to haunt us again.

But then, if Joe was still around, I would have never met Jobbers in the first place.

I'm afraid my brain latched on to this idea, and Jobbers the Thieving Kookaburra became symbolic of both my loss and my doubts about the decision I'd made to come to Australia.

I'm *not* a shiny new Alice! Not in the slightest!

And I've *tried*!

I really have!

But I'd much rather be working in a dingy hair salon next to a sewage works in the darkest, greyest part of England than be here . . . if I could only have MY JOE BACK!

So I stood there ranting at a kookaburra about how unfair life was, how much I regretted coming to Australia and how much I wanted my sunglasses, my croissant and my husband back – not necessarily in that order.

Jobbers was implacable throughout.

Christ knows what my neighbours must have thought. Another Pommy turned insane by the hot weather, I assume.

I'm afraid to say I also threw a boiled egg at Jobbers. Right off my plate and right at the little bastard. He didn't so much as flinch as it sailed past his feathery head.

He just continued to look at me in that way only Jobbers can – straight past all of my defences and right into my soul.

Which drained me of my anger, and sent me drifting into the cold waters of deep, abiding sadness.

I became such a pitiful sight that even Jobbers wasn't able to be in my company anymore. He flew off to parts unknown, leaving me sat there, staring out at the beautiful Sydney Harbour, and wishing I was anywhere else but there.

'Oh Alice, I'm so sorry,' Ben says, putting his hand on my shoulder.

'Thank you,' I reply, attempting a smile. 'That was about three weeks ago, and I haven't seen Jobbers since.'

'No?'

'Nope. It's like he decided to take pity on me once he saw the worst of me. I did come out on to the balcony last week, though, to find my sunglasses on the bistro set table.'

I reach into my handbag and draw out the very sunglasses I'm referring to.

'Well, I guess that was nice of Jobbers,' Ben remarks.

'Sort of,' I respond. 'This is the bloody cheap pair.'

We sit in silence for a few moments, me pondering the life choices I've made, and Ben probably trying to work out why somebody would call a kookaburra Jobbers.

When he speaks, though, it's about something far more troubling than a bird that's too smart for its own good.

'This is my fault,' he says, with a sigh.

'What?'

'I challenged you to go off to Australia. I shouldn't have done that. It's my fault you've had to deal with Jobbers.'

I cringe a little when I hear this. This boy is quick to look to himself for blame or weakness, isn't he? Those parents of his have really done a number on him.

'No, Ben. It's not your fault,' I correct him, in a firm voice. 'I would probably have made the decision to leave anyway, for all the reasons we spoke about last year. I don't make my life choices just based on the opinions of other people. There's a great deal I do like about Australia that I haven't told you about yet. It's just that . . . just that . . .'

'It's easier to speak about the negatives, because they stay with you more,' Ben finishes for me.

'Exactly. I haven't told you about how nice and welcoming everyone at the salon was. Or how vibrant and exciting Sydney is to live and work in. I could wax lyrical about the quality of the coffee for at least two hours.'

'That's good. Have you managed to make any friends?'

I look down at the cheap sunglasses that have a score mark in one arm, made by the beak of an irritating bird.

'Only Jobbers so far,' I reply. 'And I fear our relationship is rather defined by an angry boiled egg.' I pinch the bridge of my nose with my fingers. 'He shouldn't have caught me just after I got up. That's always my worst time.'

'How so?'

I look at Ben.

Bugger. I shouldn't have said anything.

But now I have . . .

'Dreams,' I state, matter of fact. 'Almost every night. That bloody hospital.'

'Oh, that sucks.'

'Yes, it does. And the same dream occurs over and over – me running through the doors of the A&E department to find it either empty of anyone other than Joe screaming in pain on a gurney or the building full of people who just ignore him. I plead and scream at them to help Joe, but none of them ever do. So I get to stand there and just watch his life drain away.'

'Bloody hell. I'm so sorry you had to go through that.'

'Oh, it wasn't how it happened in real life,' I point out. 'I didn't get to the hospital until about twenty minutes after he had died, and they were very nice when they broke the news. But you know what dreams are like. They like to torture you as much as possible.'

Ben nods. 'Yeah. I sometimes dream that I know how to make Harry better, but my parents refuse to listen to me.'

I wince. That sounds almost as bad as the ones I have to put up with.

'When I do have those dreams, it ruins my mood for the whole day,' I say. 'All I keep thinking about is what happened, and how nobody could stop him from dying, and the unfairness of it all, and why weren't there more, better doctors on duty who could have helped him, and why—'

The arm of the sunglasses that Jobbers had bitten into snaps off in my hands.

'Shit!' I exclaim, looking down at the broken pieces.

'At least it wasn't the expensive pair,' Ben points out.

I don't reply. I just sit there, staring at those nasty thirty-dollar sunglasses, like they are emblematic of something.

'Have you ever . . . Have you ever looked into the staffing of the A&E that day?' Ben asks. 'You sound like you have unanswered questions.'

I shake my head. 'I have the coroner's report. That's about as much as there is. And there aren't any questions, really. He was just incredibly unlucky. It happens.'

'Yeah. I'm afraid it does,' Ben agrees. And he would know, wouldn't he?

'But I can't shake the *anger*, Ben. At the unfairness of it all. I know everybody dies, and I know I'm not the only one who's suffered a loss like that, but . . .'

'The fact others are in the same pain as you doesn't negate your pain in any way,' he replies, firmly. 'After Harry died, I still had to deal with deaths at work, and none of them made me feel any better, or gave me any kind of comfort. That whole *a trouble shared is a trouble halved* thing stops long before the doorstep of death.'

I nod. 'I knew you'd understand.'

'All too well.'

'I sometimes think . . . I sometimes think that the anger is something I hold on to, because if I don't, Joe will be . . . further away from me? I don't know.'

'We think it's better to feel something than nothing,' Ben agrees. 'Even if what we feel is bad for us. I can almost forgive my parents for their attitude towards me changing jobs, because I know they are still trying to cling on to him. That their disappointment in me is down to their memory of him.'

'It's still not fair to you.'

'Maybe not. But I do it myself, as well. I love my new job, but there's still a feeling of having let Harry down in some way. That I

118

couldn't compete with him. Couldn't match what he accomplished. There are things he could do that I just couldn't.'

This is painful to hear. How can a man who can be so insightful be so way off the mark at the same time?

A bit like an otherwise sensible woman allowing misplaced and pointless anger to ruin her life?

That's different.

Is it?

'Harry asked Mel to marry him within three months of meeting her. He was just so sure of himself,' Ben says, which makes my eyes go wide.

'Do you want to ask Katie to marry you?' I reply, a little in shock.

Ben looks at me with his face crumpled up like an old piece of paper. 'Yes! I love her so much, and I know it's what I want, even though we haven't known each other all that long. But . . . But I . . . I . . .'

'You don't think she'd say yes?'

'I don't know! *Maybe? Possibly* not? Or maybe she would?'

At this point I could tell him that I think there's a good chance she'd say yes, but I don't think it would get through to him. Harry is standing right there, and doesn't appear to show any signs of moving to one side.

I have to handle this carefully . . .

While it sounds to me like Katie would indeed say yes to his proposal, it's not a guarantee. Nothing ever is in this world. And I'm not sure Ben could handle the knockback. It'd just be something else he could compare himself unfavourably with his brother about.

But then again, he clearly loves her, and it sounds like she feels the same way. And maybe taking the risk is worth it, even if there is a small chance it could go wrong.

I feel like I'm faced with a decision I don't really want to have to take.

Ben will probably take my advice on this whatever I suggest.

My decision is made when I think back to how things went with Joe all those years ago. How *right* it all was. How magical it all felt. How my life slotted into place *perfectly*.

I want the same thing for Ben. I really do.

It's worth the risk.

'If you love her that much, you should do it,' I tell him. 'Joe asked me to marry him after only a few months, and frankly, I was starting to get frustrated that he hadn't done it already. He had to plan it down to within an inch of his life, of course, to make it as romantic as it possibly could be, because that's what he did. He wanted to make sure it was perfect.'

And it was. We were in Florence, in a five-star restaurant close to the Duomo, right there on the piazza, in the warm evening weather. He had a violinist play 'Can't Help Falling In Love', and had the waiter bring over the rings on a silver platter.

Oh yes. Joe would have dealt with Jobbers much better than I ever could.

'I want to, Alice, I really, really do, but I'm not sure if I'm good enough for her,' Ben says.

This is agonising.

'I took a massive pay cut to go and work for Shelter,' he tells me, 'and I'm living in a tiny one-bedroom flat. I can't offer her much.'

'You can offer her *you*, you silly sod,' I tell him, trying to sound jokey and light, but painfully aware that I'm failing at both.

'I'm not sure that's enough,' he replies, and in my mind's eye I can see the shadow of his brother reaching out from that grave over there, and looming over Ben, with a wicked grin on its shadowy face.

I turn on the bench to face Ben properly.

'Challenge,' I say to him, bluntly.

'What do you mean?'

'It worked for you last year. So I'm doing it again this year. Call it a permanent part of our little arrangement, if you like.'

The look of realisation dawns on Ben's face as he starts to understand what I'm suggesting.

I nod. 'Yes, that's right. You accepted and completed the challenge I set you to change jobs last time, and that worked out brilliantly. So this year, I'm going to challenge you to—'

'Oh, good God, please don't say it.'

'I'm going to challenge you to ask Katie to marry you.'

'Oh, bloody hell.'

'That's right, *bloody hell*. I think she'll say yes, Ben, and I think you probably do too. It's other people who are trying to convince you otherwise.'

Ben

Oh God, *no*. That's not fair!

I should have kept my mouth shut.

Of course she was going to challenge me!

And I'd like to just shake my head vociferously, and tell her I'm never going to do that – but she was bloody right about changing jobs, wasn't she?

And Katie is perfect – or at least as close to perfect for any one human being to be. Every time I'm with her, everything else feels *lighter*.

I know she's the right person for me. She's kind, and thoughtful . . . and worries far too much about what other people think.

I want to spend the rest of my life as part of a couple that cares way too much about what other people think, God damn it.

121

'Alright, I'll do it,' I tell Alice, scarcely believing the words that are coming out of my mouth.

'Excellent!' she exclaims, clapping her hands together.

It's nice to see her excited like that.

Much better than her being sat there, wrenching her cheap sunglasses around in her hand until they break.

She's far too *angry*. I can tell that from a mile off.

I *have* to help her . . .

'Challenge,' I say to Alice, in the same tone she used with me.

'Oh,' she replies, suddenly looking a little scared.

'That's right. Fair's fair. If I'm going to do what you ask, then it's only fair you do what I ask too. That's how this game works, isn't it?'

Alice frowns. 'It's not a game.'

'Oh yes it is! *Our* game. And if I'm going to play, you are too.'

She continues to frown at me for a moment, before rolling her eyes in resignation.

'Okay, fair enough. You're probably right. What do you want me to do? Be nicer to Jobbers, in the hopes he'll give me back my Ray-Bans?'

I swallow. This could be tricky . . . but I know I'm right.

'No. I want you to seek out some help for the anger you feel.'

Alice's face drops. 'That's a bit much, Ben. I'm not that bad.'

'I'm sorry, Alice, but I think you are. Joe's death still hangs over you like a cloud, and I don't think you'll settle in Sydney until that cloud has lifted.'

One of her eyes twitches as she digests this.

'Don't ask me to do that,' she says.

'I'm sorry, but I'm going to. I may not have been the best doctor in the world, but I think I learned enough to know what help you need – and I think a few sessions with someone who knows more about this stuff than either of us would be great for you. There must be a therapist in Sydney you can go to. Just to talk.'

Alice's face contorts. 'Can't I just adopt Jobbers?'

'You can do that too, if you like. But that's my challenge, Alice.'

She's not happy about it. Any more than I'm happy about being challenged to ask my girlfriend to marry me.

That's not true, bro.

No. It's probably not, but that's how things stand.

Alice's eyes narrow as she looks at me, but I return that look with good-natured defiance. I know I'm right about this.

Just as much as she thinks she's right about Katie.

God, I hope she is.

Alice sniffs. 'I really shouldn't be getting life advice from a man dressed as an Italian plumber.'

'Well, I'm sorry, but that's all you've got right now. You can fold the whole thing into your first chat with the therapist, if you like.'

'Oh yes. I'm sure things will get off to a great start if I tell her that I'm only seeing her because Super Mario told me to do it. I'll be banged up in the Sydney looney bin before the day is out.'

'Maybe don't do that, then,' I concede. 'But as for the rest of it, are we resolved?'

'Mmph.'

'I'm sorry?'

Alice lets out an exasperated grunt. 'Yes. I guess so. But I'm not making any promises about how it'll go.'

I force out a smile. 'Neither am I. Shake on it?'

I thrust out my hand. Alice looks down at it for a moment, sizing up the commitment she's about to make. Reluctantly, she takes it and I pump them both up and down once.

If only all of my relationships were this easy to navigate.

That's the joy of keeping this one to a single day a year. It's a lot easier to navigate than *every* day.

'Can we . . . Can we stop talking about this stuff for now?' Alice asks. She then looks at her watch. 'I'm in no hurry to leave, though. I did come ten thousand miles.'

'Fair enough. Why don't you tell me a bit about what's nice about Australia? I've always fancied going there myself.'

Truth be told, I'm happy to leave our respective challenges behind for now as well. No matter how confident Alice is about what Katie's response would be, it still fills me with terror.

If she's right, it'll all have been worth it, mate.

On that, bro, I can wholeheartedly agree.

Alice

I don't think I can do it.

I don't think I *want* to do it.

Oh, God help me . . .

Year Five

*OBLONGS, NOBLONGS AND THE WORST TIME
MACHINE EVER*

Ben

This rugby kit is hideous.

On me, that is.

I'm sure for your average rugby player it's perfectly fine. For someone with bigger muscles and a wider frame it looks rugged and manly. On me, it looks like a fourteen-year-old has been dressing up in his dad's sports gear for a bet.

Look how my skinny little legs poke out of the bottom of these crisp white shorts, would you? The ratio of Ben Fielding thigh to loose, flappy shorts material is grotesquely out of whack.

And the rugby jersey hangs loosely upon my frame as well. I was assured that the entire ensemble was a medium size, but at this point I have to ask – a medium what? Water buffalo?

I can't believe I've been forced into this stupid outfit today.

But that's my parents for you. They like to get their way – and will make your life a misery if you don't eventually capitulate.

I look around the changing rooms and puff out my cheeks, letting out a long blast of air that's at least 85 per cent nervous energy.

It's not long now until I will have to leave this changing room and take the field. Everybody else has already left to go and do a warm-up, and I'll have to join them very soon, otherwise I will be missed.

I was never missed during PE at school – which was the last time I was forced into an ill-fitting sporting outfit. But I can't get away with hanging out at the back today, like I used to then.

No. In some very special and excruciating ways, I will be the centre of attention today.

Because I am Harry Fielding's little brother.

And this entire bloody event is dedicated to his memory.

Four years.

It's been *four years* since he died.

I can't quite believe it.

Partially because I can still picture him in my mind's eye like the last time I saw him was yesterday – only I don't like to do that, because as the years do pass, my memory of him focuses in more on the sick, pale thing that lay in that bed for those short few weeks.

I want to only remember the vibrant idiot, who took such glee in making my life a misery – but that Harry is getting harder and harder to picture. I can still do it if I concentrate, but it's *hard*. Especially when my brain finds it so damned easy to bring the *other* Harry bubbling to the surface at 3 a.m., when I can't sleep. The little thing in the bed, wasted and white. Damned by his own body.

Christ, I don't want to be here today.

Not like this, at least.

But he would have been forty this week. The vibrant idiot would have been entering what is supposed to be his more mature years – but I think he would probably have ignored that concept completely.

126

I would have loved to have seen how Harry handled getting older. It would have been quite the performance – featuring fireworks, inappropriate language and physical harm wrought upon some harmless bystander, probably me.

Not that I'm likely to get away without physical harm because of Harry Fielding's fortieth birthday anyway, because I'm about to take his place in a very special memorial rugby match at his second home, the Western Warriors Rugby Club.

If you want to know where strapping, middle-class, white-collar men hang out, this is the place. If you've ever wanted to steal a Jaguar, a Maserati or a Porsche SUV, you can take your pick from the plethora of them in the car park.

Just don't mention anything about mortgages, bills or worries over the future – that kind of talk is alien to them, and makes them very nervous.

What makes *me* very nervous is the position I've been put in by just about everybody I know who isn't called Katie.

The Harry Fielding Memorial is a rugby match that is played here every year, on or around Harry's birthday. And until this year I have done a good job of making sure I was extremely busy with something else every time it rolled around. This was easy when I was in training to be a doctor, but has become somewhat harder with my job at Shelter.

I mourn my brother in my own way. I don't particularly need or want to spend the day surrounded by his beefy friends, who like to do beefy things, in beefy shorts.

I am not beefy. I'm more of a *chicken* kind of guy. So avoiding coming to this annual get-together, where men run around a field with odd-shaped balls, has always been high on my to-do list.

However, this year things are very different, because it's such a landmark in what would have been Harry's life. So, I always knew that I'd probably have to attend the match, whether I wanted to or not. What I didn't know – up until literally a month ago – is that I'd be required to play a role in the game itself.

It was my father's idea. Because of course it was.

'Ben should wear the number 10 shirt this year,' he had announced, during his birthday meal at L'Preten – his favourite restaurant. Talk had inevitably got round to Harry again (in record time, it has to be said. I'd barely tucked into my cauliflower steak starter before his name was mentioned) and the fortieth-birthday rugby match was the topic.

'He'd love to see you out there in his stead, Benjamin. It'd make him very proud. And it'll make your mother and me very proud as well.' My father finished this pronouncement with a curt nod of approval at his own words.

Harry's widow, Melanie – who by this point was pretty much a member of my family in her own right – thought my father's idea was absolutely *marvellous*, and got tears in her eyes after he'd suggested it.

'I think that's an extremely good idea, Henry,' my mother agreed with a crisp smile.

This came as no surprise – I don't think my mother has ever really disagreed with my father about anything. And it was equally unsurprising that nearly everybody at the table agreed with him as well – all eleven of the buggers. My father has always been a natural leader, and people defer to him as easily as water flows downhill.

In fact, the only ones not approving of Henry Fielding's genius idea were his second son, Benjamin, and his partner, Katie.

'I don't think that's a good idea,' I said to him, trying hard not to choke on my cauliflower.

'Nonsense! It's perfect!' he bellowed in return. 'A great way for you to celebrate your brother's life.'

. . . presumably by being battered into submission by all of his beefy mates.

I said as much to my father, who, in return, harrumphed.

He's so good at harrumphing, you have to wonder if he spends hours in front of the mirror perfecting the technique.

'Don't put yourself down so much, dear,' my mother added. 'I'm sure you'll be fine – and Harry's friends will take it easy on you, I have no doubt. It'd be a lovely thing for us to see.'

There was a pleading look in my mother's eyes that I didn't like one bit. It felt a wee bit manipulative.

I tried to object some more, but when almost the whole table is against you, you eventually have to admit defeat. Which I did, right around the time they served up my salmon en croûte.

And thus, the die was cast.

And so was I, in the role of 'skinny little shit who gave rugby up when he was twelve, because he didn't like being one giant bruise – but is now forced back into it, because the guilt of not doing so would be too much to bear'.

A head pokes around the door frame of the changing room.

'Are you coming, then, Fielding Two?' blusters Davis Mitchell-Downing, a look of extreme impatience on his face.

Nobody should be able to get away with having three surnames and no first name, but Davis Mitchell-Downing was born into the kind of family where it's compulsory.

Davis Mitchell-Downing is also a car salesman, because of course he bloody is.

Mostly Jaguars, Maseratis and Range Rovers – which are all available for free outside, if you've got the right skills and temperament.

'Yeah, I'm coming,' I reply, standing up slowly. I'm willing for something to explode in my kneecap as I do this . . . but sadly, my joints remain resolutely healthy, so I trudge out of the dressing room, following Davis Mitchell-Downing like a bad puppy.

My heart sinks and my pulse races as I walk out on to the Western Warriors pitch, and into the unseasonably warm spring weather. As I do, I see that the small grandstand is packed to the rafters with spectators. They've really gone to town today, with bunting and balloons strung up around the grandstand, all with Harry's name on them. There's even a quaint little traditional-looking ice cream trolley set up to the side of the grandstand, to keep the kids happy.

Sat at the front is my mother and father, along with Melanie – and Katie.

Katie is the only one who looks worried.

Bless her, she's tried to be as supportive as she can about this debacle – the same way she is with everything else going on in my life. But Katie is not a person who is good at hiding her emotions, and I know how worried she is about me taking part in this game.

Something I don't think I could be doing without her here, to be honest.

I know she's proud of the fact I've agreed to do it, because she told me so. But that doesn't stop her worrying. Katie is the kind of person who has a heart big enough to carry a multitude of emotions in equal measure – even ones that don't really sit well together.

She gives me a big, encouraging smile as she sees me emerge from the clubhouse, which is very nice, but I know exactly how she feels about all of this.

The same as me.

I made sure her phone was fully charged this morning, so she'll be able to call the ambulance when my intestines fly out of my mouth after the first tackle.

I *am* going to get tackled, you see. No doubt about it.

Because Harry was a fly half, and fly halves get tackled *a lot*. They are the centre of the rugby team, and therefore get a lot of attention – usually in the form of fifteen stone of muscle coming at them, like a Range Rover being driven by somebody who's just nicked it, going through the car park gates.

I'd probably be alright if Harry had skulked around at the back of the team in a defensive position – but of course, my brother being my brother, he was in one of the most up-front roles possible on the rugby pitch.

Davis Mitchell-Downing is the scrum half – another one of the important players on a rugby team – and has been coaching me for the past three weeks about what I need to do.

The fly half generally has to make the decision whether the ball should be kicked, passed or carried after it has come out of the scrum.

Yes. That's right. The boy who couldn't decide whether to leave his job or not, or ask his girlfriend to marry him or not, without the help of a graveside friend, is expected to be the decision maker for the rugby match that commemorates his dead brother.

Oh joy.

And rugby is a far more complicated sport than I feel it's necessary to be. I'd be okay with football, because that's essentially just 'kick ball over there, where that net is', but rugby is on another level of complexity.

You score by making tries, and you can also score by making conversions. The points are different for each, and you can't do the second one without the first – I think. And you can score with penalty kicks – which is also for a different number of points.

You can't throw the ball (which is not shaped like a ball) forwards, but only behind you. But then you can kick it forward, that's fine. I think.

There are far more rules than that, but those are the ones I can remember.

And when one of those rules, or the myriad others that escape me right now, gets broken, all the really big lads bend over and cuddle in something called a scrum. I think.

And if your big boys win the ball, it eventually gets pushed behind to me, the fly half, who then has to do something with the ball.

That thing cannot be to throw it up into the air, scream out loud and run off the pitch, sadly.

Oh, and I should also point out that there are two types of rugby, with different rules, and I don't have a clue which one I'm playing today.

So, everything is going to go *very well*, I'm sure.

The Western Warriors Rugby team have split themselves into two sides for today's commemorative match. The other side won the toss, so my side will be receiving.

Life-saving medical treatment by the side of the pitch in my case, I'd imagine.

My heart thuds in my chest as I take up my position and wait for the fly half of the other team to kick the ball. Which he does with a blow of the referee's whistle, and the game is under way.

The ball inevitably flies in my direction, so I surreptitiously start to move away from it to the left, allowing Davis Mitchell-Downing to have a pop at it instead.

He grabs it, and starts to run up the pitch, accompanied by the rest of our team. I make a point to stay at least three or four yards further back to avoid any chance of the ball coming to me.

Davis runs up the left-hand side of the pitch until something happens, involving him being crashed into by three of the opposing team. They all then fumble around on the grass for a few moments for reasons which are beyond me, and then the referee blows his whistle and everybody crowds together.

The big beefy boys at the front then bend over into the scrum, which means I will shortly be required to do something. The ball is dropped into the roiling mass of humanity, and chaos erupts for a few moments, until the ball is ejected from the rear of the scrum. It's like watching some huge, multi-limbed alien creature giving birth.

Davis grabs the ball and chucks it at me.

'Like we discussed, Fielding Two!' he screams at me as he does this.

What we discussed is that I'm supposed to *appraise the shape of the field and make a strategic call based on that.*

The field is an oblong.

I'm not sure what that means to my strategic call, to be honest with you. Would I do something different if it was square? How about rhomboid?

I'd better make a decision fast, though, as at least two Maserati owners are coming at me full speed, with murderous looks in their eyes.

The field is oblong. Oblong rhymes with 'not long'. Something I will not be for this world, if I don't get rid of this stupid ball.

I chuck it behind me to my left, sending the Maserati drivers after it like a couple of bloodhounds.

A Porsche SUV driver on my team, who probably has four surnames and a mild cocaine habit, grabs the ball and takes off up the pitch again. I breathe a sigh of relief.

Especially when he scores a try at their end of the pitch – which means I did something right by passing it to him.

Go Oblongs!

. . . which is a far nicer name for a rugby team that Western Warriors, in my book.

Sadly the try means I must now try to kick the ball over the crossbar of the Big H.

Davis Mitchell-Downing comes over and claps me on the back. 'Well done, Fielding Two! Now get us that conversion!'

I nod dumbly, and walk up to where the rugby ball has been placed upright on the grass for me to kick.

It's pretty close to the Big H, and not at much of an angle, so it shouldn't be too hard, right?

The ref blows the whistle and I give the ball a boot. It describes an arc at the left-hand goal post, hitting it halfway up with a loud *spanging* noise, before flying straight back at my head. I have to duck out of the way, and the crowd lets out a disappointed grunt as the ball bounces awkwardly away.

Go Oblongs!

Jesus Christ on a bike.

I turn to look at the crowd, who are all pointing and laughing.

At least that's what it *feels* like they're doing.

Other than Katie, who is still trying to give me an encouraging smile, and my mother and father, who are now looking at me with a mixture of perplexity and worry.

Everybody else is probably too hopped up on ice cream and beer from the clubhouse to care how bad I am at kicking a rugby ball.

'Never mind, Fielding Two!' DMD cries at me as he runs back towards our team's half of the pitch. 'I'll take the next one!'

Yes, please, DMD. And every one after that, thank you. I don't know if you are as good as Harry was, but you'll be a damned sight better than me, I have no doubt of that.

Things continue with the game of rugby for a further twenty or so minutes, during which I get to run after everybody else up the pitch and back several times, throw the ball to someone behind me twice, kick the ball forward once, and never have any real impact on the outcome of the game whatsoever.

If they'd put a rugby sweater on a plank of wood and stuck it in the ground in the centre of the pitch, it would have probably made a slightly more effective fly half than I'm being.

I am content with this, though. Having little to do with the game means I am avoiding getting hurt or embarrassed. I don't care if DMD and the other middle-class beefies are starting to throw me dark looks – I'm happy right where I am, thank you very much.

Sadly, things take a dramatic turn for the worse with the next play of the game. Once again, the other side (we'll call them the Noblongs, if you like) are kicking the ball towards us Oblongs. I have manoeuvred myself as far away from my fellow Oblongs as I am able, in furtherance of my plan to not involve myself in the rugby match.

Unfortunately, the ball is kicked right in my direction. And there's not a bloody chance any of the other Oblongs can get over to me in time to catch the ball instead.

'Get it, Fielding Two!' DMD screams at me.

Oh dear.

My hands are held aloft, as if I'm waiting for benediction from the passing Messiah, and the rugby ball flies right towards them.

Catch it, bro! Don't let us down!

I won't! I won't!

My hands close over the rugby ball as it flies between them. Sadly I don't quite get proper purchase on it, and it bangs painfully into the bridge of my nose, instantly making my eyes water.

But the rugby ball is in my grasp! I have been successful in my catching efforts!

Now what am I supposed to bloody do with it?

Run, bro! Run for the try line!

Oh, bugger me!

I start sprinting towards the other end of the pitch, my vision partially blurred by tears of pain, and my nose throbbing mightily.

To my right, I see the Noblongs coming at me en masse.

I should probably just chuck the ball behind me and immediately curl up *into* a ball, but I can *feel* him now – right there alongside me, pushing me onwards.

Go on, bro! You can do it!

I'm not sure that I can, but I'll try, Harry! I'll try for you!

That's it! Run all the way to the end and score me a birthday try!

Okay, I will!

And, for the briefest period of time – perhaps no more than four or five seconds, it looks like I might actually make it. In front of a horde of people only here today because of how popular Harry Fielding was, I might actually make my brother proud with the one and only try I'm ever likely to score in my life.

Yes, yes!

Here it comes!

The try line starts to draw closer and I feel my excitement rise.

This will be all worth it, if I can do this! My legs may look like pencils jutting out of these shorts, but they are powering me to success, God bless them.

And then, as I sprint headlong up the left-hand side of the pitch, with my nose running and my eyes watering – but my soul lifting – I feel a presence right behind me.

A Noblong – faster than his compatriot Noblongs – has caught up to me.

Run faster!

I'm trying!

Run, bro. Run!

Unbelievably, I do indeed run a bit faster, which is quite incredible. I didn't know I had the stamina for it, or the legs.

I'm outrunning my pursuer!

Aha ha ha ha ha!

. . . I will find out later that the man in pursuit of me is one Albie Lethwitt, an expert in reconstructive surgery, who went to Imperial College with Harry, and a man who was once on course to join the British Olympics team as a 400-metre runner.

I can only feel him as a presence behind me. Everyone else can see him barely breaking a sweat as he *lets me* run up the pitch – out of some sort of pity for Harry's skinny little brother, I guess.

He's not actually going to let me score a try, though. Of course not. That would be too much.

Albie the Noblong eventually decides to bring me down, and attempts to do so by grabbing me by both shoulders – no doubt in an effort to stop me in my tracks without actually having to tackle me properly. What a very nice man.

All Albie's tentative efforts actually accomplish, however, is to knock me completely off course, and send me stumbling off to the left.

And because my little chicken legs have been pumping so hard to propel me at extremely high speed (for me, anyway – Albie probably goes faster than this when he's mowing the lawn) the stumble is impossible to get out of.

If I just drop to the ground now, I'm going to face-plant into the relatively hard spring soil. That will both be quite damaging and extremely embarrassing.

Instead I elect to try and stay on my feet, which means I continue to stumble headlong off the pitch – and right at the little ice cream trolley, set up by the side of the grandstand.

Now, you've got to appreciate that this is all happening in a few split seconds. Far too fast for my brain to keep up with. It's still trying to process how painful my nose is.

A less addled brain would convince my legs to veer me off to one side, so I can simply stumble to a halt. But my brain is very,

very addled, and therefore is of no use whatsoever. This means I do not veer off, and instead fly headfirst right at the ice cream trolley.

The poor bloke manning the thing squeals in horror and jumps away from it. The two snotty children floating around it, both holding cones full of delicious traditionally made vanilla ice cream, stare at me in equal terror.

The grandstand full of Harry Fielding's friends and family watch as *Ben* Fielding makes a beeline for the ice cream trolley, with seemingly deliberate intent.

Time inevitably slows down at this point, and from the corner of my eye, I can see Katie rising to her feet, her hand outstretched and her face a picture of shock and alarm.

And to think, only two months prior to this day from hell, *I* was the one with my arms outstretched *to her* – as I held aloft the ring in its plush velvet box.

A mere eight weeks exist between me asking Katie to marry me, and me diving headfirst into a half-empty portable ice cream freezer.

Did Katie say yes to marrying me?

Yes. Yes, she absolutely did.

Am I about to accidentally plunge my face into a freezer full of expensive traditionally made Cornish ice cream?

Yes. Yes, I absolutely am.

The first thing to hit the trolley is my left knee. The second things are my genitals.

This knocks the wind out of me completely, and bends my body double.

It is at this stage my head dives ice cream-wards.

Straight into the cold, vanillary treat I go, mashing my already damaged nose right into its sweet embrace.

And because the deep little freezer box is over half empty of its contents by now, my shoulders follow my head in, which in turn flips my legs up and over.

The poor ice cream trolley is not able to cope with all of this, needless to say. It is designed to bring happiness and far too many E numbers to the snotty children of the world – not act as a stopping measure for a ballistic idiot.

One of the trolley's back legs buckles, and the whole damn thing starts to topple over, with me wedged in it like the world's worst ice cream scoop.

For a moment, we achieve perfect equilibrium, and I hang there upside down, legs still pumping furiously. But then gravity asserts itself again, and the trolley crashes back to the ground, its final act to eject me from its freezer section – which, given the fact that ice cream is quite slippery, happens extremely fast, and with much screaming.

I slide to a halt on the grass in a ragged mess, my head and shoulders now covered in vanilla ice cream, and my arms still clasped around the rugby ball for dear life.

Alice

I have no words.

There is simply nothing I can say.

I have to believe him. He'd have no reason to make up such a hideous story for my benefit.

And the look of abject misery on his face, as he comes to the end of his mind-blowing tale, isn't something that you can fake.

What on earth do I say?

Maybe I should ask him if he was hurt?

Yes. Yes, that will do. That's a sensible question. Go with that.

'So . . . was the crowd's reception to that a little . . . icy?'

You are an evil woman, Alice Everley.

Ben's face crumples.

'Sorry, I couldn't resist.'

'Nor could anyone else,' Ben says abjectly. 'Everyone at Harry's rugby club now refers to me as Mr Whippy.'

'Mr Whippy?'

'Yes. Even my father nearly cracked a smile.'

I'm not going to laugh. Because even though this is objectively hilarious, I can see that to Ben it is anything but. All through his tale of woe he has sat there, furtively picking at his feathers.

Oh . . . that's probably something I should mention, to give the story of his descent into accidental ice cream some context. Ben is dressed as Foghorn Leghorn from the Looney Tunes.

'Were you hurt?' I now say, keeping a very straight face.

Foghorn Ben shakes his feathery head. 'No. Just my pride.'

'Ah well. That's something to be grateful for, I suppose.'

He responds with a weak smile. Which just makes my funny bone start to tingle even more.

I'm sorry, but it's completely impossible to not feel at least *some* humour from listening to a fully grown man dressed as a giant cartoon chicken tell you all about his ice cream and rugby disaster.

I'm only human.

And to be honest, I would like nothing more than to burst into great peals of laughter right now, as it would make a refreshing change from the mood I'm usually in these days.

But my friendship with Ben Fielding is more important than me being able to laugh. Seeing him here today has been something I've looked forward to for weeks. Not least because we always meet at the place where I still feel like my heart and soul lie, even all these years later.

140

I was here this morning before Ben was. A good half an hour before. Which gave me ample opportunity to speak to Joe for the first time in a year.

This version of Joe, anyway.

I'd just had enough time to depress myself fully by holding a one-way conversation with the man I'd been very happy with, before I saw Ben walking towards me dressed as Foghorn Leghorn – which improved my mood considerably.

The idiotic costumes Harry makes him dress in may be adding insult to injury for him, but I have to confess for me it's like the sun coming up.

'Actually, I think I would have preferred to have broken a leg in some heroic fashion,' Ben says, still picking at Foghorn. 'Maybe scoring the try that won the match. A broken leg heals in a few months. I will hear the name Mr Whippy being hurled my way for the next few years of my life, I'd imagine.'

'I'm sure it won't be that bad,' I counter.

His expression falls into one of disbelief. 'You've never met any rugby players, have you?'

'No. But I'm sure it won't be as bad as you think.'

Ben makes a face and moves the big yellow cloth beak sticking out from his forehead. Usually this bench is large enough for us both, but the size of the Foghorn suit is pushing me almost off.

'Anyway. Never mind all that,' I say, eager to change the subject to something a bit more positive. 'Katie agreed to marry you!'

Ben smiles. 'She did, yes.' It's nice to see it, but his entire demeanour is tempered by that silly accident at the rugby match. It's testament to Ben's personality that this is the thing he felt he needed to tell me about most, rather than the fact the woman he loves has agreed to marry him.

'You must be so happy!' I say, attempting to lift his spirits.

'I am, yes.'

141

Tell your face that, Ben.

That's unfair of me. I don't think I'd exactly look chuffed about anything, either, if I was forced into that ridiculous outfit.

'And I bet she was a great source of comfort to you about the whole ice cream rugby thing,' I venture, knowing that I'm probably on firmer ground here. I have no doubt Katie was very sympathetic. I know I would have been.

'Oh, I didn't really . . . I wasn't really . . . I just laughed it off with her, to be honest.'

'You did what?'

'You know. Laughed it off. Told her I wasn't all that bothered. Even went as far as buying us a tub of ice cream that evening, back at our flat. Ha ha ha.'

'Why on earth did you do that?'

Ben looks distraught. 'I couldn't let her know it bothered me *that much*, Alice. The whole thing was embarrassing enough, without letting on about how it made me feel.'

My eyes narrow. 'Why not?'

Ben sighs and throws up his hands. 'What good would it do me? She probably already thinks I'm an idiot. Everyone else sure as hell does. I don't want to make things worse by coming across as . . . as . . .'

'Honest?'

'. . . weak.'

I grunt in frustration and get up off the bench. Partly because Foghorn has nearly forced me off it anyway, and partly because I need to vent. 'It's not weak to let your fiancée know how you really feel about something, Ben!' I tell him in no uncertain terms. 'In fact, that makes you *strong*!'

He looks at me in utter confusion. 'But I don't want to lose her!'

'Why the blinking buggery would you lose her?'

'Because . . . Because . . . Because I'm not exactly what you'd call an *alpha male*, am I? I'm not successful, or rich, or super good-looking.'

'You think she's that *shallow*?'

'No! She's wonderful and I know she loves me for who I am.'

'Well, where's your problem?' I snap, looming over him like an angry mother hen.

'I don't want to do anything to make it *worse*. I don't want her to think I'm so weak I can't cope with a stupid little incident like diving headfirst into an ice cream trolley! I don't want her to think I can't cope with life's setbacks! I don't want her to think I can't cope with . . . with . . . .' He's struggling for the right words, and I don't know if I can supply them for him. 'I don't want her to *worry*, Alice. I *never* want her to worry. It breaks my heart.'

'Alright, alright,' I say, softening my tone. 'I understand.'

'You do?'

My shoulders sag. 'Yes. Of course I do.' I suddenly feel very tired, and slump back down next to him. 'About the not coping thing, anyway.'

'Yeah?'

I nod and purse my lips. 'That's certainly what Sienna thinks.'

'Sienna?'

'Yes. She's my . . .'

Waste of time? Waste of money? Waste of effort?

'. . . therapist. You know. The one you told me to get?'

Ben blinks in surprise. 'Oh wow. You did actually do it, then?'

I round on him. 'Well, of course I did. We had a deal, didn't we?'

He nods. 'Yeah, we did. But I wasn't sure what I'd said was enough to convince you to do it.'

Good grief. I'm not the only one here who could do with seeing a therapist, it seems.

'Well, it was . . . and she's very nice.'

'Has it helped?'

At this point I could easily lie. I could tell Ben that the eight weekly sessions I've had with Sienna Moxley (five-star-rated therapist on BetterMinds.com.au) have been a great help, and that I'm coping much better these days with my feelings of loss, grief and anger around Joe. I could tell him that my social life has vastly improved, and that I'm meeting new people, having a lovely time in Sydney, and am putting my old life behind me properly for the first time.

But then, if I lie, what the hell is the point of this relationship? I don't have to fly ten thousand miles to be dishonest with someone. I can do that for eighty dollars an hour in a therapist's office on Military Road in Sydney. Ben is meant to be the person I'm open and honest with – hence why I've been waiting for this annual meeting with so much anticipation this year.

It's my chance to vent.

At Foghorn Leghorn.

'Absolutely bloody not,' I admit, feeling tremendously relieved to do so.

At first, I thought it might be a worthwhile enterprise. Sienna was very kind, very understanding, and absolutely knew what I was going through. She told me that everything I felt was natural and normal, and that I shouldn't beat myself up that after five whole years I still hadn't moved on successfully.

Then, over the next few sessions, she tried her best to help me do that moving on – and absolutely none of it stuck.

Because Sienna Moxley could talk until she's blue in the face about embracing a new life, opening up to new people, letting go of the past, unloading my feelings of anger and accepting the truth – but then she doesn't have to live in my brain, or have my nightmares, or still have a crystal clarity of the day my husband died.

144

Honestly, it's like I have a one-way time machine in my head that constantly malfunctions, and can only transport me back to one specific occasion in my entire life – the day Joe died.

I would struggle to tell you what I had for lunch three days ago, or what cut I did on my last customer of the same day. But I can tell you exactly how many steps it was from my hastily parked car to the entrance of the A&E department, and what colour shoes the young doctor was wearing when he told me Joe was dead.

How is any therapist supposed to compete with that kind of awful clarity? She can convince my conscious mind of all the things I must do to improve my mental health, but my subconscious is having none of it.

Would you like to know how tall the doctor was, how much he weighed, what his breath smelled like and how long his hair was in millimetres?

Just don't ask me what my flight number was on the journey over here last week. Or what my flight number going back is, either.

There are now two Alice Everleys – just like there are two Joe Everleys.

One version of her is a forgetful Australian permanent resident, with a suntan, a very unhealthy flat white habit and the memory of your average goldfish. The other is a pale, thin, hollow woman, who can tell you everything you'd want to know about the patients piled up in an A&E department from five years ago.

Neither of them wants to talk to a therapist – or anyone else for that matter.

I tried to explain this to Sienna Moxley, but she insisted that both women were the same person, and I know she's not right about that at all. Pale, thin Alice couldn't manage a highly success-ful hair salon in a prestigious part of north Sydney, for instance. And suntanned, coffee-addicted Alice couldn't possibly remember that 'It Wasn't Me' by Shaggy was playing on Power FM at precisely

2.17 p.m. on a hideous day ten thousand miles away, well over five years ago.

'Bloody hell, Alice, I'm so sorry.'

'What have you got to be sorry about, Ben?'

I regret the tone of my voice the second I speak. I don't need to take my frustration out on this poor bechickened young man. It's not fair of me.

'No . . . No, *I'm* sorry, Ben,' I blurt out, trying my best to wipe that hurt look off his face. 'I shouldn't take my frustrations out on you. You've got nothing to do with the rut I'm stuck in.'

'Haven't I?'

'No. I made and make my own decisions, remember? If my stupid brain isn't able to let go of what happened when Joe died, then that's my problem, nobody else's. Not yours, and not poor old Sienna's.'

'Are you still seeing her?'

'No. It started to feel a little pointless after eight sessions. If anything, going to her seemed to *increase* the number of times I'd dream about Joe. Seems talking through my problems with someone else only brought them further up to the surface.'

I point over at where one version of Joe lies. 'Talking to Joe today has felt like it's accomplished more than seeing her did. Though I don't quite think I can afford a weekly session with him, given the cost of flights.'

'Have you got any friends you can talk to instead?' Ben asks – not for the first time.

I wobble a hand back and forth. 'I do have friends . . . though I'm afraid none of them are particularly close. I talk a lot to the girls at the salon about . . . small stuff.'

'Those aren't *friends*, Alice, those are work colleagues. Do you see anyone outside work? Anyone you can actually open up to, the way the therapist wanted?'

'My dead husband, all of the time,' I reply.

'That's not what I meant.'

'No, I know that.' I heave a sigh. 'Not really, Ben. I go to the Christmas party we have in my apartment block every year. And the guy from Coles who delivers my weekly shop is friendly.' I look at Ben. 'And then there's you, of course.'

He gives me a withering look. 'Much as I love our bizarre and wonderful little relationship, Alice, I'm not sure you can count it as a part of either of our social lives.'

I cock my head. 'Do you actually think it's wonderful?'

He nods and smiles. 'Yes, I really do. Because I can come here and see my brother in these stupid costumes he makes me wear, and the whole thing is bearable for me, because you are here. I look forward to these conversations a hell of a lot.'

I tear up a bit at this. 'Can I . . . Can I have a hand, please? Yours, I mean. Instead of Foghorn's,' I ask.

Ben yanks off his entire feathery Foghorn arm, revealing his hand beneath – which I then take in mine. 'It's wonderful to me too,' I tell him, with a rather wobbly voice. 'I can tell you things I can't tell anyone else. There's no way I could stand at work and tell the girls all about how I'm two people – one of whom is stuck in a moment from five years go.'

He considers this for a second. 'Yeah. I doubt there's anybody else I could have told about what happened at the rugby. Not . . . honestly, anyway.'

I squeeze his hand before letting go. 'Well, that's probably not all that healthy for either of us, is it?' I admit, looking up to the heavens, to see if there's any inspiration coming from there. Given that right above us is the big old oak tree, the only inspiration I'm likely to receive is from a squirrel dropping a nut on my head.

God, I miss squirrels.

. . . only because they remind you of when Joe was still alive.

Probably. But what's wrong with that?

'I live in a city of five million people, and yet I'm all alone,' I mutter, half to myself.

'My hair still smells of vanilla ice cream,' Ben adds, in an equally low voice.

At this point, the church bell rings, reminding us both that we've been sat here together for a good couple of hours now.

'You'd think the number of times we've sat here doing this, *He* might have offered up some sort of advice, wouldn't you?' I comment, looking at the church.

Ben scratches his face. 'We should have probably gone in there at some point, though.'

I nod slowly. 'Quite possibly.' I look at him. 'You think we're being punished for not being more devout?'

Ben's face wrinkles up. 'Nah. I doubt it. I figure after what we've both been through with those two over there, he probably figures we've had enough to cope with.'

'Quite possible.'

There is, deep inside me, for a brief, flickering instant, a feeling of the utmost hatred for the bloke that the pretty little church was built to worship. I have hated so many people in the depths of my mind since that day in the A&E department – including the young doctor whose hair was sixty-three millimetres long, the shouting woman with the bleeding forehead who probably took up too much of the nurse's time, the paramedic who took twenty-six minutes to reach the pavement where Joe had collapsed, and myself for not getting to the bloody hospital quicker to see her husband for the last time ever.

Might as well add God to the list.

You could have saved him for me. You could have kept him with me. You could have been there in that A&E department that day, making sure it ran a lot more efficiently. You could have—

'We're not going to get any help from Him, I don't think,' I say out loud to Ben.

'No. I think you're right.'

I reach over and take his hand again, fighting back tears as I do so.

I'm so used to fighting back tears now, I should be given a black belt in it.

'Challenge time,' I say in a wobbly voice.

He squeezes my hand in his. 'Challenge time,' he repeats.

'Please talk to Katie,' I tell him. 'Properly, I mean. Be honest with her. Tell her how you feel. She won't see it as weakness. She won't think less of you. It won't make her worry more. And she *won't* leave you. Let your barriers down, Ben. You have to.'

Ben's expression falls into doubt, as I knew it would. But I also know I'm *right*. Again. He's so much more than he thinks he is, and if this girl is in love with him, and said yes to marrying him, then I'm 100 per cent sure she sees that in him too.

'Okay, I'll try,' he promises. 'But it's hard . . .'

'I know.' My turn to squeeze again. 'But it's worth it.'

I sit up a little straighter and compose myself. 'Okay, then . . . what have you got for me? Kickboxing class to get rid of my anger? A make-over to make me feel like I'm actually living life again?'

'Make a friend,' he replies, rightly ignoring my flippant tone.

But kickboxing would be so much easier, and better for next year's anecdote . . .

I slump back again, the false winds out of my sails. 'I don't need a friend,' I say, a little sullenly. 'I have you.'

'Yes, you have got me . . . but I'm ten thousand miles away most of the time, which is no damn good. And our relationship is a very unique one. You need someone closer you can be open with. Someone you can see *regularly* . . . and talk to face to face.'

'Do I?'

'Yes, you do. And that's not something I can do, unfortunately. The same way you think I need to talk to Katie, you need to have someone close to talk to.'

'I don't think I'll ever find someone who would understand the same way you do.'

'Try,' Ben says, in the most commanding tone I've heard him use all day.

. . . he's in there. Deep down. A man who knows his own mind, and isn't beholden to his dead brother's shadow.

'Alright, alright,' I say, throwing up both hands. 'I hear what you're saying.'

'Don't just hear what I'm saying . . . make it *happen*,' he tells me. 'There's no reason that in a city of five million people, you can't find at least one person you click with.'

I wince. 'But I can't click with anyone other than Joe.'

Joe was *my person*. My only person. The only person I ever needed or wanted. That's the kind of person *I* am. I found the one. The only one. But now the one is gone. There's nobody else.

Ben points a finger at me in a very serious fashion. Sadly, the finger is still enclosed in the feathery Foghorn costume, so the effect is rather ruined. Being lectured to by a giant chicken is a difficult thing to both comprehend and accept.

'You don't know that,' he says. 'You can't tell me I shouldn't put up barriers with Katie, and then do exactly the same thing yourself.'

Damn it.

The giant chicken has uncovered my hypocrisy.

My nose wrinkles up as I try to think of a comeback that gets me out of this challenge . . . but words fail me. I can't demand he open himself up more to other people, and then refuse to do it myself.

'One friend?' I ask Ben, barely able to look into his eyes.

'Just one. That's more than enough. To start with, anyway.'

Ben holds out his hand. 'Agreed?' he says, very deliberately.

I point to his other hand. 'Pass me your chicken wing, I might as well shake on that.'

He rolls his eyes and does so. I take Foghorn's appendage in my hand and pump it up and down. 'Agreed. You talk to Katie. I find somebody to play with.'

'Excellent.'

We both take a deep breath and survey the graveyard.

'I think I'm going to go inside and offer up a little prayer,' Ben then says. 'You know . . . just in case.'

'You do remember you're dressed as Foghorn Leghorn, don't you?'

'I do. So does the vicar, though. I had to explain myself to him this morning, before you arrived.'

I nod. 'Okay, then. Let's do it. But I'm getting pictures.'

'Fair enough.'

And with that, we have once again reached the natural end point of our annual conversation.

Life can now go on . . .

A life where I have to find a new playmate, because Foghorn Leghorn has demanded it of me.

Ben's right. Maybe a prayer offered up to the big man is worth a shot.

It probably can't do any harm, at least.

Ben

Look, I didn't know the costume was flammable, alright?

I only went over to have a look at the altar. I didn't realise how close the candle was. Not until my feathery arse was on fire.

If there is a God, I doubt I'll be getting much help from Him any time soon – unless at some point they change the accepted method of prayer to 'run around dressed like a giant chicken, screaming for someone to please put your bottom out'.

Still, nobody was hurt – and it's not like I have to return the costume.

. . .

. . . . . .

Harry would be absolutely *pissing* himself.

Year Six

Coffee With Cinzano And The Love Ninja

Squeezy Alice

I should tell him about Grant.

    I know I should.

    But I know what he'll say in response.

    And I don't want to hear it.

    I just don't.

    No. It's far easier to talk about Cinzano – so that is exactly what I'm going to do.

    I'll make him laugh. I'll brighten his day with my tale of woe – and I won't mention Grant at all. Because it doesn't matter. It's not important. Ben doesn't need to know everything.

    It's my life, after all. My decisions.

    Yes.

    Yes, that's right.

    Bang goes the rental car door, echoing around what looks like a newly resurfaced car park. The freshly painted white lines glow brightly in the sun in a way they never have before.

I am irrationally uncomfortable with this change. Popping Church is meant to stay the same. It's meant to be a bulwark against the vagaries of time and progress, not an indicator of them. That's not what churches are there for. They aren't supposed to change.

Not everything *has* to change.

But the car park has. And the church gates have been replaced too.

Look how new and shiny black they are.

It's *awful*.

I stride across the newly resurfaced car park, absolutely disgusted that I don't once have to look down to make sure I don't trip on a cracked bit of concrete. I deliberately look away from the church gates as I pass through them. Bloody stupid *new* things, with their *new* paint and lack of rust.

There are quite a few people about this morning. Not surprising for a Sunday.

I think the morning service must have recently let out. I'm not used to seeing this many people here. Another change I don't like. Maybe I should ask some of them what they think of the new gates and car park. I bet they hate them too.

I walk past the small gaggle of parishioners, and as I do I catch one old lady talking – in a rather posh and tremulous voice – to her friends.

'It's not right, Elizabeth! This is a place of worship, not a fancy dress shop!'

Aaah . . .

I slow my pace a little, pretending to look at a nearby grave.

'And it's not the first time. Trevor tells me he's been here before. Dressed as a chicken, the madman was!'

The others gasp.

'And he set fire to the altar!'

No, he didn't. The flames barely had time to set alight to his tail feathers before I'd bashed them out.

'And now he's back, dressed in that ridiculous get-up! It shouldn't be allowed! Trevor must do something!'

Oh, calm down, love. If you knew why he did it, you would understand a little more.

I speed up my progress again, now keen to see just how ridiculous Ben's costume is this year.

I round the corner of the church and spot a small group of people standing around a ninja.

Oh . . .

Yes, I can see why Trevor's number-one parishioner was quite upset. A peaceful churchyard in middle England is no place for a ninja. Especially not one with a whacking great big plastic sword slung over his back.

Did I mention the ninja in question is bright pink?

Because he is.

The brightest of bright pinks. Almost unbearable-to-look-at pink.

Pinkness on such a vast and climactic level that I'm surprised it hasn't attracted more scientific study.

Instead, it's just attracted a group of disgruntled-looking churchgoers, who are clearly quite miffed that a pink ninja is standing at one of the graves in their gloriously un-pink churchyard.

I wonder if any of them realise how much he looks like a giant dildo?

. . . doubtful. I'm not sure they are the types of people who would make such an association, and I'm frankly a little ashamed that I am.

I glance at my watch as I now hurry over to where Ben is being silently assailed by the damning looks of half a dozen church folk.

It's midday, which means Ben will be trying to carry out his ritual for Harry, as he normally does.

I know him well enough to know that not even the distraction of the people standing around him will stop him from doing what he does every year at midday.

I have to intervene on his behalf before somebody pushes him, or does something else to interrupt his little ceremony. These things are important to us. They help us to feel a little closer again to the people we feel like we're drifting away from more and more as every year goes by.

I've never slept on 'my' side of the bed again, for instance. And I wear Joe's excellent hat every time I'm out in the Australian sun. It's a size too big for me, and I really should buy another one, but I don't – for the same reason Ben will ignore the people standing around him, even though every fibre of his being wants to turn around and apologise.

'Good morning, everyone!' I say as I arrive.

It's funny, in years gone by I doubt I would have done something like this without feeling deeply uncomfortable about it, but I spend my work days ordering people about now, and with that comes a fair degree of confidence when dealing with crowds. I'll have to resist the urge to ask any of them if they fancy a haircut.

'I can assure you my friend here means no insult by the costume he is wearing,' I tell them, noticing that Ben's shoulders sag with what I hope is relief.

'Then why is he wearing it?' a particularly officious little man says. He's definitely the type that would complain about people having a nice time in next door's garden.

'His late brother was something of a practical joker,' I say, electing to go with the truth, 'and my friend here is honouring him by dressing like this and standing at his graveside. It's an act of love, and not meant to cause offence.'

The small crowd all visibly relax a little at this, even Mr Curtain Twitcher.

'If you wouldn't mind leaving us, so we can spend a little time with the people we've lost, I'd be ever so grateful.' My otherwise strong tone fumbles a touch as I get to the end of the sentence.

Grief can be quite a powerful weapon of persuasion when you need it to be. It got me out of a ticket in Neutral Bay a couple of months ago, when I was crying so hard I ran a red light (it was our anniversary) and now it's proving more than ample to disperse the nosey parkers, and allow me and Ben the quality time we need alone.

I nod with some satisfaction.

Yes, indeed. I can get people to do what I want, if I use the right tone.

. . . not everyone, mind you. Some people just can't take no for an answer, but we'll get to that shortly.

By the time Ben is finished with 'We Are the Champions', the gaggle of church folk have returned down the path to the entrance.

'Oh God, *thank you*,' Ben says, pulling down the ninja hood and mask. 'I thought I was in for it when they came over. Never seen people looking so angry at me.'

I stare at him.

'Bright pink?' I eventually say.

Ben rolls his eyes. 'Yes. Because making me dress as a plain old normal ninja just wasn't enough for my brother.'

'Are you aware of . . .' – how do I put this? – '. . . the fact that you strongly resemble something that *isn't* a ninja?' I cock my head. 'At least, I'm pretty sure Ninja doesn't make them. I could be wrong. They seem to put out every other implement you can think of.'

Ben's face falls. 'You mean a sex toy, don't you?'

'I do.'

157

'Yes. I sent Katie a picture before I came here. She said much the same thing.'

I laugh at this. Maybe I shouldn't feel quite so ashamed, after all. 'And how is your wife?'

Ben smiles and says, 'She's fine, thank you. Absolutely fine.'

The smile doesn't even begin to falter – but there's something there just the same, isn't there? I think we'll get to that soon, as well.

'Shall we sit down?' I suggest, pointing over at our now weathered wooden bench. 'The tree's grown big enough that it should hide us from any more nosey parkers who might want to come and berate the six-foot dildo and his friend.'

'Excellent idea,' Ben replies, and we move to the bench. 'How have you been?' he enquires as we sit down.

I think on this for a second. 'I have been . . . okay,' I tell him. Which is largely the truth. I don't feel like I've really moved on much from twelve months ago emotionally, but then things haven't really got any worse. I'm taking this as something of a win, though I doubt Ben will be all that satisfied with my answer.

Just as well I have Cinzano to distract him with.

No, no. I haven't started bringing alcohol from the 1980s with me to the church. That would likely go down even worse than the six-foot dildo.

Cinzano is a *person* – and the question Ben asks next leads us nicely on to an explanation.

'How did the challenge go?' he asks. 'Is that why you're feeling *okay*?'

I laugh ruefully. 'Oh, good God, no, Ben. Far from it.' I clear my throat and think about the best way to start.

I didn't seek out new friends the instant I got back to Sydney last year. In fact it took me a good four months to even contemplate Ben's challenge in any way, other than to dismiss it.

But it kept niggling away in the back of my mind, as I went home to my empty apartment, and only saw people during the day at work. There's only so long you can go without having somebody real to talk to.

I say somebody real, because I have been doing a lot of talking to Joe.

Out loud.

I'll pause and allow you to digest this. Please feel free to make a disturbed face as you do it.

'No,' Ben replies. 'I get it. We're all social animals, and even when the last thing you want to do is actually *socialise*, our brains have a way of creating interactions – even if it is entirely one-sided.'

'That's a very profound statement,' I tell him.

He shrugs. 'I spend my days working with people who are divorced from society. Homelessness often leads to isolation.'

I nod. Nice to know I'm not the only one, then.

The problem has got worse for me as the years in Australia have gone by. Initially I'd just talk to Joe inside my head, and only very occasionally. But that became more frequent over time, and in the last year or so it's become out loud.

Which is fine when you're in the confines of your own apartment – but when you forget where you are and start to speak to your dead husband in your office out the back of the hair salon you manage, and one of your staff catches you in a full-blown discussion over whether to continue using the current hair dye supplier or change to a new one – you know things have reached a point where you have a real problem.

I don't think Kelly told anyone else that their boss was sat behind her desk, arguing with herself about whether the Rose Gold from Moji Cosmetics was better value than the one from Bray & Whit, but I can't be 100 per cent sure.

What I was 100 per cent sure about at that point, though, was that I'd better make some sort of effort to meet new people I could befriend. My staff at the salon don't fit the bill, as I'm not the type of person who thinks it's right for a boss to be too close with her employees (which is *extremely* handy for a person who hasn't wanted to be too close to anyone anyway, I'm sure you'd agree), so my only other option was the internet.

Or more specifically, Facebook. So I fired up an account I hadn't touched in a very long time, and searched for meet-up groups in the Sydney area.

Of which there were several, I was surprised to find out. I shouldn't have been, though. Australia has a permanent transient population with a ton of immigration, so there's bound to be a lot of these kinds of things set up for strangers to get together.

We're all social animals, after all.

I choose a group that meets up in a pub on Military Road, only a couple of kilometres from my apartment. I can just go along, see how it goes and get out fast, if I feel it's not for me.

Which is exactly what I do. And while I've been averse to socialising for reasons which we've explored a great deal thus far, I am still able to do it when forced, without *too* many problems. Again, the benefits of working somewhere busy like a hair salon. I can easily hold a conversation if I want to. And not just with the phantom of the person I love. I am not socially awkward, just emotionally shut down. I'll leave you to decide which one is worse.

There are four other people at the meet-up. And they are all quite nice. Alex from Singapore is a shy but polite young man. Stacey from Brisbane is bubbly. Elsa from Sweden is reserved. And Elijah from Connecticut is charming, and ever so American.

I fail to connect on any level with any of them.

The same cannot be said for Elijah and Stacey, who I'm sure will enjoy the fiery romance they are no doubt about to embark on. You could have cut the sexual tension with a knife. The rest of us were just background noise.

As for me, the only tension I felt was whether I'd be able to get an Uber back to my apartment without surge pricing.

Despondent, I went home – and talked to Joe about how nice everyone was, and how the Chardonnay in the Black Cockatoo had improved since we were there for the DiMarco Salon Christmas party two years ago.

It took me another month to have a crack at a meet-up again, this time choosing to go to one at Mosman Hotel instead, for fear of bumping into Alex and Elsa again. I have no doubt Stacey and Elijah were off up to no good on their own.

There was a larger group at this second event, so I didn't get to know everyone. The ones I did were by and large as nice as the guys at the Black Cockatoo. Including a tall man with kind eyes called Grant, who had recently moved to Sydney from his native Cairns for work.

Unfortunately, almost everyone at the meet-up was put in the shadows by Cinzano.

Oh boy.

Here we go, then . . .

Cinzano is one of life's . . . er . . . 'characters'. More effervescent than a champagne factory, Cinzano (or 'Cinzie', as she preferred you call her) could probably make friends with a corpse, if she so desired.

And for some bloody reason, Cinzano had decided that night that the person she most wanted to be friends with was *me*.

I put this down to several factors. One, I run a hair salon, and Cinzano had a wealth of silky, jet-black wavy hair that most women would kill for. Especially women in their fifties, which Cinzano is. Second, her family was from Portugal origi-nally (though she herself came from Perth) so felt some sort of

European kinship with me – the only other person with a background from that part of the world. Third, I bought her a drink.

. . . that's about it. Cinzano locked her attentions on to me because I gave her advice about what products to use to reduce oiliness, had once visited the Algarve on a family holiday when I was twelve, and forked out for a Malibu and Red Bull.

And when Cinzano—

Hang on . . . I should probably add here that her surname is Bella, and not 'Bianco'. In case you were wondering – which I'm sure you probably were. Bella isn't her actual surname, either, needless to say. It's Parrot.

And for that matter, her first name is not actually Cinzano, of course.

It's Joyce.

Joyce Parrot.

Joyce Parrot died the day her marriage to Barry Parrot ended ten years ago. Cinzano Bella was born from the wreckage.

Anyway, where was I?

When Cinzano decides she wants to be *bestest* friends with you, you really don't have much of a choice in the matter.

She bullied me into giving her my phone number that evening. She also bullied three other people into doing the same thing, but not with quite the same amount of energy.

'We're going to have such fun!' Cinzano told me, as she hugged me like a long-lost sister, while we were stood outside waiting for our respective taxis. 'You're so squeezy!' she added, as she cracked at least three of my ribs.

How does one take being called *squeezy*?

Is there any circumstance under which it can't be seen as a commentary on your weight?

Fortunately, Cinzano lives in Bondi Junction, across the other side of the bridge, so I didn't have to share a cab with her – as we were going in opposite directions.

But on the brief Uber ride home, I managed to convince myself that hanging out with Cinzano might actually be *good fun*. Yes, yes. If I was going to make friends, it might as well be with a person who could offer me an *exciting* time.

Go the *whole hog*, so to speak.

It's funny how we make these kinds of rationalisations for decisions we feel forced into, isn't it?

I got a text from Cinzano about twenty minutes later, as I was making myself some toast.

LUVLY to MEET u, Squeezy ALICE! We'll HOOK UP soon!

I don't know for sure how psychopaths construct a text message, but I'd be willing to bet it's in a similar fashion.

Two days then go by before Cinzano texts me again. I guess she needed the time to murder the other three people whose phone numbers she got at the meet-up?

FANCY a COFFEE, Squeezy ALICE? High SOCIETY in ROSE Bay do a luvly FLAT white!

Oh, my GOD. I AM going TO get MURDERED.

I put the doubts and silliness aside for a moment, and properly consider the offer. I've had at least half a dozen customers come into the salon in the last few months and recommend the coffee at High Society in Rose Bay – and this is the first time I've had the opportunity to visit it as anything other than a lonely loser.

Okay, the person I'd be visiting with will probably be harvesting my kidneys by lunchtime, but at least I will have died having sampled what apparently is the best flat white in the Sydney area.

I agree – against my better judgement – to meet Cinzano at 11 a.m., and receive a flurry of emojis in response that I think are completely at random, but who can be sure?

As you can imagine, it's with some trepidation that I jump on the ferry and make my way down to Rose Bay. It's a gloriously sunny day in Sydney, so my mood is lifted a great deal by that as I cross the harbour. I also think that my mood might be lifted by the fact I'm finally making some sort of effort to see new people in a social setting. This is a very big deal for me. And regardless of how it goes, I'm proud of the fact I'm going through with it.

Cinzano is dressed in a pantsuit from the 1970s. This pantsuit is a vibrant mixture of pink, white, red, green, yellow and blue stripes.

There's every chance it can be observed from orbit.

Her wealth of black hair cascades around her shoulders like a waterfall, and her make-up choices would suit the evil queen from *Snow White*.

None of it should work. But it absolutely does. Largely because Cinzano has the personality to pull it off.

She also orders me the flat white I have longed to try, and her a long black with milk. The barista tries to say that this is in fact an *Americano*, but Cinzano's having none of that. It's a long black with milk that she wants, nothing else.

Because there's every chance her outfit would set off the sprinkler system, we sit outside under an umbrella to keep the sun off, and as soon as my arse has hit the seat, the performance begins.

Cinzano can talk.

No, sorry, I mean Cinzano can TALK.

About Australia, about Portugal, about coffee, about food, about the weather, about sport, about chickens, about ducks, about cars, about trucks, about nice things, and bad things, and all things in between.

It's like having the entire internet shouted at me.

Cinzano is animated to the point of being sued by Disney. The hands fly, the legs fly, the head flies, the hair flies – and the flies avoid her for fear of being whacked out of the air.

I am stunned.

It's as if I've been saving up all of my social interactions from the past four years into one intensive, concentrated session.

I say 'interactions' but I don't really do much interacting. Trying to butt in on Cinzano is rather like attempting to stop an aeroplane propeller with a lightly cooked sausage.

I learn an awful lot about her during her conversation with herself. I learn that she's really called Joyce Parrot . . . and gain more detail than I ever could have wanted about the reasons for the breakdown of her marriage. Barry the bastard was putting his lightly cooked sausage in places he shouldn't have been.

And there's a strident quality to Cinzano's thick west Australian accent that I find fascinating. She doesn't necessarily speak loudly, but she's shouting at the top of her voice all the same. It's the tone, you see. It cuts through anything. Including the conversations of all the more softly spoken Sydneysiders around us.

11 a.m. fast turns into midday. By 1 p.m. I'm starving hungry, but don't even get the chance to voice this before Cinzano orders us both smashed avo on toast. She doesn't ask me if I *want* smashed avo on toast, you understand. I just end up with it in front of me, as Cinzano regales me with the story of how she adopted a duck.

I wish I had the time and the energy to explain further about the duck adoption, but it took Cinzano a good three-quarters of an hour to go through the whole thing with me. It was a tale so epic and bizarre that my mind wasn't entirely able to grasp it, but I think it involved a journey to Mordor at some point.

By the time 3 p.m. rolls around, my arse is as numb as my brain, Cinzano is on her seventh long black with milk, and I start thinking of the ways I'm going to punish Ben Fielding for putting me up to this in the first place.

'Sorry.'

It's while Cinzano is barraging me with a story about how she once met Delta Goodrem in the ladies' changing rooms at Target that I come up with an escape plan.

Or, should I say, I make a great show of looking at my watch, before blurting out, 'I have a doctor's appointment!' just as Cinzano is telling me how Delta Goodrem is a lot shorter in real life than she looks on TV. And a lot more brunette, and a bit fatter.

'Oh, do you?' she says, her face dropping into one of extreme sympathy in an instant. 'What is it, Squeezy Alice? Is it something serious?'

Oh, good God, now I have to make up a reason for going to the doctor.

'It's nothing, really,' I say in a hushed tone. 'Nothing that important.'

Her face drops even more with the burden of all the sympathy she's carrying. 'Is it your bits?'

'Pardon me?'

'Is it . . . you know . . . your *bits*?' She points down towards her crotch in a gesture that I'm sure she thinks is surreptitious and not at all obvious, but in actual fact resembles someone conducting air traffic control.

Fantastic. I've sat here for four hours with this woman, and the only thing she's got round to asking me about is my vagina.

Don't pretend you're not fine with that. The last thing you really want to do is to talk to anyone about your life.

I shake my head. 'No. It's my . . . my head. I've been getting a lot of headaches recently.'

'Oh no! Do you know why?'

Yes, Cinzano. The combination of that pantsuit and the story about the adopted duck. They're enough to give a corpse a headache.

'No. Nothing serious, though, I'm sure.'

Cinzano leans across the table and grabs my hand. 'I'm there for you, Squeezy Alice! If you need anything, I'm *right there.*'

Up to and including being sat beside my bed at three o'clock in the morning, looking at me intensely, I'd imagine.

'Thank you, Cinzano,' I say.

'It's Cinzie to you!' she shrieks.

Oh God. I have to get out of here. The looks we're getting could stun a horse.

Or an adopted duck.

Cinzano and I part with another one of her rib-breaking hugs, and I hurry back to the ferry terminal, occasionally throwing looks over my shoulder to check she isn't following me.

By the time I get home, I am exhausted.

Still, I have no desire to hold another conversation with my dead husband for the time being. I have no desire to hold a conversation with anyone ever again, to be honest with you.

'Is that the last time you saw Cinzano?' Ben then asks.

I go slightly bug-eyed. 'Ha! I wish!'

Cinzano in fact bullies me into *two more* meet-ups with her. One that goes on for about three months, and a second that I'm still not 100 per cent sure is actually finished. For all I know, my poor brain has rebelled against reality and created a fantasy of me continuing my life Cinzano-free, while my body still sits there being bombarded by information and anecdotes, with a thin line of dribble coming from my mouth.

Still, if that's not the case, and this is the real world, I eventually managed to pluck up the courage to turn Cinzano down for a fourth meet-up, citing a busy work schedule.

I had to do the same for her fifth request . . . and sixth, seventh, eighth, ninth and tenth.

I made an awful lot of imaginary visits back to the UK in that time period, let me tell you.

'But she finally got the message?' Ben asks hopefully.

Nope. No message was received unfortunately.

Not until the police nearly had to get involved.

'The police?'

Yes. But only because Cinzano decided to come to the salon one afternoon.

How the hell she managed this I don't know. I never had the chance to tell her where I actually worked, during one of our three-month-long conversations. I can only assume she just trolled around the upmarket hair salons of Sydney until she found the right one.

And when she did, she came striding on to the salon's floor, demanding to speak to her Squeezy Alice. I was out the back doing the stocktake. But I could still hear her voice alright.

How many hair salons had she walked into demanding to see her Squeezy Alice before she got to mine? Who can say?

The Australians like their stories of legendary nutters, and there's every chance a new one has now been coined about the multi-coloured banshee who roams the streets of old Sydney, crying for her Squeezy Alice to come and save her from the Americano monster.

I have never been quite as embarrassed in my life as the day a security guard had to extricate a lunatic from my hair salon. Luckily, the small complex of boutique shops DiMarco's is in has someone permanently engaged to provide that very service, and even more luckily Cooper was across the way chatting up the girl who runs the overpriced clothes store opposite the salon.

Unluckily, Cooper is twenty-three, and a string bean with arms, so Cinzano was able to put up a pretty decent fight.

'Squeezy Alice!' she screamed, making me wince – not just because she insists on calling me by that stupid name, but also because I know damned well that everyone else will now be calling me it behind my back. 'Stop this! We're friends!'

'Er . . . we can't be, Cinzano!' I retort, as Cooper's weedy little arms try to drag her out of the front door of the shop. 'I . . . I . . .' What kind of excuse can I make up?

'She's moving back to the UK!' pipes up Madeline the stylist from beside me.

'Yes!' I shout in agreement. 'I'm going back to the UK!'

'Why, Squeezy Alice?' Cinzano intones, her face a picture of utter regret.

Yes, why, Squeezy Alice? What reason can you give her?

'She's been thrown out of Australia for gambling offences!' cries Madeline.

'What?' I round on her with a look of horror on my face.

Madeline looks equally horrified, but shrugs her shoulders and says, 'Held an illegal blackjack tournament, she did. Skimmed off the top as well.'

I stare at Madeline with disbelief. 'Please stop helping,' I tell her in a desperate voice.

'Oh, Squeezy Alice, how could you?' Cinzano exclaims, now halfway out the front door thanks to Cooper's efforts. The three customers we have in this morning are all looking like they wish they were anywhere else. I have to nip this in the bud. I have to get her out of here as quickly as possible. Which I guess means—

I affect an expression of the deepest and most sincere regret. 'I couldn't help myself! I was *weak*, Cinzano! I'm no good to you as a friend!'

'Is that why you said you were never around for coffee?'

'Yes! That's absolutely right. I am . . . I am a bad person!'

'And a convicted felon in three states!' Madeline pipes up.

'Be quiet!' I hiss at her.

'Time to leave, madam!' Cooper insists.

'Yes! Leave, Cinzano! There are much better people for you out there than me!' I wail, and start to make shooing motions with my hands.

Cinzano looks at me with a mixture of pity and disgust. 'You could have told me about your problems when we talked!' she tells me.

'When?' I snap back, rather unintentionally.

But Cooper has finally got on top of the situation, and Cinzano is fully out of the salon now. Without another word exchanged between us, she is frogmarched back out on to Military Road, and the last I see of her is her wild hair flailing in the wind.

The last I see of her in real life, that is. I continue to have nightmares.

They are still preferable to the ones I have about Joe.

I turn slowly back to Madeline. 'What was *that* all about?' I plead.

She contrives to look apologetic. 'Sorry, Alice. My cousin from Auckland got thrown out for doing all of that stuff a couple of years ago. I figured it'd be a good excuse for you.'

I'm suddenly aware of the stares my customers are giving me.

Sigh. This is going to take a lot of explaining – and possibly several free haircuts.

Ben chuckles with laughter, making the plastic sword strapped to his back wobble about. 'She sounds incredible,' he says with disbelief.

I nod. 'Sydney is home to a lot of characters. She was most definitely one of them.'

'And you really haven't seen her since?'

'Nope. Though every time I see a woman with thick black hair I go into panic stations.'

'Yeah, I bet.' Ben scratches his chin ruefully, and then thinks of something else. 'Did you try the meet-up again?' he says, hopefully. 'Was there anyone else you met who might have been a better fit for you at the same meeting? Anyone at all?'

I stare at him for a second. 'No. No one else, unfortunately.'

Because there wasn't, was there?

I haven't been on another meet-up since Cinzano, and there certainly *wasn't* anyone else I enjoyed talking to at the one I met her at.

Also, as a way of apologising, Madeline asked me if I'd like to come out with her and her friends to their favourite bar on Military Road . . . and I almost went. I *almost* did. It might have been nice.

. . . but then I know they'd ask me about myself. Because that's what you do when you go out for drinks, isn't it? You talk. You get into conversations. You talk about your life. And Madeline would ask me about my past life in the UK at some point, and I'd have to tell her about Joe.

So I didn't go. Even though part of me wanted to.

And there really has been no one else.

No one else at all.

Definitely *not* Grant. Tall, kind Grant, with the sad eyes – who had moved from Cairns to Sydney for work.

No. I didn't see him again, either, despite the fact he gave me his phone number too, and said he'd love to meet up with me again – just the two of us this time.

But the phone number went into the bin, and I went for coffee with Cinzano instead, because *oh, my God* that was so much easier than even contemplating meeting up with kind, sad-eyed Grant again.

'That's a shame,' Ben says, searching my face for any hint that I might not be telling the whole truth.

But I'm *not* lying. I *am* telling the truth. There was no one else – because the phone number written on the paper serviette went into the bin, and I went for coffee with Cinzano, and the story about her is the only one that matters, and the only one I want to tell today.

Grant doesn't matter.

Because Joe still *does* – so very, very much. And I'd rather be saddled with a reputation for being a gambling fiend and a felon in three states than ever sit across a table from another man who isn't my Joe.

And the nights when I have nightmares about Cinzano (particularly the one where Paul DiMarco is in the store, firing me for running an illegal blackjack tournament out the back of his salon) are always better. I'd dream about Cinzano every night of the week if it meant I didn't dream about that bloody A&E department, and how I'm always late. Always too late. Always too. Bloody. *Late.*

'Alice? Are you okay?' Ben asks, leaning forward a little to look into my downcast eyes.

I try my best to snap out of it. Something it takes me more and more time to do the older I get. 'Yep. I'm fine. Just thinking about how horrible that day in the salon was.'

'Yes, I'm sure.' He bangs a pink fist on his pink knee. 'I should never have challenged you to do that.'

Oh, no. Here we go . . .

Harry's come out to play, and has squatted himself on Ben's shoulders, the way he always does.

I want to tell Ben that no, he's wrong. He was right to challenge me to find new friends, because at least I caught a glimpse of what it's like to have a social life again. If Cinzano hadn't been a lunatic, who knows what kind of friendship we might have had? And if I hadn't thrown that serviette with a hastily scrawled phone number away in the bin because I'm terrified of actually being open with another human being, who knows what kind of—

'And what about the challenge I gave you?' I say firmly.

I need to turn the tables. I need this to *shift*.

Ben lets out a long-drawn-out breath. 'I talked to Katie,' he says.

'How did it go?'

'Pretty well. She was very understanding, like you'd said she'd be.'

'Of course she was.'

Then his face falls. 'But something awful has happened. Something I don't know what to do about at all.'

Oh no. Maybe it was *me* who shouldn't have issued the challenge. 'What is it? What's going on?'

He looks at me mournfully. 'Katie wants to have a baby. It's a disaster.'

Ben

How the hell can I be a father right now?

. . . actually, I don't literally mean *right now*, right now. Because anyone wandering around a graveyard dressed as a pink ninja should of course be precluded from ever having children.

But when I'm not doing something so bloody hare-brained, I am still ill-suited to bringing a child into this world.

My wages won't support it, for starters. I'm doing well in my job, and am now a senior caseworker at Shelter. I get the satisfaction of helping many homeless people into more stable and happy lives – but unfortunately that doesn't come with a great pay packet, as you'd probably expect from a charity. Getting clients like bright-eyed Sam Chaney into a dry, comfortable new council flat, or grumpy but lovable Alan Brady off the white cider, makes me feel like a million bucks – but doesn't *pay it*, unfortunately.

Katie's teaching wages are better than mine, and without her contribution we wouldn't be able to stay afloat. We do okay, and can just about afford the mortgage we have on our two-bed terrace – but the idea of introducing another human being into that unsteady equation makes my blood run cold.

My job tends to show me just how difficult life can get, if you allow it to get away from you too much. So many of the people we help only became homeless due to financial hardship. These are by and large decent, honest, hardworking folk who either made poor decisions, or were battered by the vagaries of the economy. I've had men and women who went from kings to paupers through my door, more often than I can remember. And while I've taken great satisfaction getting them back on their feet, I also see each and every one of them as a cautionary tale.

Having a baby right now is not the right thing for Katie and me to do. We can't afford it, and I can't afford to . . . well . . .

'Fail,' Alice says, in a matter-of-fact voice.

'Exactly!' I reply, clapping my hands together. 'Things are more or less well balanced at the moment, and I'm coping with life okay. But I know myself well enough to know that trying to be a dad would throw me off completely.'

'Because of how expensive it is.'

'Yes.'

'And for no other reason.' The doubtful tone to Alice's voice is unavoidable.

'That's right,' I tell her, very deliberately.

'Hmmm.'

I shuffle on the bench a bit, suddenly feeling very uncomfortable.

This is not because of the pink ninja suit. It's actually *very* comfortable. A little *too* comfortable.

When I got dressed in it this morning I actually felt like it could be something I'd wear around the house, were it not for the fact it's bright pink and comes with a hooded mask. The pyjama bits are nice and loose, though. Very good for the testicles, I've found. The material is quite soft and pliable, and I have to admire Harry's choice of manufacturer.

I don't admire my inability to speak plainly with Alice, though. This is the first time I've ever felt like this with her, but then again this is the first time I've ever felt a bit *silly* about how I really feel.

Oh, I've *looked* silly more times than I care to remember around her – but *felt* silly? Not so much.

It's much easier to tell her that I don't want a baby because I can't afford it than it is to tell her it's because I don't think I'd make as good a father as my brother would have.

And I know *he'd* have made a good father, because he had to substitute for mine so many times. I'm reminded of the main occasion he did this every time I stand at that grave and wait for 'We Are the Champions' to conclude, but there were plenty of other occasions, weren't there? When our father was busy with a surgery, or a convention, or a golf game, or simply locked away in his study, doing whatever fathers like mine did when they were locked away in their studies.

That's where he was when I popped in to see my parents this morning.

Up in his bloody study again. Sat there in his incredibly ancient and yet still immaculate tweed jacket and trousers, hunkered over his desk, with those little round glasses perched on the end of his nose. Didn't come out to say hello once.

'He's busy with his memoir,' my mother said apologetically.

I wonder if the memoir will feature anything about how bad a father he was to two boys? I very much doubt it. My father has never been one for self-reflection.

I guess in a lot of ways Harry had it worse than me. I had a cool older brother to substitute for the attentions of a father who never wanted to give any. What was it like for Harry himself?

Hard, but character-building, I have to assume. That's why he was so strong.

Yes. He would have made a cracking father. If for no other reason than he knew how to buy a really comfortable ninja suit. Which is probably right up there on the wish list of most small boys when it comes to fatherly requirements and expectations.

I'd have picked a much more *sensible*-looking black ninja suit, which would have probably felt like walking around in a cheese grater.

I wonder what I'd write in a memoir of my life?

Would I have enough self-awareness to know that having such an emotionally and physically divorced father is also a reason why I don't want to be one?

What if I'm like him?

What if I can't cope?

'Okay, I don't want to be a dad because mine was terrible,' I splutter to Alice.

'Welcome back,' she says drily. 'I wondered where you'd wandered off to. I was about to call for a rescue party.'

'Sorry. I've had a lot on my mind.'

'Sounds to me like you've only had *one* thing on your mind, actually,' she sniffs. 'Which . . . I'm very much hoping you've discussed properly *with your wife*.'

I have to laugh at this. Alice can be very direct when she wants to be. I'm surprised she got caught up with that Cinzano woman as badly as she did.

'Yes, Alice, me and Katie have talked about all of it. Extensively. Over *many* conversations. I wasn't about to let you down now, was I?'

'And how does she feel?'

I make a face. 'She understands where I'm coming from, but is frustrated that I can't see where we should be going *to*.'

Alice nods. 'Always a very astute woman, your wife.'

'Yes, she is. But that doesn't change the situation. We still haven't got enough money to have a kid.'

'And you haven't got enough confidence, either,' she says, sympathetically.

'Nope. I can come to a graveyard dressed as a giant pink ninja dildo, but I can't work up the courage to have a baby.'

'I'd imagine the second one is far harder than the first,' Alice agrees.

Which perks up my curiosity a little. 'Did you . . . Did you and Joe ever think of having children?'

This is *not* a deliberate tactic to change subjects. I am keen to hear anyone else's insights about children these days – especially those who never had them.

Alice shakes her head. 'No, we were never that type of couple. Maybe that could have changed, but . . . well, you know.'

I nod.

'But I doubt we would have changed our minds, to be honest,' she continues. 'It's one of those fundamental things in life – and I don't think that many people really alter their opinion of it as the years go by. I've known couples split up because one wanted children and the other didn't.'

My blood runs cold.

'Take that look of abject horror off your face,' Alice says. 'I don't think that's the problem you and Katie have.'

'Then what is?'

'You both want children, but only one of you is ready for it.'

'That feels about right.'

Alice raises an eyebrow. 'You ever consider that maybe Katie's outlook is better than yours? That she understands the way things are a little more accurately? Can't you trust her feelings, instead of yours . . . and go for it?'

'It doesn't work like that,' I admit. 'Not in my head, anyway.'

'Why?'

'Because I have no doubt about her parenting abilities, it's just mine I'm not confident about. Having kids is such a huge responsibility, and I don't want them to end up like Long Jonathan, if I'm a bad father.'

'Excuse me?' Alice says, a bit taken aback.

'Sorry . . . Long Jonathan is a homeless man I know through work. Guy in his early twenties, he'd been on the streets since he was seventeen, thanks to parents who were eventually unable to take care of themselves, let alone anyone else. Lovely chap, once you get to know him.'

'Oh, come on, Ben. I doubt you'd be *that* bad a father. You come from much better stock!'

I give Alice a sideways look. 'Long Jonathan's parents were a wealthy middle-class couple with their own interior design business.'

Alice looks stunned. 'Really?'

'Yes, *really*. Things fell apart when the business partner they had ran off with most of their capital. The company went under, and they went bankrupt. His father started drinking heavily, getting more and more abusive as he did, and his mother suffered a hideous spiral of depression. Jonathan had to get out, and found himself with nothing and no one. Trust me, Alice, homelessness can happen to anyone, from any background.'

'Well, that doesn't mean anything like that would happen to *you*,' Alice says, with a somewhat snippy tone. People don't like their preconceived notions challenged, and get uncomfortable when they are. I don't blame Alice, though – it's a very common prejudice I come up against in my line of work.

We're all prey to the vagaries of the world around us, and none of us know how fast things can go downhill if we're hit with an out-of-the-blue disaster.

That's what makes me so afraid to have a kid. What if I'm one of those people who can't cope well with catastrophe? Will I also have a seventeen-year-old son out on the streets, while I drink myself to death?

'It can happen to any one of us, Alice,' I point out, knowing how right I am.

'Well, I still don't think it would happen to *you*,' she insists. 'Do you think that type of thing could happen to someone like Harry?'

'Of course not.'

'I thought you said it could happen to *anyone*?'

'That's not what I meant. I meant . . . It's not . . . Oh God, I don't know.'

Even in my certainty about the pitfalls of life, I cannot imagine Harry falling into any of them.

I think there may be a *slight* chance I have my brother up on a pedestal.

Jesus, you bloody think so, bro?

'Well, there you go, you're *wrong*,' Alice continues to push. 'Harry would have made a damned good father, and so would you!'

'That's not how it works, Alice, I—'

'Challenge!' she cries to the heavens.

'Oh, bloody hell, *really*?' I reply in dismay, knowing what's coming.

'Yes, *really*.' She points a finger at me. 'Try for a baby, Fielding!'

'I can't do that!'

'Yes, you can!' Alice says, eyes bulging as she continues to point at me with one arm stiffly stretched out and a finger hovering right in front of my face. 'You, Benjamin Lionel Fielding—'

'My middle name is Henry.'

'You, Benjamin Henry Fielding, will, over the course of the next twelve months, attempt to knock your poor bloody wife up!' Alice exclaims.

'I can't just—'

'Up the bloody duff!'

'It's not that—'

'Pregnant and happy!'

'I don't think—'

'With child!'

'Alright, alright, give it a bloody rest!'

The finger continues to point. 'Will you do it?'

'Yes, yes! I'll bloody do it!'

'Good!' The finger points skyward and a triumphant expression crosses Alice's face. 'So shall it be done!'

Good grief. Have I just agreed to have a child based on a silly challenge laid down for me by a friend? Is that the only way I can even begin to push past my hang-ups?

Mind you . . . I'm not the only one with a hang-up, am I?

'Challenge,' I say in a quiet but insistent voice.

Alice sits up again and squares her shoulders. 'Go on, then, lay it on me,' she says.

I look at her in what I hope is a meaningful way. 'Find Grant with the kind eyes again, and go out on a date with him.'

Aah . . . *Yes.* That's what I was expecting. That look of shocked surprise . . .

Because I saw the way her face changed when she mentioned Grant in the middle of her story about Cinzano.

And I may be a shit prospect as a father, but I know how other people *tick.*

'W-what are you t-talking about?' Alice stutters.

'You know what I'm talking about. *Who* I'm talking about. Find him again, Alice. And if you do, go out with him. Just see where it leads, okay?'

The look of protest burns in her eyes. She wants to tell me I'm wrong. She wants to tell me that she has no idea what I'm on about.

Alice

'I can't, Ben!' I cry, tears coming unbidden and unwanted. 'I can't do it to him!'

'Who? Joe?'

'Yes!' I wail. 'Yes, yes! I can't do it!'

Ben pauses, searching my face with a look that makes me feel deeply uncomfortable.

Stop looking into my soul, damn you.

'Joe would want you to find someone new, Alice.' The tone he uses is gentle, but it still cuts me to ribbons. 'He'd want you to be close to another person.'

'But *I* don't want to find somebody new!'

'Are you absolutely sure about that?'

'Yes!'

181

I don't need or want anybody else, damn it. That part of my life died when Joe did, and I have no interest in trying to recreate it with another person. Why can't Ben see that?

So why did you take Grant's number back out of the bin and put it in the kitchen drawer when you got back from coffee with Cinzano?

Because . . . Because . . .

'I don't want anybody else . . . but it's nice to feel *wanted*, isn't it?' I say out loud, half to myself and half to Ben.

'Yes, it is,' he replies. 'Everybody needs to feel wanted, Alice. And there's nothing wrong with that.'

'No, but—'

'No, but nothing. If you're going to insist I put my worries aside and have a *baby*, you can at least find a nice person like Grant to go on a *date* with.'

Which is fair enough, even if I partially hate him for saying it.

Doesn't he see how right Katie is to want to have a child with him, though?

It shouldn't need me to challenge him to do it!

Ben

Doesn't she see how right I am that meeting a new man would be good for her?

It shouldn't need me to challenge her to do it!

Alice

'Right! Fine! I'll see if I can track him down.'

'And if you can't?'

'Then I don't know!'

'. . . you'll find someone else instead. As long as you try to make a meaningful connection with someone who doesn't call you Squeezy Alice.'

I have to laugh at this. What else can I do?

As far as I was concerned, my experience with Cinzano was the beginning and end of my attempts to find new friends in Sydney – but Ben clearly has other ideas.

All I can say, though, is that I'd better come back here next year and find out he's impregnated his wife.

Damn.

I wish we'd never started these silly challenges in the first place.

It was your idea.

Yes, yes, I know that!

'Can we talk about something else?' I plead with Ben. 'We've both made our promises for the year. I don't think we need to run it into the ground.'

'Agreed,' Ben replies. 'Would you like to go and get a coffee somewhere? I'd love a long black with milk.'

Year Seven

SAUCEPANS AND SPIDERS

Ben

'Are you really sure about this?' Katie asks, watching me climb
awkwardly into this year's stupid costume.

'I think so,' I reply, extremely unsure of myself.

Because how can this be appropriate?

How can this be right?

How can I stand there today, dressed like this, after everything
that's happened?

'He'd understand, you know,' Katie says, sitting down on the
bed next to me, placing a gentle, comforting hand on my back. 'If
you didn't do it.'

'Yes. He might. But then again . . .' I trail off.

Harry probably *would* understand. Because there's no way he
could have thought about something like this happening when he
tasked me with these ridiculous annual pilgrimages. It would have
been the farthest thing from his mind. A complete impossibility.

Surely he wouldn't have expected me to go to the church this year, would he? I know I wouldn't expect it of him, if our roles were reversed.

I shouldn't go.

I really shouldn't. Katie is right.

'It'll be fine,' I promise her. 'I can do it.'

She sighs. 'Okay . . . but if Alice isn't there for any reason, you bloody *call me*, Ben Fielding. I'm not having you down there on your own today.'

I nod and give my wife a long hug. The longer the hug, the longer I can stand up.

'I'll see you later,' I eventually tell Katie, getting up off the bed slowly. She gets to her feet as well, gives me a kiss and watches me leave the bedroom, that look of concern never leaving her face.

Just get out of the car and get it done, bro. Because whatever else has happened, you're still here for me, aren't you? And she told you to come. Said it would be wrong if you didn't, so get out of the car and get it done.

Yes. Our mother did tell me to come.

In fact, she *insisted* on it.

Which is probably the only reason I managed to get down here in this incongruously awful outfit.

Honestly, your timing is either perfect or the worst thing to ever happen, Harry.

Still, I'm here now, and whether I like it or not, I *am* dressed as The Undertaker from the WWE – no matter how grossly inappropriate that costume is for both this location and the past year I've been through.

The black, full-length leotard rides up into my crotch as I stumble across the back car park. I am dismayed by how much my little paunch shows underneath it.

I would have preferred this to be a much earlier costume, to be honest, when I had the body for it.

Not that I ever really had the body for a skintight, black, full-length bodysuit, giant black leather duster coat, long black wig, purple gloves and a big black undertaker's hat. Only one man in history ever had the body for it, and even he probably felt self-conscious every now and again.

I just hope nobody asks me to conduct a service while I'm in the cemetery.

I've been to enough funerals this year, thank you very much.

And I see that Alice is already here.

There she is, standing at Joe's grave, looking down at him, and lost deep in thought.

She doesn't appear to have changed a bit.

Not like me.

My little paunch is testament to that.

Things were so different the last time we were here together. It feels like far more than a year has passed.

I take a deep breath, and walk slowly towards her. She's so lost in thought I almost feel like I'd be rude to interrupt her, but it's nearly midday and I have to get this stupid ritual out of the way.

I don't want to have anything to do with it. Not this year. But I know I *have* to. Because she *told* me to. And I don't want to let her down. Not at the moment. Not when she's still so fragile.

'Hi Alice,' I say in a soft voice, causing her to start out of whatever mild trance she's been in. She looks at the watch on her wrist.

'Oh God, I didn't realise how long I'd been here!' she exclaims in some surprise, before smiling and giving me a hug.

It's not Harry, but it'll do. It'll do just fine.

'How are you, Ben?' Alice says as she steps back and gives me a look up and down.

'I'm . . . I've been better,' I tell her.

Her face falls. 'Oh, I'm so sorry to hear that. Can you tell me what's happened?'

I point at Harry's grave. 'Of course. Just let me . . . let me get this over and done with, okay?'

'Sure,' she replies, and steps away, going over to our bench, while I go to stand at the end of Harry's final resting place.

I deliberately do not look at the fresh grave that lies a few feet behind it.

Alice hasn't noticed it, or if she has, it hasn't registered on her at all. But then, why would it?

'We Are the Champions' begins, and this year I can picture that 'father–son' sports day with more clarity than I think I ever have before. And for the first time in years, I start to cry as I stand there, and wait for it to be over – thinking about how proud and how sad I felt that day on that podium, with my brother standing next to me, and my father nowhere to be seen.

Yes. Harry would have made a fantastic father. That fact never changes.

Neither does the fact I am still not one.

My eyes travel to the grave behind Harry's again, and I am so very glad that The Undertaker costume doesn't come with make-up, because it would be halfway down my face by now.

The song finishes, and I wipe away the tears with the purple glove on my right hand.

Now all I have to do is turn around and tell Alice what's happened.

It's the hardest thing I've ever done in my life.

As soon as she sees my face, Alice is up off the bench and over to me. 'Oh Ben! What's happened?' she exclaims, hugging me once more.

I sniff, squeeze my eyes together and slump into her.

'My father's dead,' I tell her, in a dull tone.

Alice

I don't want to let go of him.

I just want to stand here and hold him while he sobs into my shoulder.

I'll ask him how it happened soon, and hopefully he'll want to talk about it, but for now, all I want to do is hold him. Because sometimes that's all somebody really needs.

And I can do it for him this time. Because I'm not grieving now – or at least, my grief is a smoothed-over rock from being handled so much. It's still heavy, but it's much easier to hold these days.

I let Ben cry for a little while longer until the worst is over, before detaching myself, and moving him over to sit down on the bench.

'Oh God, I'm so sorry,' he says as we do this.

'You've got nothing to be sorry about. And I'm so sorry you've lost your dad. Is he . . .'

I look up and around the graveyard for a second.

'Yeah,' Ben says, picking up on my meaning. 'Behind Harry.'

'Must have been strange and awful coming here for yet another funeral,' I say.

He nods. 'It was. Felt wrong in a weird way as well. Probably because I was dressed in a sensible suit . . . and you weren't here.'

'I doubt I would have helped much.'

'Maybe, maybe not. But at least you could have met Katie.'

I smile. 'That would have been lovely.'

He pauses for a moment to take off the massive black hat, along with the very cheap-looking black wig.

'Who are you supposed to be this time?' I ask.

'You never watch any WWE wrestling?' he replies, not sounding all that surprised.

'No, that one passed me by, I have to say.'

'Harry and I used to love it when we were kids. Not a WrestleMania went by without us glued to the television. I'm dressed as one of the most famous wrestlers of the lot. The Undertaker.' He makes an awkward face.

'Oh God. That's a bit on the nose, isn't it?'

He smiles ruefully. 'It sure as hell is. Harry's timing is, as ever, *impeccable.*'

'You think he would have changed the costume if he'd known?'

'Oh, good lord, no,' Ben says, allowing himself a full-throated laugh. 'Katie said I probably shouldn't come dressed like him, though.'

'Not surprising.'

'She doesn't quite get why I continue to do this, I don't think.'

'I'm sure she does, Ben. It's just that maybe this time around things are a bit too . . . I don't know . . . *raw?* Must be hard for her to see you this upset, and maybe she thinks the silly costume just makes things worse. I wouldn't worry about the argument.'

'It's not the only one we've had recently,' he admits, drawing a concerned look from yours truly. 'I'm afraid . . . I'm afraid I didn't do the challenge this time around.'

I can barely take the look of apologetic dismay on his face. 'It's okay, Ben. I totally understand.' I heave a sigh. 'I have to confess, I wish I hadn't done mine, either.'

'Why's that?'

I shake my head. 'No, no. You first. You sound like you need to talk about all of this a lot more than you need to hear about me showing my undies to a bunch of backpackers.'

'Excuse me?'

I shake my head again. 'Later, Ben. What happened with your dad?'

Ben rubs his eyes and slouches back into the bench. 'The worst thing about it was the last thing I said to him,' he begins.

Ben

'I'm not going to pay any attention to a man telling me how to be a father, when he's barely been one himself!' I spit as I storm down the stairs from my father's attic study.

'Ben! Don't speak to your father like that!' Mum shouts from where she's standing at the bottom of the stairs, hands clutched around the ornate, polished newel cap that I'd spent many years of my youth trying to avoid crushing my knackers on as I slid down the banister.

'What else am I supposed to do? When he just comes out with something like that over the roast potatoes?'

'He didn't mean anything by it!' she insists, going rigid.

Going *more* rigid, I should say. My mother's natural state of being has always been pretty rigid.

'Of course he bloody did!' I retort as I round the landing and start down towards her. 'You don't just come out with something like that in conversation by accident!'

'He was only trying to fill the silence a bit, Ben. You coming here without Katie today made us both feel a bit uncomfortable.'

My eyes go wide with incredulity. 'Oh, I'm so sorry my marital problems have made you feel *a bit uncomfortable*, Mum. Imagine how they make me feel! More than "a little" uncomfortable, I can assure you of that! In fact, I feel like I'm permanently lying naked on a bed of nails with a hippo on my chest!'

My mother's face slides into a look of distaste. 'Don't be so graphic, Ben.'

I reach the bottom of the stairs and try to think of something else to say, but she's got that 'you're being a silly little boy' expression on her face, which always means that anything I try to say now will just be dismissed as me 'acting up'.

It doesn't matter that I'm a man in his thirties. I'll always be eight and 'acting up', as far as my mother is concerned.

I'll also always be a *disappointment*, as far as my father is concerned. That much was proved to me once again about an hour ago, when, just as I was pushing a roast potato around the plate, he said, 'It's a shame you and Katie are having issues, Benjamin.'

'Yes, I know,' I replied sullenly.

'Your mother and I really would like to have a grandchild to play with at some point before we die, you know.' His eyebrow arched in that way it always does when he is disapproving. I saw it a lot when I was kid. Harry probably saw it a lot more, given his predilection for practical jokes. But there was always an indulgent quality to the expression thrown at him that I never received.

'Please, not this again,' I snapped. 'That's got nothing to do with why Katie isn't here today.'

Which was no word of a lie. We had an argument this morning about me not wanting to go to her niece's third-birthday party. That had nothing to do with me still not wanting to have a baby.

. . . and if you believe that, I have a bridge to sell you.

I know full well I'm holding Katie back from having what she wants, and that I'm being grossly unfair to her because of it. She's an amazing woman who deserves to have equally amazing children.

I am *not* amazing.

This is the problem.

'Hasn't it?' my father replied, the eyebrow arching like a hyperactive, mid-air dolphin.

'Oh, leave him alone, Henry,' my mother chided. 'He clearly doesn't want to talk about it.'

And she was right.

Not for another hour anyway.

But when my father made his excuses and went back up to his bloody study, I lost my temper and followed him up there to have it out with him.

The following confrontation was pretty typical of the kind I've had with him over the years. Me, getting more and more frustrated with his attitude. Him, getting less and less interested in continuing the conversation.

I didn't let him off the hook this time, though. I even went as far as yanking the antique syringe out of his hand before he had chance to start tinkering with it – which was historically the signal for the fact he no longer wanted to have this kind of discussion.

If my father wasn't happy, he'd immediately pick up one of his vast collection of Victorian medical antiques and start to fiddle with it. He did it when I told him how much I hated being a doctor. He also did it when I told him I wasn't coming back for Harry's memorial rugby match again after the last disaster. I wasn't going to let him do it today.

So instead I'm the one stood there holding a massive copper syringe that would have been poked into a great many people about 100 years ago, waggling it at my father as I tell him how sick I am of hearing him bang on about having no grandchildren.

He remains completely stoic, as always – even though I'm dreadfully mishandling an antique that's probably worth more than my car.

Luckily for the continued existence of the syringe, he doesn't bring Harry up once. I think if he had done that this time around, the damn thing would have gone right out of the small, round window that never lets in enough light up here.

But he does tell me that I'm being very silly, and that being a father is a responsibility that would do me some good.

I try to tell him – *again* – how I don't feel I'm ready for it, which is when he says, 'I never felt I was, either, Benjamin. But I was strong enough to get through it. And you can be too. I am more than happy to give you some advice – man to man. It's about time you grew up, my boy. Started earning a decent wage. You can't bring a child into this world on . . . whatever it is they've got you on at that *place*. You've had your fun, but you have to knuckle down sometime.'

'What the hell is that supposed to mean?'

My father looks down at me from over his little round glasses. 'You know what I mean, Benjamin. Being a good father is all about *sacrifice* . . . up to and including getting a job you might not necessarily want, but have to have, to provide properly for your family.'

The blood thumps in my head. 'And my job isn't good enough for that, I suppose?'

'No, Benjamin. Not if you want to be a *good father*.'

This is when I screamed the last words I would ever say to him, dropped the antique syringe back on to his Chesterfield desk with a loud clatter, and stormed back downstairs to my perturbed mother.

'I'm going home. Thank you for the dinner,' I tell her in a flat tone.

'Oh . . . don't leave with it like this, Ben.'

I throw my hands up. 'He's started tinkering! You know there's no point trying to talk to him when he's started *tinkering*.'

She doesn't have an answer for that, because she knows I'm right. Once my father starts to tinker, you could point a howitzer at him and demand he respond, and you'd probably still get nothing out of him.

'Try anyway, would you? He's been a little . . .' She trails off. I spot something in my mother's face I've never seen before – genuine worry about my father. My mother doesn't do genuine worry about my father. It's like being worried about a rock.

'A little what? Distant? Because he's been distant with me since the day I was born!'

She starts to protest again, but I'm having none of it. All I want to do is grab my car keys and get out of here. There's no sense in being around either parent when this type of incident occurs. It did me no good to stick around when I told them I was quitting as a doctor, and I see no reason for it to be any different this time.

Because there's always a next time, isn't there?

Always a chance to calm down, cool down and then speak to them again at a later date.

Okay, it'll be a good few weeks until I want to be anywhere near my father again. Partly because of what he said at the dinner table, and partly because what he said at the dinner table was actually 100 per cent accurate. He's right about me and Katie arguing almost constantly about having a kid, and it absolutely *is* affecting my marriage to an intolerable level.

I just don't need my father reinforcing all of that to me, while he fiddles with a Victorian amputation saw.

So I leave.

. . . and it's the worst decision I'll ever make.

Because three weeks later, the cerebral aneurysm that's been very slowly building in my father's brain at the base of his skull decides to rupture.

I get the call from my mother in the aftermath of another argument with Katie. This one about saucepans.

We need new saucepans, I recognise this fact. But I also recognise that the set of saucepans Katie wants from Dunelm are over a hundred quid, which is far too much money for us to spend on saucepans. I don't want to spend over a hundred quid on saucepans, because I still don't want to have a baby.

It's all perfectly logical in my head.

Logic evaporates out of the window when my mother tells me that my father is now in the hospital, being treated for a massive bleed on his brain.

She waited to let me know what was happening until she had a proper and accurate diagnosis. Ever the doctor, my mother. Even in times of the greatest crisis.

And her phone call is a time machine.

The absolute worst time machine there's ever been, because it instantly transports me back nearly eight years to when my mother told me about Harry's diagnosis of stage 4 leukaemia.

I'm afraid Katie has to take over the call at this point, because I'm unable to hold the phone anymore.

Please not again, please not again, please not again . . . my brain decides to start playing on a loop.

The argument with my wife is forgotten (for now) as she drives me to the hospital. I want her to speed up as much as she can, and slow right down at the exact same time.

Because I can't do it again.

. . . only I *can*, because that is what we do in circumstances such as these.

Don't ever let anyone convince you human beings are *weak*, because we can move towards pain, loss and suffering when we have to, without missing a beat.

If someone thinks humans are weak, show them what we do for love.

Because I *do* love him.

Even when he's up in his study polishing the brass bedpan he bought in a junk shop for five quid, and forgetting he's supposed to be helping me learn to ride my stupid bike.

Even when he's berating me for not being more like my older brother.

Even when he's telling me to have a child.

I love him.

And the last thing I told him was I thought he'd been a terrible father.

And the last time I'll ever see him is when he's intubated, lying on a hospital bed, while the doctor treating him lies to me about his chances.

I left medicine behind a long time ago, but it never really leaves *you*.

Not when the people around you still get sick. The only way I could ever move completely past my medical training would be if everybody I care about became invulnerable overnight.

And the doctor is talking about the surgery they're going to try, and it all sounds perfectly reasonable, and it's exactly what I would have been telling a distraught family.

I'd also have known that a rupture that massive was impossible to cure, and that my father only had a few hours to live – two days at absolute most.

But I stood there and nodded along, the same way I did when my father talked to me about Harry's diagnosis. The only difference this time is that I now have the same look of resignation in my eyes that he had back then.

Harry was doomed. And now so is my father.

Life is poetry. It rhymes.

My brother, Harry, died at twenty past four on a sunny Friday afternoon in the living room of my parents' house. My father, Henry, died at seven minutes past three in the middle of a wet and windy Tuesday night in a private hospital room.

Only it was all exactly the same.

Exactly.

'I'm sorry this is so depressing,' I say to Alice, feeling my throat run dry. 'So . . . close to home.'

'You've nothing to apologise for,' Alice replies, in a thick voice.

She's in the time machine now as well. I've transported her back, just as efficiently as my mother did with that phone call.

'Maybe not, but I know how hard hearing it is for you.'

'Not as hard as experiencing it was for you,' she points out, which is more than fair enough.

Because grief *compounds*. Which is something I never realised before (but then again, why would I?). A first horrible loss makes the second one even worse, because you have *precedent*.

I'd still be mourning my father now, even if Harry hadn't died, but would I be mourning him quite as much as I am? Would I be as consistently upset? Given what kind of man my father was, and the relationship I had with him?

I just don't know.

But if I'm honest, I don't think so.

'Does it make me an awful human being to say that?' I ask Alice.

'No,' she says, wiping away a tear. 'Someone dying doesn't change who they were when they were alive, or the way you felt about them.' Her expression goes tight. 'How has your mother been?'

'Inconsolable, of course.'

Alice looks a little awkward. 'No, I mean how has she been with *you*?'

Unfortunately, I get her meaning straight away. 'Could be better, could be worse,' I admit.

Alice's expression turns unreadable.

'I'm being there for her as much as I can be,' I continue, feeling the need to fill the silence. 'Obviously it's hard, because I also have Katie to worry about. And I think she's getting a bit upset with me for spending so much time with my mother, which just adds to the tension between us.'

'I doubt that's what Katie is upset about, Ben,' Alice says.

'Oh, so what do you think it is?' There's a slight edge in my voice that I don't mean to be there, but Alice is getting into some long weeds now, and I'm not sure it's an entirely safe place for her to be.

She looks at me and shakes her head. '*Saucepans*, Ben. She's upset about the saucepans.'

I take her meaning. 'Yes. I'm sure that's it,' I agree, as we both circle the actual issue from a great height.

'I'm sure you'd be perfectly capable of getting those saucepans,' Alice says. 'And I have no doubt you'd be absolutely fantastic at using them.'

'You think? I'm worried I'd drop one of them, or wouldn't be able to afford to buy the ingredients to cook with them properly,' I reply, figuring that we might as well drive the analogy into the ground at this point.

'You don't do yourself enough credit. I'm sure you'd make a great cook.' Alice rolls her eyes. 'And even if you weren't as good as you'd like to be, you have Katie there to help you. Both with the cooking and the cleaning.'

I look a little confused. 'Now all I can picture is a baby in a saucepan, and I'm not sure it's a mental image I need right now.'

Alice chuckles. 'Then picture me with my arse out, surrounded by backpackers,' she replies. 'The horror of that should drive any other imagery out of your head instantly. It certainly works for me.'

'How the hell did that happen?'

'Spiders,' she says, staring off into the middle distance of memory. 'Spiders and a date I should never have gone on.'

For an instant, I couldn't breathe.

I certainly couldn't speak.

This was a situation I thought I'd never find myself in, and the enormity of it forces my brain into some sort of temporary shutdown.

'Hello? Anybody there?' Grant says, in his gentle Australian accent.

Put the bloody phone down. This is stupid. Just put the bloody phone down, like you have a thousand other times over the past few weeks. You should never have got as far as actually dialling his bloody number!

'Hello,' I reply, voice weakened by the import of what I'm attempting. 'Is that Grant?'

'Er, yeah. Who's this?'

A mad woman.

A mad woman you bumped into once at a Facebook meet-up over a year ago, who hasn't been able to pluck up the courage to call you until now. But she kept the stupid bloody serviette you wrote your number on, because it's weirdly symbolic of another life she could have if things were . . . different.

'Um . . . my name is Alice. We, er . . . We met quite a while ago? In the Mosman Hotel bar? You gave me your number.'

There's silence on the other end for a moment.

Great. He can't remember who I am . . . or he *does* remember who I am, but now has to break it to me that he's been happily married for the past nine months, after a whirlwind romance with Cinzano Bella that resulted in three arrests.

'Oh wow! Hi Alice, it's really nice to hear from you.' He allows a warm laugh to escape. 'Truth is, I didn't think I would.'

'No. Sorry, I haven't been . . . up for anything like this before now.'

You're still not! You're STILL NOT.

Put the phone down!

He laughs again. 'Anything like what?'

'Oh . . . you know. Meeting people. People like you. For a drink. With people like you.'

Great, now I sound like Jarvis Cocker having a seizure.

I take a deep breath, trying to get a hold of myself.

You run probably one of the most prestigious hair salons in the city, you mad bitch. This is nothing. *Just calm down, and stop acting like a teenage girl! You can do this.*

'What I'm trying to say is, would you still like to come out for a drink with me sometime?'

Well done.

Now let's just hope he says no, so we can get on with our life the way it should be.

'Um . . . yeah. I'd love to,' Grant says, destroying any hope I had of this being over quickly. 'When were you thinking?'

'Thursday night?' I squeak.

People who run prestigious hair salons should not squeak.

'Great. How about we try the Mosman Hotel again, just the two of us this time?'

He's suggesting familiar ground to make me feel more comfortable.

The man with the kind eyes and gentle voice is also considerate.

What an absolute disaster all round.

'That'd be lovely. Eight p.m.?' I say, in a somewhat robotic voice.

'Yeah, that's great for me. Look forward to seeing you then, Alice.'

'And you, Grant. Have a nice rest of the day, and see you Thursday.'

'You too! Bye for now.'

'Yes, bye for now.'

I hang up, and stare at the wall.

This only lasts for about five or six hours.

I've just asked someone out on a date for the first time in twenty years. And it's all Ben Fielding's fault.

'Hey!'

Well, it is.

There's absolutely no way I would have done this very stupid thing, unless I'd been challenged to do it by my friend.

The fact I'd already kept Grant's number in the kitchen drawer for months is completely irrelevant.

'You never told me about that.'

No. Because it was completely irrelevant.

'It *feels* quite relevant.'

Regardless of what is relevant or not, I am now committed to seeing a man I have met once, over a year ago. The level of instant regret I am feeling is quite palpable.

With an expression of absolute disgust on my face, I look down at the empty wine glass on the kitchen counter in front of me. My fourth empty wine glass of the night.

Hence the bloody phone call.

The wine was a gift from Paul DiMarco, to celebrate my fourth year at his prestigious hair salon – that absolutely should not be run by someone who squeaks.

Four years of my life that has been a combination of extremely fulfilling and utterly devoid of meaning.

Or, to be more accurate, devoid of meaningful *relationships*.

Paul bought me a very expensive bottle of Pinot Noir – which I absolutely hate. But he wasn't to know that, because he hardly knows me at all.

Didn't stop me necking four glasses of the stuff as I clutched Grant's phone number in my hand, though.

Everyone clapped politely when Paul handed over the wine, in a ceremony that took place right after closing time at 5.30. They all looked happy for me, but there wasn't what you'd exactly call much *enthusiasm*.

It was at that precise moment I realised that all of these kind and lovely people were most definitely work acquaintances, and not friends. Friends whoop, cheer and holler when you achieve something. Work acquaintances clap politely. And this is Australians we're talking about here. They don't go in for the reserved displays of public affection the British do. If they love you, they have no problems letting you *bloody well know all about it, mate*.

I am not close to any of these people. Not Paul DiMarco. Not Ulla, my super-reliable and chatty head stylist. Not Jacob the colourist, who always gets me my flat white from the coffee shop around the corner. Not Madeline the stylist, who got me out of a pickle with good old Cinzano last year, but had to make up ridiculous lies about my life because she knows nothing of the reality. Not any of the other myriad friendly and amenable staff I've gathered around me for the past four years.

None of these people knows a damned thing about me, and that's entirely my fault. The front I maintain is harder than diamond.

Standing there – with a smile plastered across my face, a bottle of very expensive wine that I don't like clasped in my hand, and surrounded by loads of people – I have to say I've never felt so alone in my life.

The polite applause stayed with me through the rest of the day, the drive home and the four glasses of wine I drank before I worked up the courage to finally dial Grant's number.

Having put the phone down on him, I am instantly and completely consumed by suffocating guilt.

I've just asked another man to go out on a date with me.

I shouldn't be doing this. It's an utter betrayal of Joe's memory. *Don't be bloody ridiculous.*

But I *want* to be bloody ridiculous. He's only been gone seven years. How can I even be thinking about dating another person? Seven years should be nowhere near enough for me to have got over his death! What the hell is wrong with me?

I should call Grant up again, tell him there's been a terrible mistake that only happened because of four glasses of awful wine, and cancel the date.

Then I can go into work tomorrow . . . and the next day, and the next day – and then we'll eventually reach ten years since I started at the hair salon. Then Paul DiMarco can give me another bottle of wine I don't like (but how would he know that when he barely knows me at all) and everyone who doesn't know a thing about me can politely applaud again.

'I'm sorry, sweetheart,' I say out loud to my empty kitchen. 'I need a little more now. You can understand that, can't you?'

'Of course he'd understand that,' Ben says.

Which is of no help whatsoever, because that's a conversation I won't be having for several months yet, and doesn't help me at all right now, as I stand at my kitchen counter trying not to cry.

'I love you with all my heart,' I tell Joe, 'and I always will, but I think I just need *a little more now*. It's been such a long time.'

Seven years is nothing, you cruel bitch!

'I hope you can understand that, and not think less of me.'

I receive no answer, which I know I won't, because I never do. But there's always a small part of me that's disappointed anyway.

A fifth and final glass of dreadful red wine follows the other four – which is just about enough to help me blot out the guilt, and I fall asleep on my couch in the same clothes I was wearing earlier today, while they all clapped politely at a stranger.

'Do you enjoy the sun?' I ask.

'Er, yeah,' Grant replies.

'Very sunny here,' I remark.

'Um . . . yeah.'

'And hot.'

'Yep.'

'And also large.'

'It is.'

'Very large,' I point out.

'Yeah.'

'And hot.'

'Er . . . yeah, it is.'

Good lord. I am to small talk what Donald Trump is to astrophysics.

I'm so out of bloody practice with this kind of thing, it's approaching levels of embarrassing that no other human being has ever come close to. My nerves are going to be the death of me. Or the death of this date, at least.

Grant is quite frankly doing incredibly well to still be sat across the table from me. I'd have been up and out of here like a shot a good ten minutes ago. It must be like having a date with a malfunctioning robot who can only spit out obvious facts about Australia.

But I have to keep up this idiotically banal small talk, even though I sound like a stone-cold moron. Otherwise he might ask me the one question I'm dreading more than any other.

Which is . . . *why?*

Why did you come to Sydney, Alice?

Why did you move away from your home and everyone you know?

And I know he's going to ask it. That's one of the reasons I'm so nervous. Because I honestly don't know if I'll be able to tell him the truth, without ruining this date in one way or another. I honestly don't know if I can open up like that.

Oh, I'm only here because the man who owns my heart for all eternity went and died on me, Grant. Sorry about that. Should I get the bill for the drinks now?

Why.

Why, why, *why.*

I know it's coming.

But maybe I can get in there first, and soften the blow a bit . . .

'So, what made you move down here from Cairns?' I ask him as I take a sip of my mojito. Actually, it's more like a gulp.

'Oh, I had a good job offer I couldn't turn down,' he says. Then his face clouds a little. 'And I lost my wife a couple of years ago, so thought it would be nice to try somewhere else.'

I blink a couple of times.

No, Grant.

That's *my* line.

I'm the one who admits that they're a widow.

Didn't you get the script?

Something has gone very wrong here . . .

'Oh, I'm so sorry,' I find myself saying, fully on automatic. I have to put the mojito down as my hand has started to tremble a little.

'Thank you,' Grant says, and smiles. There are tears in his eyes.

No, Grant!

I have the tears in my eyes! That's *my* thing!

The entire dynamic of this date has just shifted completely in my head. I came here thinking I'd have to battle myself. I had no idea Grant might be going through exactly the same thing.

'I . . . er . . . I . . .'

I swallow and take another gulp of mojito.

SAY IT.

'I lost my husband seven years ago,' I tell Grant, now feeling like I've just turned this conversation into the worst game of one-upmanship in history.

Aha! You think you're grieving, mi laddo? Two years is nothing! I've been a basket case for seven *years now! Seven whole years!*

'Oh, I'm so sorry to hear that,' Grant replies in that kind and gentle voice of his.

Don't bloody cry, you mad cow!

Throw the mojito over your face. You can just tell Grant you suffer from a serious problem with your motor functions, or something. Anything is better than letting him see you cry!

'Oh God, I'm really, really sorry,' I tell him as I try to dab the tears away.

Good job you wore the waterproof mascara.

I *always* wear the sodding waterproof mascara!

Grant's hand reaches out across the table and takes mine. 'You have nothing to apologise for. I know exactly how you feel.'

And then we begin to talk.

No . . . sorry . . . I mean we begin to TALK.

Because all the asinine bullshit goes aside, and instead we start a conversation about the losses we've both had to endure, and how that was the driving force for us both to leave our respective homes and come to Sydney.

And it's an absolutely *awful* conversation to have on a first date, while at the same time being the absolute *best* conversation I've had for many years – other than the ones I have every 8 July with Ben Fielding.

'Thanks.'

'No worries.'

I need a mirror, you see. I need a person who knows what I know, and feels what I feel. For me to open up to someone, I need to know that they feel the pain, and how difficult it all is. No amount of therapists, work colleagues or well-meaning strangers works. It has to be someone who *knows*.

Who bleeds every time they dream, and moans every time they wake up.

And Grant knows. Oh, he knows, alright. I can see myself reflected in his eyes, and the mirror is very clear.

Needless to say, there's no kissing or hugging at the end of this date.

I feel more like I've been in a three-hour therapy session (one that's actually been of some benefit), and you don't tend to hug or kiss your therapist. I certainly didn't with mine, anyway.

But I do promise to see Grant again – because I haven't felt this connected to another human being in years.

I don't know whether romance is on the cards at any point, but at least I feel like I've made an honest to goodness *friend* finally.

There's no hug or kiss on date two, either. There is a lot more conversation about Joe and Grant's late wife, Clara, though. You'd think long conversations about ex-partners and the grief that comes with losing them would be the kiss of death for a date, but it's just the opposite for the both of us.

On date three we do hug at the end, and it's the most lovely thing in the world. Partly because we're standing at a ferry terminal beside the Sydney Harbour Bridge – and you don't get backdrops like that for every hug you have, let me tell you. But mainly because Grant feels as gentle as he sounds.

We didn't talk about the past on this third date anywhere near as much. In fact, most of it was centred around the future, and what we both want from our lives from now on.

Fancy that! Me actually engaging in a conversation about the future with another human being! What is happening to me? I don't do that. I don't *ever* do that. All I think about is the *past*.

And yet, there I was, chatting away about one day owning my own hair salon, in a small town on the northern New South Wales coast. Somewhere with a cute little beach, an even cuter coffee shop and neighbours who all know each other's name.

I didn't even bloody know that was what I wanted in my future until I'd said it.

It's like being with Grant has unlocked a part of my brain that's been active underneath the surface all this time, but has been kept quiet by all the stuff going on up top.

Remarkable.

I let Grant kiss me on the cheek at the end of date four. It connects me for an instant to the Australian national grid. And connects me to Australia as a whole, far more than I ever have been in the years I've lived here.

Date five is a little different from the drinks and meals we've had around that fabulous harbour so far. On date five, we're going to go for a bushwalk in one of the national parks about an hour's drive outside the city.

This marks a major step up in the amount of time I'm going to be spending with Grant in one go, and feels like an escalation in our nascent relationship that I'm extremely nervous about.

Not least because one of the things Joe and I loved to do was visit the national parks of the UK, and this is all starting to skirt a bit close to home. Going for drinks or a meal is pretty typical early date stuff, but this bushwalk feels more, I don't know . . . *personal*, I guess?

And then there's the fact this will be my first proper visit to the Australian bush in the four years I've been here. I've never had anyone to go with before, of course. And there's the whole issue of the giant bloody spiders.

I have been blessed with relatively little exposure to Australia's most famous creepy-crawly. I've had to get my neighbour to extricate one huntsman spider in the time I've been in my apartment, and Madeline has always taken care of anything that has managed to crawl its way into the backrooms of the salon.

I have deliberately avoided going too far into the Australian countryside – preferring nice, well-tended city parks. So this is going to be a first for me.

It won't be a first for Grant. He was bushwalking in the tropics from the age of five, and everybody knows that most things in Cairns want to kill you stone dead as soon as they look at you, so he's well used to dealing with Australia's lethal fauna.

But my greatest fear – as I stand outside my apartment block, covered in sun screen and wearing what I hope is a sensible combination of cargo shorts, a cute plaid long-sleeved shirt and a brand-new sun hat – is what kind of hat *Grant* will be wearing.

Because if he turns up in a bushman's hat like the one Joe never got to wear, I may fall to pieces right here on the roadside.

Dark Alice has been talking to me a lot these past few days, in the run-up to the date.

Don't you feel bad doing this with another man?

Don't you feel sad this isn't with Joe?

Don't you think he'd be upset to see you do this without him?

Don't you—

Grant pulls up in a big Ford ute. He's wearing an AFL baseball cap.

Great. I can still go on this date, then.

'You look fantastic,' he tells me as I get in the truck. Which is very nice of him, given that I'm dressed for a bushwalk and not a meal in a fancy restaurant.

'Thank you,' I reply. 'You look very Australian,' I tell him with a smile, earning me a chuckle.

And he does. Like me, he's wearing a plaid shirt, but his is blue and black – and the pair of big hiking boots and Dickies' work shorts go very well. Aussie men look right in outdoor clothing the way British men never seem to. Joe's white little legs always looked slightly embarrassed when he forced them into a pair of shorts.

Don't you think he'd be jealous of the way Grant looks?

'Shall we go, then?' I say, maybe a little too loudly.

And an hour and a half or so later, we're walking along a gravel path between towering eucalyptus trees. The weather has been kind to us today. It's blue skies and only about twenty-four degrees. Perfect walking weather.

So much so that the park is pretty full of other folks taking full advantage of it. This is an extremely good sign, as it indicates that there are no murderous spiders about. If there are little kids running around, then it probably means I'm safe.

Probably.

I still look up at the branches of every tree we pass under, though.

'You okay?' Grant asks me as I peer into the nether regions of a nearby scribbly gum.

'Yeah, I'm fine. I'm just being a typical Pom when it comes to the wildlife.'

'No worries. I'll get anything away from you, if it comes looking for lunch.'

'Thank you,' I tell him, sounding a little more confident. It's very nice to have a man by your side who will deal with the spiders.

Don't you think Joe could have dealt with them for you too?

'What's that big rock up ahead?' I say to Grant, again a little too loudly.

'That's where we're headed,' he tells me. 'Grey's Rock. It's a lovely spot to chill out, looking at the view. When we get there, it'll be picnic time!' Grant points at the large rucksack on his back, containing the surprise picnic he's put together for us.

Don't you remember the last time you went on a picnic?

. . . just be quiet, please.

And for the next couple of hours, she is, thankfully.

While there are some similarities with the kinds of trips out I took with Joe, you can't really compare the tame, easy British countryside with the glorious and eclectic Australian one. And the view from Grey's Rock really is quite exceptional.

These are new memories I'm making, not recycled ones.

For instance, there are no squirrels.

This is Australia. Any squirrels would have been killed off years ago. They just don't have the muscles, the venom or the sheer bloody-minded vindictiveness to survive here.

Luckily, most of the things that do want to end your life in the most spectacular way possible are not situated on Grey's Rock, which is a single, enormous tree-covered promontory sticking out from the bush like a particularly enthusiastic hitchhiker's thumb.

It takes a good half an hour to climb the steps to the top, but once you're here the view is breathtaking, and the picnic area is expansive. Fancy an outdoor barbecue, looking down towards Sydney, and out over the gloriously blue Tasman Sea? Then this is the place for you.

Australians put outdoor barbecues everywhere. If the moon landings had been conducted by Australia instead of America, you'd be able to have a sausage sizzle in the Sea of Tranquillity.

Sadly, Grey's Rock is the main attraction in these here parts, so my picnic with Grant is not carried out alone . . . but we just have about enough space from our fellow hikers to be able to enjoy it more or less in peace.

Grant's Australian-ness extends way past his clothing and into his culinary choices. This is not the picnic of a pretentious man, nor one who requires the finest ingredients from M&S to enjoy an outdoor spread.

We have smashed avo. We have beetroot. We have Coles cooked sausages, Tim Tams and Bega cheese. There are savoury Shapes and Arnott's biscuits.

Yes, *of course* there's Vegemite. The universe demands it.

There is also beer.

Posh beer, mind. None of your bog-standard four X. Nope. We've got Great Northern Crisp, all the way from Grant's stomping ground up in Far North Queensland.

Which tastes *incredible* up here on Grey's Rock. So much so, I drink a full three bottles of it in the ninety or so minutes we spend looking out over the New South Wales scenery. This is way more than I usually drink (unless I'm working up the courage to make phone calls), but the piles of picnic food ensure I'm not three sheets to the wind by the time I've drained the last one.

I am, however, in dire need of a pee.

This was not something that occurred to me before I started to neck the first bottle.

Needing a pee up here demands entry into the small public toilet located close to where the rough-hewn stairs end, over on the other side of the Rock's plateau.

The toilet consists of a single cubicle, and is constructed of breeze blocks painted green, with a corrugated tin roof.

It also screams SPIDERS.

Loud enough for me to have to cover my ears, even from here.

And while I have felt quite comfortable so far on this excursion, knowing that Grant would be there to scare any of the little bastards away – I can't exactly expect him to do that while I'm sat on the dunny, now can I?

I take a deep breath. 'I'll be back in a minute,' I tell Grant. 'I just have to use the toilet.'

'Yeah, no trouble,' he replies. 'I'll start packing all this stuff away while you're gone.'

I nod, and scurry across the picnic area, past several very happy-looking young people with backpacks, and arrive at the smell of the toilet.

This happens a good ten seconds before I get to the toilet itself – which rather indicates how badly this day is about to go downhill for me.

I kick the green wooden door of the toilet open, and immediately wish I had a priest with me. Hell has erupted on Grey's Rock, you see. In the shape of whatever it is smeared up the side of the stainless-steel toilet bowl.

Gagging, I move away from the toilet.

I'm just going to have to hold my pee in until we get back down to the car park. I can't use that toilet – even if the stench does tend to dictate that no spiders will be in there. Even they can't be dumb enough to bathe in that horrifying miasma.

But the walk back to said car park is a good hour at the very least – and I am *busting*.

Looking past the toilet, I spy a thick collection of eucalyptus trees and various bushes a good twenty feet away.

My heart sinks.

And my bladder strains.

There's nothing else for it. I'm going to have to pee right here, in mother nature's glorious bounty.

Damn it.

Making sure that no one is watching me, I make an effort to saunter nonchalantly away from the hideous toilet, and towards the big, thick patch of bush that I'm about to christen.

I duck behind it successfully, and start to unbutton my shorts.

With them pulled down, along with my underwear, I attempt to squat and relieve myself. Only the shorts are going to be in the bloody way, if I'm not very careful.

I sigh, noting not for the first time that my life would probably be a far more convenient place if I had been born with a penis.

I do not want pee on my shorts when I return to Grant. I do not want pee on any item of clothing when I'm entirely on my own in my own apartment, let alone out in public on a fifth date with a kind, gentle man who knows a good beer when he sees one.

So I stand up again, awkwardly pull the shorts off over my hiking boots and recommence my mission of relief.

Aaaah . . .

That's better.

And it's the perfect crime. No one has seen me, or heard me, I don't think. All I have to do now is—

If we go on to Wikipedia and type in the search 'Australian spiders', we are provided with a detailed run-down of all the taxonomic species of arachnid that live in this fine and beautiful country.

They come in all shapes and sizes. In all varieties of harmless and deadly.

However, I'm sad to report that the Wikipedia page for Australian spiders is not complete, because they have clearly missed one species of spider off completely.

The one that is currently sat on my discarded cute shorts, looking at me with evil intent, and carrying a flick knife.

Okay, it's *not* carrying a flick knife, but everything else is 100 per cent true. There is evil intent in the seven thousand eyes it has clustered around its beady little head, of that I have no doubt.

And judging from the thickness of those hideously hairy little black legs, it easily has the muscle power to leap from my discarded shorts and on to my face.

I cannot imagine what this particular spider is called, but judging from the fact Australians like to give their animal species pretty prosaic names a lot of the time (for instance, a Brown snake is called that because it's brown) I can only assume this is the fabled Big Black Bastard Spider.

Thus far, it has not moved from where it sits upon my cute shorts. How long it has been there, I cannot be sure. There's every chance it's just watched me pee, which for some reason makes this situation even worse.

I stare down at it, absolutely frozen to the spot. A small, high-pitched squeal escapes my pursed lips.

The spider still does not move.

Neither do I.

Which is great. If I just stay crouched like this, with my underwear around my ankles, for the rest of my natural life upon this planet, everything will be *fine*.

Unfortunately, the muscles in my legs are having none of that, and start to twitch involuntarily, making me judder a little.

This is all the spider needs to launch its attack.

It scurries towards me, across my cute shorts, at roughly the speed of terror.

I let out a scream, and rise quickly to a standing position, whipping my underwear up at the same time. This does not appreciably make my situation any better, as the spider is still coming towards me.

My rational brain would tell me just to step away a little, wait for it to get off my shorts, and then grab them up.

My rational brain has gone on holiday, though. It's sat on a beach somewhere, sipping a mojito, and eternally glad it isn't anywhere near an eight-inch black spider.

Therefore, my irrational brain is the only one I'm left with, and it has decided that the best course of action for me is to run away. Especially as the spider has now reached the edge of my shorts, and is clearly getting ready to spring off them and attack my face.

I burst from the bush I've been hiding behind, to see that the entire picnic ground is now looking in my direction, thanks to the panicked scream I just let out.

Joe is about ten feet away, coming towards me with a concerned expression on his face.

'Are you alright?' Joe exclaims, and I immediately run towards him, the panic forcing all thought out of my head. I have to get away from that spider. I don't care that I'm showing off my knickers to a load of complete strangers.

Joe will save me. Joe will know what to do.

'Are you alright?' he repeats as I reach him. 'Are you bitten?'

'Oh God! Oh God! A spider! A spider! It's so large and horrible, Joe!' I wail.

His face creases into a look of confusion and dismay.

'What did you just call me?' Grant says.

. . . and reality asserts itself once more.

This is Grant. This man is called *Grant*, and I'm in Australia, running away from a large, probably deadly Australian spider. He's not Joe.

But that's what I've just called him, in my state of sheer, unbridled panic.

216

'Oh no,' Ben says, his face falling. 'You didn't, did you?'

I nod slowly. 'Oh, I most certainly did,' I reply, a hot flush of embarrassment rising across my face.

'How did he take it?'

'Oh, he laughed it off. What else could he do? But nothing was the same after that. The walk back down to the car park was excruciating. We barely spoke.'

'Did you get your shorts back?'

I roll my eyes. 'No, Ben. I didn't think my humiliation was quite complete enough, so I elected to spend the rest of the day just in my pair of big, white Kmart knickers.'

'Sorry. Stupid question.'

'It was, rather . . . but I can kind of understand it. I didn't really want to put them back on again, after that big black bugger had been on them – but Grant went and retrieved them for me anyway, while I held the half-empty rucksack over me, to protect what was left of my modesty.'

Ben swallows hard. 'Have you . . . Have you seen Grant again since?'

I pinch the bridge of my nose. I can feel a headache coming on. 'No, Ben. I haven't seen him since. If it was hard enough for me to call him to see if he wanted to go out on a date, I doubt there's enough terrible red wine in the entire world to get me to contact him after accidentally calling him by my dead husband's name.'

'Oh, that's just so awful.'

'Yes, it is, isn't it? But it showed me one thing, I guess.'

'What's that?'

I look at him. 'I'm not ready to move on, Ben. Joe is still with me every day, and it's him I want to turn to when I'm in trouble. Poor Grant deserves someone who will turn to *him*.'

'You can't look at it like that,' Ben insists. 'It was just a slip of the tongue. You were in a panic, like you said. I'm sure it's fixable!'

I smile ruefully. 'It's been three months since it happened, Ben. I'm pretty sure it's not something that can be fixed now.'

Ben deflates in front of me when I say this. It seems like an appropriate response, so I do much the same.

We're just two deflated old balloons, sat here waiting to be cleared away after the party has long ended.

And I've been deflated since that day on Grey's Rock, if I'm being honest.

The past few months have dragged me along with them, and I barely remember doing much outside styling hair and sitting in an empty apartment, waiting for something to happen that never does.

The girls at work asked me how my fifth date went with Grant, of course. I just lied and told them it was fine, but that we didn't really connect with one another, once we were together for longer. An easy lie. An easy way to avoid the kinds of questions I just can't answer, when they're asked by people who don't understand death. Not like me.

. . . I think I might be a bit depressed, truth be told. You know . . . just a *little bit*?

I got a taste of a life less lonely, and went and screwed it up. That kind of thing gets under your skin, let me tell you.

'Well, what a truly *wonderful* year we've both had,' Ben says, proving that there's still some air left in the balloon yet.

'Yep,' I agree – although he's had it far worse than me when you look at it objectively. I may have ruined a burgeoning romance because I'm still stuck fast in the old one, but at least I didn't lose a loved one.

Yes, you did. That's kind of the whole point, isn't it?

Oh, do be quiet.

'I don't think,' Ben continues, 'that I'm really up for any kind of challenge this year, Alice. If it's all the same to you.'

I nod in agreement. 'That's fine with me,' I tell him.

'Maybe, instead of a challenge, we could just . . . just have another hug?'

I nod again. 'That would be lovely.'

And so we do hug again – because sometimes that's all that's really needed, or even *possible*, at times like these.

Ben

It would have been nice to be able to give Alice some words of advice or encouragement, like I usually can at the end of these little get-togethers. But this time around, I have absolutely *nothing*.

It sounds like the last thing she needs is more advice from me, anyway. The last two times she's agreed to do what I challenged her with, it's ended in disaster. I think I was absolutely right to suggest we don't bother with any of that malarkey this year.

I very much doubt I could rise to any challenge she set me, either.

Best we just leave all of that well enough alone for this year – and maybe forever. Not sure it's done either of us all that much good, to be honest with you.

Hugging is much nicer.

It's also much easier, with far less wear and tear on the knees, and the heart.

'So, what do we do now?' Alice eventually says as we sit apart again.

I shrug. 'I have absolutely no idea. Just try to . . . get through it, I suppose.'

'Can we . . . Can we maybe keep in touch with each other a little more from now on?' Alice asks, in a shy voice. 'I think I'd like that now. Hell, I think I *need* that now.'

'Of course we can,' I reply, feeling stupid that I hadn't suggested it myself.

'Thanks,' she says with a relieved look on her face.

For an instant, I regret agreeing to it.

Not because I don't want to hear from Alice a little more during the year, but because I'm not sure being in contact with me will do her all that much good.

It might not do me all that much good, either, if I have to worry about the advice I'm giving.

But, too late now. I'm going to be a bigger part of Alice's life, and she's going to be a bigger part of mine. Whether that's a good idea or not remains to be seen.

With any luck, things will be a little easier in the coming twelve months.

It sounds like we could both do with a year that's a little more settled down. Maybe then we can both start to come to terms with the way the world is treating us at the moment.

Yes.

That's something to look forward to.

Things just need to be a little more settled down, and the both of us will be fine.

Fingers crossed 2020 is a much better year than 2019 was . . .

Year Eight

EMAILS AND EGGS

Ben Fielding < ben.fielding26@outlook.co.uk >

To: 'Alice Everley'

Subject: How are you?

Hiya!

Sorry I haven't been in touch very much recently. With the way things are, work's been an absolute nightmare, as you might imagine. People living on the streets doesn't stop just because nobody else is using them!

Couldn't let today go by without an email, though. Just really sorry we couldn't see each other like normal. Would have been nice to have our regular catch-up, as always ☺

I guess I can tell you this, though: I've now been made a senior caseworker. The bump in salary is very much appreciated, but that's one of the reasons I've been so busy. Other people might be working from home, but I've been out and about more than ever – staying as safe as possible, though, don't worry!

The promotion came as a real surprise, because I don't really feel like I'm able to do as much as I'd like to help all the people that come through our doors. It never seems to be enough, you know? There's this one girl, Tanisha, whose story breaks my heart. I'm trying my hardest to help her, but I never seem to be able to do enough. I see her sliding back into the misery she was trying to escape.

The same goes for a sweet but quiet guy called Rafik. And good old Larry Bristow, with his jokes. And Sasha, and Alan. And . . . and . . . and . . . I see them all slipping back, because I just can't do *enough*.

. . . sorry, you don't need me wailing on at you about my work problems!

How are you doing? How's the whole thing been over there? I guess you haven't been working? How is that affecting you? I really hope you are okay.

Lots of love,

Ben

Alice Everley < everley.alice@gmail.com.au >

To: 'Ben Fielding'

Subject: RE: How are you?

Hi Ben,

It's lovely to hear from you! And don't worry about not getting in touch earlier, I totally understand. I can't imagine how difficult your job is now . . . but congratulations on the promotion. I'm sure it's well deserved – and I'm sure you do a lot more good than you think for the people you help. Katie must be very proud of you. And I hope your mum is being nice about it as well? And yes, please stay as safe as you possibly can. I know you're the careful type, but I also know you have a habit of putting other people first a bit too much, so watch out for yourself please!

Things have been very weird here, as you might imagine. They closed the border completely today, so no one can get into New South Wales, and no one can get out! It's funny how one of the largest countries on earth starts to feel very small all of a sudden.

The salon has been shut this entire time, but it looks like we might be re-opening soon. I thought that when it shut it might send me right off the deep end. The thought of being in my apartment all of the time frankly terrified me. But the weirdest thing has happened. I'm actually feeling . . . pretty good? I know that sounds deeply strange, but I've spent the last few years more or less on my own most of the time, so this change hasn't really hurt me all that much. In fact, I've probably been getting out and about more than I ever have before. We're allowed to exercise, so I've been exploring areas of Sydney I've never visited. The whole thing has been very calming for me.

That's sounds awful, doesn't it? I know you guys have been hit hard by it, and of course I'd prefer it if it had never happened at all, but the lockdowns have been (oh God, how do I say this) a bit of a relief for me. The pressure to *do more* has completely gone away. It feels like everybody is living my life now.

Having said that, I really do miss my regular trip to the UK to see you. Doesn't feel right to just be sat here, and not flying. I can't believe I actually miss the idea of plane food and a stopover in Singapore ☺ Still, hopefully it won't be too long until things are bit more back to normal. You might get a visit from me at a different time of year! Do you think we could meet up then instead? I'd really like that.

Love and hugs back,

Alice xx

To: 'Alice Everley'

Subject: RE: How are you?

Hiya,

Don't feel bad about feeling that way about this whole stupid thing. You're not the only one, by any stretch of the imagination. And I can imagine that it must feel a little better for you, if things haven't improved on the social front. I'm sorry they haven't, but maybe that's just as well, given what's been happening?

Katie was very proud of me, yes. Which was lovely, as, if I'm being honest, things have been more than a little fraught between us recently. Some of that's down to the pressure on us as keyworkers in all of this mess, but the 'old' problem is still there. Stress never helps with that kind of thing. And we're both *very* stressed right now. There hasn't been any . . . you know . . . *intimate stuff* going on for quite some time now. My fault. Not hers.

225

But can you even imagine trying to have a kid at the moment? Just another reason why I'm glad we don't! Doesn't really bear thinking about.

My mother has been a bit *distant*. She seemed pleased when I told her about the job, but she wasn't exactly over the moon. These days, though, I'm not so sure that's because she disappointed in my life choices, but rather because she still misses my father so much. The last few months have been super hard on her, as you'd imagine. I'm trying to cut her as much slack as possible. And I'm going round to see her as much as I can. She has her friends, but that's not quite the same thing as family, is it? So I've been making the effort to pop round and do something with her as often as I can. We have discovered a penchant for jigsaws. Last week we completed a two-thousand-piece one of a toucan wearing a top hat. It was quite something to behold.

And yes, of course I'd like to meet up with you before the year is out, and judging from what we're being told on the news, that might be possible. Maybe around Christmas? I don't know. We'll have to see how it goes!

Lots of love, Ben x

Alice Everley < everley.alice@gmail.com.au >

Subject: RE: How are you?

Hi Ben,

I'm really sorry things are still problematic for you and Katie. I really hoped after the chat we had late last year that things might be different. But then again, the world turned upside down almost straight after that, so I guess all bets were off when it came to the issues in everybody's lives. I'm pleased she was happy about your job, but please don't let things spiral, okay? You and Katie are so good together, and your problems can be worked out, I promise.

Give your mum time. She'll 'come back', so to speak, but she's got to get through her grief the same way we have.

Pfft. Hark at me trying to give advice about how people get over grief, when the only reason I'm in a good mood these days is because everyone else around me now feels as cut off as I do. I'd put a 'rolling eyes' emoji in here, but I have no idea how to do it . . .

Christmas would be a lovely time to meet up ☺ Let's hope we can do it.

Can I ask, though: did you go to the graveyard as usual anyway? Were you allowed? And if you did, was it . . . normal? Has anything changed about it? I always like to think of it as the one thing that never does change in my life – even if everything else is going to hell!

Love and hugs,

Alice xx

Ben Fielding < ben.fielding26@outlook.co.uk >

To: 'Alice Everley'

Subject: RE: How are you?

Hiya,

I'll try not to let things get any worse with Katie, Alice. I really will. But it gets more difficult all of the time. She hasn't changed her mind, but neither have I. I'm just never in the right place for it. Especially not now.

Thanks for saying that about my mother. I hope you're right. And don't be so hard on yourself. I still wake up crying sometimes when I've had a dream about Harry. We were out riding on our bikes in the last one I had, and I woke up with an ache in my heart that hasn't really lifted since.

No. I didn't go to the church like normal, even though we were allowed to do stuff like that, I think. It just didn't seem right under the circumstances – even though I could have easily got away with the bloody costume he had lined up for me this year. If ever there was a year I would have been glad nobody was around to see me, it would have been this one.

But I did miss doing it, a huge amount. I always come away from our meet-ups feeling a little better about myself. You always know the right thing to say.

Lots of Love, Ben x

Alice Everley < everley.alice@gmail.com.au >

To: 'Ben Fielding'

Subject: RE: How are you?

Okay, I have to ask. What was the costume? I don't think I can go through the rest of this weird year without knowing. Please tell me!

Love and hugs,

Alice

Xx

Ben Fielding < *ben.fielding26@outlook.co.uk* >

To: 'Alice Everley'

Subject: RE: How are you?

Well, Alice. Let's just say that if I'd worn it and
had a great fall, all the king's horses and all the
bloody king's men couldn't have put me back
together again . . .

Alice Everley < *everley.alice@gmail.com.au* >

To: 'Ben Fielding'

Subject: RE: How are you?

HUMPTY DUMPTY.

OH, MY GOD.

Ben Fielding < *ben.fielding26@outlook.co.uk* >

Subject: RE: How are you?

Tell me about it.

. . . but I would have been happy to wear it, because it would have meant we could have met up as usual.

Take care, and hopefully see you soon. At Christmas if not before.

Lots of love Ben xx

Alice Everley < everley.alice@gmail.com.au >

To: 'Ben Fielding'

Subject: RE: How are you?

You too. Get in touch any time ☺

Love and hugs,

Alice

Xx

Year Nine

THE DREAMS AND THE GHOSTS

Alice Everley < everley.alice@gmail.com.au >

To: 'Ben Fielding'

Subject: Are you okay?

Hi Ben,

Just thought I'd drop you a quick email, as haven't heard from you in quite a while. I'm sorry we weren't able to meet up at Christmas like we planned. This stupid thing doesn't want to end, does it? Sorry I haven't been more in touch. I have my reasons, unfortunately.

How have you been? Hope you are really well, and the job is going okay.

I'm not all that great, truth be told. Things are starting to get back to normal here, but it's been a hard year. The isolation finally got to me in a way it didn't in 2020. I found myself living in the past again, way too much. For a while it wasn't so bad. The memories weren't so strong – but the longer you stay with yourself without much company (even the work kind) the more you start to turn inwards.

The dreams about Joe are worse again. They went away completely for a bit, but they're back with a vengeance now. I spend most nights in that damned A&E department again – only, dreams being dreams, it's now an emergency room here in Australia. But it's still the same. That feeling of dreadful certainty. The helplessness. The cold.

Every. Damned. Night.

Will I ever get past this?

Please let me know you're doing better than I am. At least that'll make things a bit easier ☺

Love and hugs,

Alice

Xx

Alice Everley < everley.alice@gmail.com.au >

To: 'Ben Fielding'

Subject: Can you let me know you're okay?

Hi Ben,

Please could you just get in touch to let me know you're okay. It's been ages since I last heard from you. I think all of my emails have been reaching you? You don't have to talk much if you don't want to, but I do need to know that you are alright.

Love,

Alice

Ben Fielding < ben.fielding26@outlook.co.uk >

To: 'Alice Everley'

Subject: RE: Can you let me know you're okay?

Hi Alice,

Sorry I haven't been replying. Please don't worry about me. It sounds like you have enough on your plate. And there's really not much you could do even if you were here.

They really don't want to stop haunting us, do they?

Lots of love, Ben x

Alice Everley < everley.alice@gmail.com.au >

To: 'Ben Fielding'

Subject: RE: Can you let me know you're okay?

No. They don't.

I hope things get a little better – for both of us. I'm not sure I can take many more years of feeling like this. How can I still be so angry about it? How can I still miss him so much?

Oh God . . . What are we going to do?

I miss talking to you so much, face to face. I really hope we can meet up soon.

Love and the biggest hugs,

Alice

Xx

Year Ten

THE PAST AND THE FUTURE

Ben

'I don't want you to worry about it,' Harry says, pointing a very serious finger at me.

'You don't want me to *worry about it*?' I reply, absolutely flabbergasted that he'd think I'd be able to do anything other than worry myself sick.

'No. Of course I don't. Look at me,' he demands, throwing his arms wide. 'I'm strong as an ox. If anyone can fight this off, it's *me*.' He picks up the rucksack and pulls out the blue-and-white rugby jersey. 'Do you really think someone who was going to die from blood cancer would be off out to play rugby?'

'Don't say that.'

Harry makes a face. 'Look, I know you're not keen on the rugby, bro, but you don't have to be like that about it.'

I roll my eyes. 'You know what I'm talking about. Don't talk about . . . *dying*.'

He throws up his arms. 'That's what I'm trying to tell you! I don't want *you* thinking about me dying, because it's not going to happen! I'll be fine.'

I make a face. 'You sure you should be playing today? After what happened last week?'

Harry flaps his hand. 'Oh, that was nothing. I was tired. Out of sorts.'

I roll my eyes again. 'You fainted in the middle of dinner, Harry.'

'Yes, yes. But I'm okay now.'

'You're not *okay*,' I say through gritted teeth. 'You've been diagnosed with *leukaemia*.'

'Yes. I have. But plenty of people survive it.'

I can't meet his gaze when he says this. Because he's a doctor, and I'm in medical school, and we both know the truth. We both bloody *know it*.

I open my mouth to protest again – but he has that look in his eyes. The look that tells me I'm getting a Chinese burn if I carry on the way I'm going.

He grabs the rugby jersey, and stuffs it back into his rucksack. 'Right, I'm off. Just . . . chill out about the whole thing. We'll get through it, like we always do.'

I nod.

What the hell else can I do?

What the hell else can I do, apart from *watch*?

◆ ◆ ◆

I let go of the death grip I have on the hem of the blue-and-white rugby jersey I'm wearing, and rest my head against the wall.

It's better if I stay here.

Better if I just stay *here*, and let them get on with it without me.

That was the mistake I made the first time.

I got up and joined in.

I *took part*.

I tried to fill in for *him*, and look where it got me?

Upside down in a load of melting ice cream.

Was that *five* years ago?

Was it *really*?

Because it feels like five minutes.

And it only feels like ten minutes since I was sat at my brother's bedside for the final time, while he told me that he loved me, and that he was scared, and that he was sorry.

I hate that the clarity is still there. Even after all these years.

Ten years.

An entire decade.

And all I want to do is sink into the bottle of gin I bought in Tesco on the way home from work last night – even though I promised Katie I'd cut back – but here I am again in this bloody changing room, because it's *ten years* since Harry Fielding died.

And they feel the need to hold another bloody memorial rugby match in his honour.

I didn't have my parents guilting me into taking part this time.

My mother didn't need to say a thing to me.

Because how could I not be here?

The inertial guilt would be way too much. I'd hate myself just about as much as everyone else would, if I'd stayed away.

I would have preferred it if Katie hadn't come, though.

She doesn't need to see me running around a rugby pitch again, with my gut leading the way. At least five years ago I still had something of a spring in my step. These days, I'm slightly afraid I'm going to keel over the second the whistle blows.

But Katie was insistent she come along, no matter how much I tried to dissuade her.

Maybe after all the arguments, she *wants* to see me get humiliated again. She'd probably enjoy watching me dunk myself into a truck full of vanilla ice cream this time around.

I have no idea what my mother thinks or wants. But then, I never do these days. She was certainly very pleased when I made no effort to argue about taking part today, so maybe she also fancies seeing me upside down in ice cream?

Who's to say?

In fact, I feel like there's a *lot* of people who are keen to watch what idiocy I get up to on the rugby field again. I can't count the amount of them who have made a point of telling me they'll be here today.

Bastards.

I was especially dismayed to learn that some of the guys from work will be in attendance. My boss, Claire, and my fellow senior caseworker, Remmy, are both going to be sat there in the stands 'cheering me on'. I should never have mentioned anything about it to them. But the last thing I expected was for them to then turn around and say they'd be coming along to lend me their support.

Aaaargh.

Davis Mitchell-Downing seemed as delighted as anyone to welcome me back to the hallowed ground of Western Warriors. I haven't seen him in nearly five years, and yet he welcomed me back like a long-lost brother – instead of the reluctant stand-in for one.

I am deeply suspicious about his motives. There's no reason for him to be this positive about me once again taking to the rugby pitch. Not after last time. Maybe this is payback for five years ago, as far as he is concerned.

My hand involuntarily grips the hem of the rugby jersey again, and my knuckles start to turn white.

I can't take this again. I should never have agreed to come, no matter how many people are here to 'support' me.

I'm going to make a fool of myself in front of dozens of people. Show them what an idiot I truly am. *Again.*

But . . . look and see: Davis Mitchell-Downing is once again poking his head around the doorframe.

'Are you coming, then?' he asks me – and I struck by the most powerful déjà vu I've ever experienced.

Everything is the same.

. . . only that's a lie, of course. I'm *twice* as terrified as I was last time, and *twice* as out of shape. Maybe there are two ice cream vans I can plough into this time around.

'Yeah, yeah. Just . . . give me a second more to . . . gird my loins.'

'No worries! See you out there in a second,' Davis says, before disappearing again – which is a better response than I would have thought I'd get, to be fair. He's being a lot softer with me than he was last time – which rather suggests I'm pitiable enough for even someone like him to be gentle with me.

You'll be fine, I hear Harry say in the vaults of my mind.

No, I won't.

Yes, you will, bro.

You weren't.

You weren't, Harry.

That day you went out to come here and play your silly bloody rugby match was the last time I think I ever saw you truly well. Still the Harry I knew and loved.

You weren't *fine* after that.

Nothing was *fine* after that.

And there was nothing I could do.

That's why I'm sat here, about to force myself out on to that rugby pitch again – because you weren't fine, and there was nothing I could do.

But I can do this.

No matter how it makes my soul crawl into a corner, I can do this.

Because you can't.

I rise to my feet, letting go of the jersey as I do so.

Whatever happens, it's better than nothing, isn't it, Ben?

Better than not being here.

Better than not *being*.

I run the sleeve of the jersey over my eyes to wipe away the tears, and walk towards the door.

Back along the corridor that leads out on to the rugby pitch, I am surrounded by ghosts.

Happily, they blow away as I walk out into the fresh, sunny day that will see me humiliate myself in front of the large crowd that are—

Oh.

There are actually a few empty seats. Quite a few.

I don't know whether to feel happy about this, or a bit upset.

On the one hand, it's fewer people to see me dive headfirst into something inappropriate, but on the other hand, it's a bit upsetting to see fewer people here to commemorate Harry.

That strange combination of feelings stays with me as I walk over to where Davis and the rest of the Warriors are waiting for me.

Looking back at the crowd, I can see Katie and my mother at the front. They both have expectant looks on their faces, which troubles me somewhat. They can't be foolish enough to think that this is going to go well, can they?

'Ben!' Davis Mitchell-Downing barks as I draw close. 'You ready for this?'

'I guess?' I reply, sounding anything but.

He holds up a hand. 'Slight change of plans for today, I'm afraid.'

My heart sinks. This whole malarky is bad enough without something *different* being sprung on me. I can't cope with that.

'Boulders can't play, due to his ligament surgery taking longer to heal that he'd have liked, so I'm going to have to ask you to take his place.'

My mouth drops open.

Boulders is otherwise known as Morgan Ponsonby. And, in a case of the greatest amount of reverse nominative determinism you've ever heard of, Morgan Ponsonby is a brick shithouse of a man.

Nobody that large should be called Morgan Ponsonby. It'd be like naming Niagara Falls the Canadian Dribbles.

'I can't do that,' I point out, entirely accurately. I am a head shorter than Morgan Ponsonby, and about five stone lighter. Me taking his place in the scrum is like trying to plug the hole in the side of the *Titanic* with a half-eaten bowl of jelly.

'Nonsense!' Davis exclaims. 'You'll be *fine!*'

Just like Harry wasn't.

'I'll guide you through what you need to do,' Davis assures me, and before I can protest further the referee blows his whistle, and the two sides split up to go to their respective halves.

Like a man going to the gallows for a second time, I am now a combination of utter terror and abject surprise at finding myself in such an unlikely situation.

I'm going in the scrum?

Even Harry never did that!

But the whistle to start the match has just been blown, and I don't have any time to worry about it all now, because I have to guide my gut up the pitch to where someone else from my team has caught the ball.

Bizarrely, he doesn't seem to make much of an attempt to run towards the goal line of the opposing side. Instead he just ambles forward a bit until he is tackled to the ground, and knocks the ball forward.

This of course sets up the scrum.

Alarm bells are now going off in my head. That looked incredibly *contrived*. These men are doctors, lawyers, posh car salesmen and rugby players. They are not known for their theatrical prowess.

They obviously want to get into a scrum as fast as possible, which means they want *me* in the scrum as fast as possible.

What is going on here?

What are they going to do to me?

'Come on, Ben,' Davis says, putting an arm around my shoulder. 'All you have to do is bend down next to Jennings and Wilkeson, and pop your arms up around their waists.'

'Then what?' I say, the panic rising to overwhelm me.

'Er . . . then, well, the ball will be stuck in, and you have to kick it back. Easy.'

It is not bloody *easy*. It is anything but *easy*.

I attempt to wrap my arms around Jennings and Wilkeson, which is like trying to bear-hug two chest freezers.

Once in that position, the opposing scrum locks heads with us, and I am suddenly comprehensively claustrophobic.

I have sweaty, hairy heads on either side of my own, and am being grasped in ways and in areas that should be off-limits to anyone other than a close loved one or medical practitioner.

But now all I have to do is wait for the ball, feign attempting to kick it somewhere, and then get out of this horrific multi-limbed embrace as quickly as possible.

Only there's no ball . . .

A good thirty seconds have gone by, and I can feel my legs starting to cramp in protest.

'What's going on?' I wail to my fellow scrummers.

'Er . . . problem with the ball probably,' Jennings counters. 'It happens sometimes.'

Jennings is so close to me, it's like I'm having sweet nothings whispered into my ear by a woolly mammoth.

'Can we get up, then?' I plead, feeling something start to twang in my back.

'Um . . . give it a second,' Wilkeson pipes up.

'Why?' I wail.

'Er . . . because that's what we were told to do,' Jennings says.

'Told to do? What do you mean, told to do?' The alarm bells, which are now loud enough to give me tinnitus, clang around in my head at terrifying velocity.

What are these bastards going to do to me? What do they all have planned for me that I don't know about?

'Break the scrum!' I hear Davis exclaim, and I almost start crying with relief.

I can't take any *more*. Not now. Not at the moment.

The scrum rises from its bent-over position as one, and splits up once we're all properly upright again.

That's when I look over at the crowd and see—

Alice

It takes him a few moments to properly recognise that it's me.

That's not much of a surprise. I'm pretty sure I'm the last person he was expecting to see this morning.

And it's odd to see him looking the way he does. I'm so used to being around Ben when he's wearing an idiotic costume that to see him dressed relatively normally is something of a revelation.

Mind you, he does look tremendously awkward in that rugby outfit anyway, so I guess we're not really all that far away from the way things usually are, when you get right down it.

And it's an outfit he's only wearing because of Harry, which is par for the course too.

Aah . . . *Harry*.

I feel like I've learned a lot more about you in the past few weeks than I have the entire time I've known Ben.

Arranging everything today has meant I've had to talk to a lot of your friends. And they paint a somewhat different picture of you than your brother does.

For starters, you actually appear to be a human being. First among equals for sure, but not nearly the paragon of absolute virtue that Ben seems to think you are. Davis Mitchell-Downing dis-abused me of that notion during our phone conversations, and the two we've had in real life, since I got here last week.

Would you be pleased by what I've got planned for your brother, Harry?

I'd like to think you would.

But do I also think you'd be a little jealous of having a rugby match dedicated to you altered like this?

Yes, I think you'd feel that as well, wouldn't you?

But your brother *needs* this, Harry. And *I* need to give it to him just as much. I need to do this. I need to be here. I've kept myself apart too long.

He's been my friend for all of these years . . . and you haven't.

So sit back and just try to enjoy it, okay? And if you see my husband, tell him I still miss him, please.

I walk slowly across the rugby pitch towards Ben. He half stumbles towards me, with a look of disbelief on his face. Which is precisely the look I wanted to see. It means he has no idea what's about to transpire, and that's just the way things should be. That's the way things have to be. This has to be a shock for him, otherwise it won't work.

'Alice? What . . . What are you doing here?' he asks, face a picture of confusion.

'Oh, you know. I was in the neighbourhood and thought I'd pop in,' I say flippantly.

'What? In the neighbourhood?' He looks around to check he hasn't suddenly been transported to a rugby field in Australia.

'I'm here to see *you*,' I tell him in a more serious tone. 'And I'm here to show you something. Something you really need to see, Ben. Because I don't think you have, in all the years I've known you.'

Ben swallows hard. 'I have no idea what's happening.'

I laugh. 'Don't worry, you will.'

I look around and see that both Katie and Ben's mother, Tabitha, have come out to stand in front of the grandstand just as planned.

If I've got to know the late Harry Fielding a little better thanks to all my plans and plotting over the past few weeks, I've got to know his living, breathing relatives even more.

And both Ben's wife and mother are *sad*. For reasons I don't really think Ben understands.

I don't think Ben understands much of how people actually feel about him at all, which is why I'm 100 per cent glad I came up with this rather fanciful idea – and that they've backed me on it fully, right up to this moment.

I doubt he'd think they would, which is horrible.

'Come on,' I tell Ben, and grab him by one hand.

'What is going on, Alice? Why are you at Harry's match?'

I give him a meaningful look. 'I'm here because this isn't Harry's match, Ben, not anymore. He's been celebrated enough, I think.'

Am I more than a little angry at a man who's been dead for ten years?

Yes. I think I am, actually.

'What do you mean this isn't Harry's match?'

'Ben, just let Alice explain,' Katie says.

Ben looks at his wife. 'Do you . . . Do you *know* Alice? *How* do you know Alice?' His face is a picture.

'We've been talking to her a lot, son,' Tabitha says. 'I'm afraid it's all been kept from you.'

I wince a little. Of the two of them, Tabitha has been the one a little more wary of this master plan of mine. Which I guess is fair enough. Not sure most people would react all that well to some weirdo from Australia popping up to stage an intervention in their son's life.

It's a bit of a shame she's standoffish with me, though, because I'd like nothing better than to give her a hug. She knows what it's like to lose a husband. Worse, she knows what it's like to lose a son. I wish I could do more for her, I truly do.

But if the one thing I *can* do is help her surviving son be a happier person, then that'll have to be enough for now.

I may be haunted by my own ghosts that I'm too weak to exorcise – but that doesn't mean I won't do everything in my power to exorcise the ones haunting the people I love.

I now run the most prestigious chain of hair salons in the Sydney area. This is all a walk in the park compared to that.

Ben looks at me, stunned. 'What have you been doing with my family?' he asks, the anxiety writ large across his face.

Right, that's quite enough of that. I'm not here to make him feel worse about himself. He does that to himself without anyone's help.

Let's change that . . .

'Ben, I want you to do something for me,' I tell him.

'What?'

'I want you to look past me, Katie and your mum, and up into the grandstand, please.'

'Why?'

I roll my eyes. 'Just do it, please. And take a long look at some of the people sitting there.'

He nods, a bit dumbly, and turns his attention to the crowd of people that he probably thinks are here today for his brother.

They're not.

I've bloody well made sure of *that*.

Ben

It takes me a minute.

My brain is so frazzled by recent events that it needs that time to actually focus on what – and who – my eyes are looking at.

Seeing Alice in this context was so shocking, I'm not surprised I'm this discombobulated.

And she knows Katie and my mother?

How did she get in touch with them?

What's she been saying to them?

What have they been saying to *her*?

That'll all have to wait for later, though, because now my brain is rewiring itself a bit, and I start to notice two things: one, that the crowd in the grandstand is now much larger. In fact, every seat is full. And two, that I recognise almost all of the new faces.

'Long Jonathan? What . . . What are you doing here?' I say in disbelief.

Because that *is* Long Jonathan, isn't it? I can tell by the pointy nose.

It's a good job the nose is so pointy, because otherwise he's unrecognisable in a rather neat black suit.

So is Tanisha Lambert. Who smiles at me in a way I never thought I'd see, given everything that's happened to her. She looks about ten years younger than the last time I saw her.

And there's Larry Bristow, the old boy who was on the streets after his wife died, and the drink took him. I first saw him looking like a drowned kitten in a black plastic bag, when we went to visit him for the first time in the arches under the railway bridge. Now he's wearing jeans and a pressed shirt, and is also smiling broadly.

And that's Alan Brady . . . and that's Sam Chaney . . . and that's Rafik Hammad . . . and that's Ellen Porter . . . and—

I turn to look at Alice. 'What is this, Alice? Why are they all here?'

She looks me in the eyes.

'They are here because of *you*, Ben Fielding,' she replies. She's crying for some reason. I don't really understand why.

'Me?'

'Yes, *you*,' Katie says, stepping closer.

'Now, do us a favour, and just stand there and listen, will you?' Alice tells me, before turning and gesturing to Long Jonathan – who stands up, fumbling in his jacket pocket for a second, before producing a piece of paper and staring down at it intently.

'I am here because you,' he begins in a cracked voice, clearing his throat. '. . . Because you helped me when nobody else would. They all thought I was a lost cause, but you didn't. You saw *me*, instead of just a drunk kid with no hope. I now live in a lovely flat just off Burrows Avenue, and I am very happy. Because of you.' He looks up at me. 'Because of you,' he repeats, and smiles.

'Thanks, Jonathan, that was very nice,' Alice says.

I'm flabbergasted. How does Alice know Long Jonathan, of all people?

'Now you, Tanisha,' Alice calls out.

Tanisha stands up. She's not holding a piece of paper. 'Hey Ben!' she says and waves.

'Hi Tanisha . . . how are you?' I reply in a slightly lost tone of voice.

'I'm great, Ben! And it's all thanks to you!'

'Is it?'

'For sure! If you hadn't got me into that shelter, I'd never have got away from that bastard, Leo. He would have found me' – her face darkens – 'and he would have hurt me again. But you stopped that, Ben! You saved me!'

I blush furiously. 'Oh, I wouldn't go that far.'

'I would!' she insists, with a determined tilt of her head. 'I have a *good* man in my life now, and a baby boy.' She beams at me. 'I'll show you pictures later!'

'Oh . . . okay,' I respond, more than a little taken aback at this massive change in someone who I last saw with a face covered in slowly healing bruises.

Tanisha sits back down, and Alice bids Rafik Hammad to stand up. He also has a short speech prepared on a piece of paper.

It turns out they all do.

One after the other, people I have seen come through the doors of Shelter over the course of the last half decade rise to their feet to tell me how well they are doing.

Because of me.

But that's not right, is it?

It's not because of *me*.

I've just been doing my job all of these years. They are the ones who have turned their lives around. Rafik was a drug dealer who is now working for Sainsbury's, and is getting married next month. Alan Brady lost everything in the global financial crisis, but is now in sheltered accommodation, and helping his fellow residents with their taxes. Ellen Porter had to sell herself just to have enough money to get a hot drink, but now she's helping counsel other women.

They are the ones who have done all this. *They* are the ones who have made the difference.

It wasn't me!

'No!' I hear Alice say from beside me. I turn to face her. She looks angry. Oh dear. 'No, Ben Fielding!' she continues. 'You're not going to wriggle out from this! I can see that brain of yours trying to convince you that you didn't save all of these people, and I'm not letting it get away with it!'

'*We're* not letting you get away with it!' Katie says in a determined voice.

'No, we're not,' my mother agrees, in a much softer tone. There are tears in her eyes, and a look on her face I can't quite fathom.

I hold up a hand to the crowd. 'But I didn't do all that much, really,' I say.

'Yes, you did!' Tanisha cries out. 'I'd be dead without you!'

'So would I!' Ellen repeats.

'And me!' Long Jonathan agrees.

'Me too!' Alan Brady shouts.

'Me as well!' Larry Bristow adds.

'I'd have killed someone without you there,' Rafik says, hushing everyone else instantly. All eyes turn to look at the tall, thin man, whose tattoos are still there, even if the look of hate on his face isn't. 'I was a . . . a bad person, Ben. I hurt people. If you don't believe anyone else today, believe *me*. You got me off the street. Away from a lot of really bad people. You saved me, bro, and you saved a lot of others too, I think.' He swallows hard, voice choked with emotion. 'Don't you dare say you didn't. Because if you do, you make it all . . . less real. It won't mean as much, man. Don't do that.'

Tanisha whoops with approval and claps her hands.

Embarrassingly, this starts a full round of applause that ripples at first through all of my old clients, and then gets taken up by the rest of the grandstand.

I just stand there dumbfounded.

What else can I do?

251

Then, there's movement from beside me, and I see my mother turn from the applauding grandstand, move closer and put her arms around me.

I can't remember the last time I had a hug from my mother. Was it when my father died?

No. Not even then, I don't think.

It was when Harry died.

Yes. That's it. A few seconds after he drew his last breath, and the living room was full of the sound of machines winding down, and nothing else.

She hugged me then.

But this is a *fiercer* hug. A stronger hug.

And as she hugs me, she says something in a low voice that I have to strain a little to hear over the noise coming from the crowd of people witnessing this.

'Your father and your brother would be very proud of you, son,' she says. '*I* am very proud of you.'

Oh dear.

I'm afraid the dam bursts at this point.

You could put a thousand people in front of me who can tell me I saved their lives, and it wouldn't have been able to break through the walls of self-loathing I've erected over the years.

But my mother telling me she's proud of me bulldozes those walls away, as if they were made of rice paper.

I start to sob in her arms.

The hug gets tighter.

Until she moves a little to allow Katie to come in as well.

You did *save them, bro. Each and every one of them.*

I couldn't save you.

Nobody could have.

You could have done so much more.

Not more than you have, little bro. Not more than you.

I look up through a haze of tears to see that Alice is standing just a little apart from us, her hands folded across her chest and a gentle smile on her face. There's also a slight look of satisfaction in her eyes from a job well done.

How the hell do I ever repay this?

Katie and Mum disentangle themselves from me, and my wife looks at me with a determined expression on her face. 'Do you see now, Ben? Please tell me that you do. Because if all of this doesn't show you the kind of man you actually are, I don't know anything ever will.'

I look up at the crowd again. 'Yeah,' I say, more than a little out of breath. 'I get it.'

A hand rests itself gently upon my shoulder, and I look around to see something that must count as some sort of wonder of the world. Davis Mitchell-Downing has tears in his eyes. Actual, real tears.

Good lord.

'He talked about you lot, you know,' Davis says, his manful brow creasing like a collapsing suspension bridge. 'Harry, I mean. Always said things were better when you were around.'

'Did he?' I reply, a lump in my throat.

'Oh yes. I had to give him a sweaty rubbington one time, because he was getting too emotional about you. Loved you, he did.'

I'm choosing not to dwell on whatever the hell a 'sweaty rubbington' might be, and I'm instead concentrating on the rather incredible and lovely thing Davis Mitchell-Downing has just said to me about my brother.

'Three cheers for Ben Fielding!' Davis Mitchell-Downing then crows at the top of his voice.

My cheeks flame red.

He could have just left it at that nice comment about Harry . . . but then I don't think people like Davis Mitchell-Downing really operate like that.

'Hip hip . . . hooray!' he cries, and about half the crowd join in.

The second cheer is much louder, and the third is so loud that I feel like my brain is going to crawl down my spine and hide somewhere dark, because of the cringeworthiness of it all.

Even Alice is perplexed by it. This clearly wasn't part of her plan.

And what a plan it must have been.

How did she get all these people here today? How did she track them down?

The fact my boss is here must have something to do with it.

How long did all of this *take*?

Alice

'Let's just say I'm glad I have plenty of international minutes on my phone contract,' I tell Ben, and take another bite of the finger sandwich.

The caterers who supply Western Warriors for their social events know how to make a good prawn cocktail sandwich, it has to be said.

And an *expensive* prawn cocktail sandwich as well – but I have Davis and the rugby lads to thank for helping me stump up the cash for all of the food we are now eating in the Warriors bar.

Hell, it was their suggestion we do this after the match in the first place. Rugby lads are never ones to pass up an opportunity for some drinking during the day, I've noticed. I'd like to see how friendly they'd be with the AFL blokes back home. I'm sure they'd get on like an industrial estate on fire.

'When did you *start?*' Ben continues to question me, from where he's stood, slightly leant against the bar, with one arm around Katie's shoulder. He looks more relaxed than I've seen in a long time.

And he also seems adamant about knowing how I put this all together – thinking it must have been some sort of grand master plan. But it was a lot more prosaic than he thinks.

'Well, it started with tracking down Katie at the school where she works, and went from there,' I tell him.

I knew from the tone of those emails (and the fact that communication from him was extremely sporadic) that Ben was in a very bad place, and I equally knew that trying to talk to him about it wasn't going to do any good. After all, all the conversations we've had over the years face to face didn't do much to change his outlook, so another one over the phone wasn't going to shift the dial at all. It might have made me feel a little better, but would have done nothing for Ben.

Turning to Katie for her advice was my best option, not least because she was in the same time zone as Ben and his depressive state.

'And I was more than happy to help,' Katie interjects with a smile.

'You were, which was a relief,' I say with a nod, 'because we'd never actually met, and I didn't quite know how you'd react to me butting in on your lives.'

Katie waves a hand. 'It really was fine, Alice. From everything Ben had told me about you, you felt more like a long-lost sister-in-law getting in touch than anything else. It was lovely.'

My lip wobbles a bit at this. What an extraordinarily nice thing for her to say.

I remember Ben telling me how open his wife was about her feelings, and getting a small dose of that today shows me why he loves her so much.

Katie agreed with me that Ben would never come out from under the cloud without a big shock to his system, and was very happy to help organise today's little surprise. His stubbornness about his own sense of self-worth was as obvious to her as it was to me, so we needed to pin him down and shock him into a change of attitude.

We both agreed it would be a good idea to turn the rugby match into something Ben could feel good about from now on. It felt suitably symbolic.

Once Katie was on board, and we'd started organising via lunchtime calls for her, and late evening calls for me, we turned to the next person on the list whose help we knew we'd need.

Ben's boss, Claire, was a little reticent to begin with, but warmed up to the whole idea once I'd laid it out for her.

To be honest, none of this would have been possible without her. She had to approach Ben's old clients to see if they'd want to be a part of today. It's testament to how liked he is that they all said yes straight away.

I don't particularly want to detail every step of this whole thing to Ben, but he's not really giving me much choice. It almost feels like he's trying to unpick what's happened today, so he can find fault in it. And by find fault in *it*, I mean find fault in *himself*, of course.

His treacherous brain probably wants me to admit I had to pay people to come here today and celebrate his accomplishments, so he can feel worse about himself again – but I'm not going to even give it an inch.

Ben Fielding is just going to have to accept that the people gathered in this social club right now are here because of the man he is – whether he likes it or not.

'Gosh,' he says in a slightly stunned voice when I'm done explaining all of this to him. I doubt this will be the last conversation we have about it, but I hope it's the last for now, as I'm dead on my feet. I still feel jet-lagged, even though I've been here over a week. Rushing around trying to organise an intervention for your best friend will do that.

'Alright, that's enough of the twenty questions, mister,' Katie says, reading the exhausted expression on my face perfectly. 'Alice has told you everything you need to know, so just be happy she's here, and everything went off as well as it did.'

I give her a grateful smile.

I think her and I are going to be quite close in the future . . . with any luck.

It's a shame Ben's mother left about twenty minutes ago, as I'd like to get to know her a bit better too.

Tabitha made her excuses by saying she felt very tired. I think it's probably more that the events of the day have been a bit too much for her, which I can't blame her for at all. I think there are more conversations between her and her son needed in the near future, but just the fact she's openly said how proud she is of him is a step in the right direction. I wasn't really expecting that to happen, but I was delighted that it did.

'So, what are your plans for the rest of the time you're here?' Katie asks. 'We'd love to have you over for dinner.'

'Yes! That'd be marvellous!' Ben agrees.

'I'd love to,' I say, with a smile. 'I have all this time here, so I'd love to see you both a bit more.'

I haven't taken any official leave from the salon now for a very long time, so Paul was happy to let me have this extended break for several weeks. While I'm here, I'm going to visit with my friends, take a look at some old haunts – and go along to one hospital accident and emergency department . . .

I have to exorcise my demons.

I absolutely *have* to.

I don't want there to be an ulterior motive for this extended visit to England. I want it just to be about helping Ben, and being there for someone when they need me. But there is an ulterior motive. A big one. The biggest one of all.

'Other than that,' I continue to Ben and Katie, 'I'm just going to enjoy the English countryside, and enjoy some summer temperatures that don't feel like you're next door to the sun.'

'That's all?' Ben says, eyes narrowing slightly.

I look at him for a moment longer than I probably should. 'Yes, yes. That's all.'

He doesn't need to know what I have planned at the hospital. I don't want to ruin the good mood we're all in today. He doesn't need to know I'm

Ben

Lying.

She's lying, and I really don't know why . . .

She has something planned that she doesn't want to tell us about, and there's a part of me that wants to push it until I find out what it is, because I don't like the look behind her eyes one little bit.

But with Katie by my side, and a room full of happy, upbeat people, I don't think it's the right time.

I hope it will be at some point in the near future.

'I'm glad you're staying until . . . well, you know . . . that day,' I say to her with a slightly clouded smile.

'Me too. If for no other reason than to see what Harry has made you dress in this year,' Alice replies.

I laugh.

I genuinely *laugh*.

For the first time since my late brother started me off on this ridiculous tradition, I don't feel any dread or sadness about having to dress up and stand at his grave.

It's going to take me a lot more time to fully digest what's happened here today, but if Alice's plan was to shock me out of a stupor I've been in for far too long, it worked.

As I look around this room now, I am stunned by the changes I see in people who were in a terrible place the last time I laid eyes on them.

I am even more stunned by the fact they all came along today to see me.

Alice couldn't have picked a better event to pull this stunt at. I've spent years dreading these rugby matches held in Harry's honour, because they just underlined everything he was that I wasn't.

But now? Well, my memories of them are going to be very different from now on, aren't they?

God bless you, Alice.

Thank you for everything you've done for me. I will never be able to repay you . . . but I do want to know what that look behind your eyes is. Because I really don't like it *one little bit*.

We all spend another hour or so in the Western Warriors bar, during which Tanisha invites me to her birthday party in a fortnight – which I will most certainly go to, and Davis Mitchell-Downing invites me to join the rugby club – which I most certainly will not. I am gratified that his opinion of me was much higher than I ever thought it was, but I don't think I need to ruin the tentative friendship we have by making a mockery of his favourite sport.

I will feel better about myself in general after today, I think – but that will not extend as far as thinking I can be any good at rugby.

There are some things I am more than happy to admit Harry was better at than me.

But nothing all that important anymore, eh, bro?

No, Harry. Probably not.

In the car park, the hug I give Alice is warm and long, but the hug Katie gives her is even longer. This is probably the one thing that actually fills my heart more than anything else I've seen today.

. . . I'll keep that to myself, though, I think.

With promises made for Alice to come over for dinner next week, we part company with her, and make our way home. During the ride I am a little quiet, ruminating on the day's events.

'You okay?' Katie asks me.

'Yes,' I say – more or less honestly, for a change. 'Just processing it all, really.'

. . . and probably thinking about that look in Alice's eyes more than I should be.

When we get home, though, something rather wonderful happens.

I believe the creatures of this planet refer to it as 'sex'.

It's been so long since Katie and I have indulged ourselves that I'd almost forgotten how to do it. It's like riding a bike, though – it all comes back to you. Especially when the bike ride is quite *brief*, given how long it's been since we last hopped into the saddle.

Afterwards, while Katie makes what will be the best cup of tea I've ever had in my life, I ruminate some more on what happened at Western Warriors. I think I'll be doing this a lot in the weeks to come. Not least because all of my neuroses are still present and correct at the moment, and I'll need to remind myself of the *truth* on a regular basis, until my brain accepts the way things *are*, instead of the way it *wants things to be*.

I've been too hard on myself, haven't I?

Yes, bro. You absolutely have.

Gosh.

Good old Davis was right, you know. Things did get better when you came along, bro.

They did?

Absolutely.

Blimey. What a silly boy I've been, eh?

So what are you going to do about it?

I think about this for a moment, before replying.

Probably stop talking to you, for starters. You're not really Harry.

No, I'm not.

You're me.

Yes, I am.

I have to let him go, don't I?

Yes, you do.

Tears prick my eyes.

But I love him so much. And he loved me too. I'm not sure I can do it.

Of course you can. You just have to get up, go downstairs and have a cup of tea with your wife.

Then what?

Then start living your life. *Because ten years is way too long to be mourning someone else's.*

Just get up?

Just get up.

Which I then do . . . and go downstairs to have the best cup of tea I've ever had in my life.

Alice

And so, here I am again.

For the fourth time in as many weeks.

God help me.

I have tried to enjoy my time here in the UK, I truly have. But I'm afraid it's actually been one of the hardest things I've ever done.

Because this isn't home anymore.

And all the time I've spent with Ben and Katie in the past month cannot in any way compete with the visits I've made to this bloody hospital.

Because I couldn't let it go.

As much as I wanted to. As much as I just wanted to take this time to reconnect with people, see all the places from my past and drink as much PG Tips as I can get my hands on, I couldn't let it go.

So I've now made more visits to an A&E department than a drunk rock climber.

I have to *know*.

I have to know *why*.

I have to exorcise this demon that's been haunting me for a decade.

Why did my old life have to end here in such a terrible fashion? Why did Joe Everley, a fit young man in his mid-forties, die here in this miserable place?

I know what they told me at the time. I know what the reports said. But it's not *enough*. It's never really been enough. Because the nightmares have never left me. Because the feeling that something went very *wrong* here has never left me.

So I've been back here repeatedly, and I have been determined to find out more – no matter how many strange looks I get, nor how many medical staff refuse to talk to me on the many occasions I've tried to strike up a conversation. I'm afraid I've probably created a reputation for myself of being a very annoying busybody who won't stop walking up to random people to ask them whether they worked here ten years ago.

It only needed one of them to say yes they did, and then for them to agree to say something. And it only needed me badgering almost all of them for four weeks to find that person.

Zuzanna approached me the last time I was here, by the coffee machine that had just swallowed my last pound coin. A petite nurse with a kind face and a heavy Eastern European accent, Zuzanna had clearly heard about the mad woman with the faint Australian twang, sticking her nose in where it didn't belong, and asking way too many questions about what happened on a January night here a decade ago.

Everybody else told me either they were not working here back then or couldn't remember.

Zuzanna was different.

Zuzanna *was* here that night, and bloody well *could* remember – because it was far from an ordinary shift.

And she agreed to speak to me at the end of her next day shift, in the hospital cafeteria.

Which is right now.

Oh God, it is *right now*.

My heart thuds slowly and deliberately in my chest as I enter what is actually a very nicely appointed café. It's only about a quarter full, given that it's late evening.

I see Zuzanna nursing a coffee over in one corner, against a window that looks out over the hospital car park. The same car park I continue to have dreams about to this day. Only it's far smaller and easier to get across than the one that leaps into my mind during REM sleep. It doesn't expand out to infinite proportions every time I try to run towards my dying husband.

With my hands gripped so tightly I have to be careful not to dig my nails into my palms hard enough to need Zuzanna's professional attention, I cross the café and sit down opposite her.

'Hello,' I say in a voice that I hope sounds a little stronger than I feel. 'Thanks for meeting with me.'

'It's not a problem,' she says with a rather lacklustre smile. The bags under her eyes attest to someone who probably doesn't want to be in this building for one moment more than she absolutely has to be.

I am instantly reminded of Ben, all those years ago, when he was training to be a doctor.

'You said you think you can tell me a little more about what happened that night?' I ask. 'The night . . . my husband died?' My mouth is so dry I wish I'd bought a drink at the counter.

Zuzanna nods – a little uncertainly. 'I do not want to get any-one into trouble,' she says.

I shake my head. 'I don't want that, either. I just want . . . an answer, you know? Something that tells me if and why my Joe . . .' I trail off. She knows.

Zuzanna nods again. 'I can understand that. You are not the only person who feels this way about . . . what happens to their loved ones. And for once I can actually say something.' There's a wealth of knowledge behind those eyes that I neither want nor care to find out more about. 'Most never get to know, but I know what happened that day, and I will tell you.'

'Thank you so much,' I say, and have to fight back the impulse to reach across the table and hold her hand. Zuzanna cuts a forlorn figure, and I can see that this kind of conversation is hard for her.

'It does not mean that anything could have been done for your husband anyway,' she points out to me. It is a statement I should pay far more attention to than I actually do, I have to confess. I'm on the edge of some sort of revelation here, and don't want any-thing to ruin it.

'What happened?' I ask, the desperate urgency in my voice palpable.

Zuzanna instantly looks like she regrets ever agreeing to this meeting – and who can blame her? I wouldn't want to sit across from a woman in the kind of heightened state I apparently am.

Noting the alarm on her face, I force myself to sit back in my chair and relax a little. 'Sorry. I understand everything you're saying. It's just that I've been living with this for quite a long time.'

She smiles awkwardly, takes a sip of her coffee and locks eyes with me for a moment, before they slip away to look out of the window. 'We were understaffed – as usual,' she says, with a dismayed exhalation of breath. 'That's always the main problem, Mrs Everley. No matter what else. That's *always* the main problem.'

I nod.

I get that. I truly do. But there's more, isn't there? There's something else. I can see it trapped behind her eyes.

'And?' I urge, eagerly.

Zuzanna breathes in deeply. 'I only remember that day because of what else happened. It was very unusual.'

'Which was?'

'Somebody on our staff had a problem while they were on shift. We had to help them.'

'Who was it who had the problem?'

'One of our doctors. One of our *best* doctors. Down from surgery to help out, because we were so understaffed. He was the doctor who saw your husband for his initial triage. He was someone everybody loved, and our attention was drawn away briefly from the patients to him.' She holds up her hands, palms out. 'It was only very brief, I promise!'

'But long enough,' I reply, and I can feel the blood actually being drawn from underneath my fingernails now.

'Yes, I think so. Information slipped between the cracks. Not just about your husband, but for many people in the A&E that day. We were all so stressed, and so tired, you see. Any distraction was bound to make things ten times worse.' Zuzanna swallows hard and continues. 'And as I say, it was because we were so understaffed anyway.' I nod absently, but I'm having trouble hearing her now. I've gone somewhere else. 'And losing him made things all the worse,' she continues. 'I don't think we could have done anything to save your husband anyway, but you ask if things could have been better that day? If we had problems over and above the usual? Then I answer yes. Things could have been better. *We* could have been better. I am very sorry.'

'Thank you,' I manage to say, the lid on my anger very near the point of flying off. 'Thank you for being honest with me.'

You stupid, stupid woman. Why didn't you do your bloody job? Why didn't you all do your bloody jobs?!

Calm the hell down.

This wasn't Zuzanna's fault. It wasn't *any* fault of theirs. Including the doctor.

Yes, it was. Yes, it bloody was. Yes, yes, yes!

'Did your . . . What happened with the doctor?' I don't care, but I have to look like I do, don't I? I have to look and sound like someone who doesn't want to jump across this table and claw her eyes out. I have to sound *normal*. I have to ask normal questions, the way a normal person would, in a normal conversation.

Zuzanna's eyes cloud. 'I do not know for sure. I did not see him again.'

'What was his name?' I ask, still not caring, but trying to give the appearance of such.

The answer Zuzanna gives utterly and completely destroys my life.

The second time that's happened in this bloody hospital.

Ben

So, this is what I'd look like with long hair, is it?

You know what, I kind of approve.

I knew I should have grown it out when I was a teenager.

I certainly couldn't do that now. The small, but ever widening bald patch on the crown of my head attests to that fact. And I doubt I could have ever got my hair as long and as flowing as this wig.

Or as ginger.

It really does look quite *magnificent*, though.

As do the leather jacket, black leather trousers and ripped t-shirt.

I have never been into rock or heavy metal, so have never dressed in this manner before, but I do feel like I've missed out on something, now I finally have.

Harry was the one who was into that kind of music, so the fancy dress costume he's making me wear this year does make some sort of sense. I've been at this a decade now, and I get the impression he was starting to run out of inspiration by this point.

Last year's cowboy costume wasn't exactly original, either – but then nobody saw me in it anyway, given that there was nobody here when I performed our ritual.

And okay . . . the Humpty Dumpty outfit was a lot more in keeping with previous years, but the pandemic properly put paid to me ever wearing that one, didn't it?

So sorry, Harry!

I laugh out loud as I saunter across the car park of the church – my long, fake red hair blowing in the wind. I really dodged an egg-shaped bullet on that one.

'Eggsellent,' I say out loud, to no one in particular, and laugh out loud again.

I should probably be in a more sombre mood, given where I am and what I'm about to do, but give me a break . . . I've been doing this for ten years now, and any unpleasant activity gets easier after ten years. You always inevitably get used to something, don't you?

And I am well used to dressing up like a berk, and spending an afternoon in a graveyard with my best friend, Alice.

. . . only this time we probably won't need an afternoon, as I've seen a lot of her recently anyway, given that she's been here in the country ever since the rugby match that changed my life.

I still have no idea how I'm ever going to repay her, but I won't give up thinking about it until I do.

Maybe I can get an idea of how to go about it from today's conversation. I've been looking forward to it all week, knowing that I am in a far better place for it than I have ever been before – all thanks to her.

There must be something I can do to repay all of Alice's effort and kindness – and today marks the first chance I'm going to get to glean what that might be.

Today will be all about *her*. Once she's got over laughing at me in a pair of skintight leather trousers, that is.

The churchyard is a little fuller than it normally is on this day. The nice weather has obviously brought people out to spend some time with their late loved ones. That's fine, though. I doubt a fake rock star walking among them will worry them too much.

I'm fully prepared to bat away any complaints, anyway. I've never been all that comfortable with telling people why I come here dressed in these outlandish costumes, but this year I don't think it'd be something I'd have an issue with.

I spy Alice sat on our bench in front of Harry and Joe's graves, which immediately brings a smile to my face. I figure I might do a little dance on the spot while I get through 'We Are the Champions', which should make her giggle.

I draw closer to her, thinking she'll look up and see me (the bright red wig is a little hard to miss) but she continues to stare at Joe's grave with a stern look on her face.

Oh no. She's obviously had a bit of bad time of it being here today. I'll have to do my best to cheer her up.

The little wiggle dance during the song should help. Even I could laugh at my somewhat saggy bottom bobbing back and forth in these trousers.

'Hey Alice!' I say to her in a bright voice as I reach her. Helping her out of whatever dark mood she is in starts with being upbeat myself, I think.

Alice doesn't immediately answer, but she does look up at me. The stern look does not disappear. In fact, if anything, it gets even harder.

'Are you okay?' I say, the smile dropping off my face.

'No, Ben. I'm not *okay*,' she replies, her eyes flashing.

'What's wrong?'

Alice slowly gets to her feet and steps a little closer to me. Is she going to give me a hug? That doesn't seem to line up with the vibes she's generally giving o—

A burst of hot, stinging pain hits me on the side of my face.

She's just slapped me.

Alice has just full on *slapped me* in the face.

My hand flies to the red patch blossoming on my left cheek. 'What the hell?!' I cry in sudden anger, and complete shock.

'You bastard!' she hisses at me. I'm sure it would have been a scream if we hadn't been in a churchyard with a dozen other people. 'You absolute *bastard!*'

The hate in her eyes is terrifying, and terrible.

'What the hell's wrong? What have I done?' I exclaim, the heat in my check not dissipating one little bit.

'You know *exactly* what you've done!' she rages, and points a trembling finger at my chest. 'You knew! You must have known!'

'Must have known what?!' I snap back. This isn't Alice. This is some monster that's possessed her.

'That *he* was there that day!'

I shake my head in utter confusion. 'Who? Who was there? Where?'

'Your bloody brother!' she barks. 'Your precious bloody brother, *Harry*!'

I rip the ginger wig off my head. 'Start making some damn sense, Alice!'

Alice takes a sharp inhale of breath. 'Harry was there the day Joe died! In the A&E department! You must have known!'

The heat from my cheek is instantly replaced with an icy cold that suffuses my entire body. 'Harry was there the day Joe died?' I reply, barely able to form the words. 'How did you . . . Where did you find that out?'

'I spoke to a nurse who was on shift the day it happened,' Alice spits. 'She told me your brother had "an emergency" and that's why Joe wasn't taken care of properly!' She fixes me with a grim stare that makes me want to turn my face away from her. 'What was it, Ben? Another one of your brother's stupid practical jokes? Is that why you've never been able to tell me about it? To admit it? Because you knew all along that precious bloody Harry Fielding was responsible for my poor Joe's death!'

The words cut me to pieces.

My brain, addled by all of this as it is, tries to process the idea that Harry was in the same hospital on the same day that Alice's husband was admitted.

It's possible. Of course it is. Harry always put himself forward for extra A&E shifts when he could. He could have been there that day.

But what are the *chances*? What are the *odds*?

Something starts to crumble beneath my feet.

I shake my head rapidly back and forth. 'I didn't know, Alice. I promise!' I take a step forward, but she instantly backs off.

'Get away from me!' she snaps, and turns, stalking off with her arms held out downwards and ram rod straight.

But then she spins again and marches towards me. It's my turn to back off. So much that I nearly stumble on the raised concrete edges of Harry's grave.

'Are you seriously trying to tell me that you had no bloody idea that your brother was working in the same hospital, on the same day?!' she rages.

'No!' I repeat, this time with more vigour in my voice. I don't think I deserve this treatment, to be honest. 'I had no clue! I didn't follow Harry's every move, you know!'

Alice doesn't know what to say for a moment. Part of her wants to accept that I'm telling the truth, but I'm not sure it's the part that's winning. 'It's impossible!' she eventually snaps. 'Did you *know*? When we first met here all those years ago? Were you only here to see me because you knew what he'd done?' The suspicion in her eyes is heartbreaking.

'What? No, of course not! Why would you think that?'

'Because it's all *impossible*, Ben! That we'd just meet the way we did. And that they'd be *next door to each other in the bloody graveyard*!'

And for a moment, I can only agree with her.

A dark part of my mind wonders if there's some sort of hideous *deliberateness* behind the cruelty of it all. You take two distraught people who think they are complete strangers, give them ten years to become friends and then show them that their lives have been tangled together far more than they ever realised.

Rationality then reasserts itself (and in the weeks to come I will look back on this moment with a small feeling of pride that it does) and I shake my head again.

'It's not impossible, Alice,' I tell her firmly. 'Harry was a doctor. Joe was sick. They both worked and lived in this area.'

'No! No, it's impossible that you didn't know!' she wails, but there's a crack in her belief now. I just need to widen it.

'I didn't know, Alice. I'm sorry about all of it, but *I didn't know.*'

'How could you *not*?' she now pleads. She's desperate for this all to make sense somehow . . . but I don't have the answers she needs. 'How could he have done this?'

She's also desperate to find somebody to blame.

I fix her with a look that I hate. 'Harry would *never* have deliberately compromised a patient's safety,' I tell her, in a tone of voice you could use to carve out a decent memorial.

That gets through.

'You don't know that, Ben.'

'Yes, I do. I absolutely *do.*'

Do you, bro? Do you really? I did like a joke at the most inappropriate of times, didn't I? Can you say for certain that you're right?

Alice stares into my eyes, and instantly steps away from me again. 'No. No, you don't know for sure. You don't know he didn't do something that compromised how they treated Joe. You don't know!'

'Yes, I do!'

'No!' Her finger stabs at me again, shaking with fury. 'You don't! I've known you for *ten years*, Ben. I know when you're not sure about something! I've sat on that damned bench and watched you be not sure about yourself for so long, I know that look like the back of my hand!'

I go to open my mouth again to argue, but she's right. As much as I want to believe Harry wouldn't have done anything that could have affected Joe, I don't know it for certain.

I need to think about all of this. I need to find out more. I need to take Alice away from here and get her to see some reason.

'Please, Alice. Let's just go somewhere together and figure this out,' I say, stepping towards her once more. 'We can find out what Harry actually did. We can sort all of this out.' My hand reaches out to take her by the arm. It's meant to be a conciliatory gesture. It's absolutely the wrong thing to do.

'Get away from me!' Alice snaps, forcing me away with a furious push.

I stumble once, hit the edge of Harry's grave, and fall back on to the last resting place of my only brother with a sickening crunch.

Alice looks down at me in horror for a moment, realising what she's done.

Then she turns and runs.

I need to get up.

I *should* get up.

I should go after her.

I should—

Alice

I should get up from my desk and go back to work.

I can't just sit here in the semi-darkness of my office all day. I can hear how busy things are getting, and I know the girls will want me out there to help them.

But instead, I just sit here, staring out of the window behind my desk that looks out on to the yard at the back of the salon, and out on a grey spring day in Sydney that would be better suited to the UK.

I shudder.

I'm never going back there, I don't think.

Not now.

Not after what happened.

Because what do I have there now? A few old friends I barely have anything in common with after being away from them for nearly a decade . . . and *nothing else* – apart from bad memories, and even worse regrets.

At least here I have my work, and my colleagues, and, usually, the kind of weather that can always put a smile on your face.

Not today, though. Today is very *British*, and I don't think there will be a day with weather like this I won't dread for the rest of my life.

I should get up from my desk and go back to work.

But I don't.

Of course I don't.

I haven't done for the past three weeks.

I've hidden in here as much as possible, claiming that I have a lot of admin to do. Which is the truth – I always have admin to do. But not enough to justify the amount of hours I've spent sat in my office, trying my very best to stay away from people as much as possible.

And that's all I'm going to do from now on. Stay away from people.

Because where does it get me when I try something different? Where does it get me when I try to reach out to someone? Try to connect with them? Try to be close?

Betrayal, that's where.

Or death.

One of those two options. Both of which are terrible.

No. Staying away is better. Staying away is safer. It always was and it always will be.

My staff know there's a problem. It would be a little hard for them not to. But they don't do or say anything about it. My natural aloofness towards them over the years guarantees that I'm not bothered by their concern now. They know when to leave me alone.

So I have been *alone*.

And I will continue to be *alone*.

There's simply no better choice for me. The alternatives are far too horrible to contemplate. If nothing else, if I were around people for any length of time, I would inevitably have to tell them why I am so damned depressed.

And I don't want to talk about that. I don't *ever* want to talk about that. I just want enough time to go by so that it doesn't hurt so much. So that I can forget.

That's the way it's supposed to work. Time goes by, and you forget. That's what they say.

Just because it hasn't worked for me before, does not mean it can't happen for me in the future.

The far, *distant* future, that is.

In the more immediate future is an evening of television I won't pay much attention to, and food I won't taste.

This is fine, though. Neither thing will ask me how I'm feeling. Neither thing can betray me, or die on me.

I say goodnight to everyone as they troop into my office one by one to say they are off for the day. Madeline *almost* pauses to ask me how I am. My blood runs cold as she stands there for a moment longer than she should. But then she just smiles and turns to leave, thank God.

I lock the salon up, set the alarm and walk out into the August drizzle, trying very hard not to think about how it feels so incredibly British.

It was gloriously sunny day when I left that country last month. . . . I think I prefer the drizzle.

The radio DJ tells me on the way home that a new report has been published stating that people who take two showers a day live longer. Maybe I'll have a bath tonight.

I barely notice Jobbers as I pass by him on the path that leads to my apartment block. I'm sure this annoys him a great deal. Jobbers likes to be the centre of attention, but I don't have the energy to make *anything* the centre of my attention at the moment, no matter how loudly it laughs at me.

I pass through the main entrance door to the apartment, which is still broken, and propped open with a stack of *Sydney Today* free newspapers. Obviously the body corporate meeting didn't do much good last night, then. I didn't attend it – for reasons which hardly need explaining. No need to anyway, when Clive will fill me in as soon as is humanly possible. I hope he doesn't ask me how I'm doing when he does, though.

Inside my apartment, I prepare two things. A spaghetti Bolognaise ready meal direct from the freezer in Woolworths, and a large glass of red wine.

Given how pissed off Jobbers looked, and the state of the weather, I elect to consume these inside, staring out of my bifold apartment doors at the drizzle falling on to the harbour.

As I finish the spaghetti Bolognaise, which tastes roughly like the cardboard box it came wrapped in, and drain the last of the wine, I am forced to reflect that I may be at what is called my 'lowest ebb'.

When my doorbell rings, indicating that Clive just couldn't wait any longer to tell me how badly the body corporate went, I heave a sigh and get up. I might as well spend twenty minutes commiserating with my neighbour about how long it's been since the apartment front door worked properly.

Then I'll have a bath, watch *The Block* and try to go to sleep.

Maybe the weather will be a little better tomorrow, so that my office won't feel quite so dark as I sit in there all day, hiding from the rest of the world.

I open my front door. 'Evening, Cli—'

The words die in my mouth.

'Hi Alice,' Ben Fielding says. 'Can we please talk?'

Ben

I am hungry and exhausted by the time I reach Alice's apartment. I haven't slept since the night before last, back in the UK.

Was it the night before last, though? Or was it last night? I've never experienced this level of jet lag before. It's hard to know what day it is.

I wanted to sleep on the plane, but the thought of having this conversation kept me awake the entire flight. Not least because I was deathly afraid that I wouldn't even get as far as the conversation even *starting*.

There's every chance Alice will just slam the door in my face and refuse to speak to me, which will mean I'll have wasted two grand and thirty hours of my life flying to Australia for no reason.

But she wouldn't answer the phone! Or reply to any text messages!

How the hell else was I supposed to talk to her?

How the hell else was I supposed to explain things to her? Tell her about what I've discovered in the weeks since she's been gone?

I simply had no choice but to come here, and hope against hope that she'd give me the chance to speak face to face.

And so here I stand, exhausted and hungry, at the front door to an apartment block that I would never have found without a pleading phone call to Paul DiMarco, placed two days ago long distance.

Or was it three days?

Who can tell?

He didn't want to tell me where Alice lived initially. And who can blame him? A complete stranger ringing you up at your company main offices, asking for the address of one of your most senior employees, is not the kind of thing that you have a positive response about.

It took me a good twenty minutes of explaining who I was, and what had happened, for him to trust that I wasn't some kind of lunatic stalker.

The thing that probably convinced him I meant well was the explanation I gave for why Alice had been acting so aloof from everyone all this time, and why she was so glum since getting back from the UK. Paul had easily picked up on her even greater insular mood on the occasions he'd seen her, and was pleased to be provided with a reason for it.

I felt like I was heavily intruding on Alice's privacy as I went through the circumstances of my relationship with her to Paul, but I had no choice. And I couldn't exactly make things any worse between us by confiding in her boss, could I?

Paul eventually relented, telling me Alice's address, and wishing me luck. I won't forget the trust he placed in me that day in a hurry.

The trust that means I can stand here now, looking at the horror on Alice's face, and trying to frame my next words very, *very* carefully . . .

'What . . . What the hell are you doing here?' Alice says, stepping back from her own front door and putting a hand to her mouth.

'You weren't answering your phone or text messages,' I reply, which is not necessarily the most convincing of reasons for flying halfway around the world – with a six-year-old in the seat across the aisle from you with a terrible head cold.

'No. I . . . I don't want to speak to you. You know what happened!'

'Yes, I do. And I'm not just going to leave it like that. Please, for the love of God, just let me speak for a few minutes. You can give me that much for coming all the way here, can't you?'

There's a look on her face that suggests she is quite willing to deprive me of those few minutes, no matter how far I've come. I'm going to have to say something more.

'I've found out what happened that day,' I tell her in a very blunt voice. '*Properly*, I mean. The day Joe died. Don't you want to know?'

'I know enough.'

'No, you don't!' I snap, and immediately regret it. Getting angry is not going to get me inside this apartment and out of the Australian drizzle. 'Please, Alice. Just let me talk. You can throw me out after that, if you like.'

She stares at me for a second. 'I can't believe you're here.'

'Neither can I,' I concede. You have no idea how surreal it was to see the Sydney Opera House and the bridge two hours ago. You should only ever see epic stuff like that when you're on a nice holiday, not when you're trying to fix a relationship with someone who hates you. 'But I am, and I have a bloody good reason, so let me in, will you? If for no other reason than we were friends for so long.'

She's still hesitant, but I've got through to the sensible parts of her brain, I think.

'Five minutes,' Alice says. 'I'll give you five minutes.'

I nod. I won't need that long. 'Thank you. I don't think I could have walked away with nothing after all of that. Especially not when that bird looks just about ready to dive-bomb me.'

Alice's eyes turn flinty. 'Jobbers is a good boy.'

Christ, I really do have to fix this.

Alice then leads me through to what is a rather spectacular open-plan kitchen and living area. 'Bloody hell, you weren't kidding about the view, were you?' I say, looking out through the bifold doors that stretch across the front of the whole room.

'No,' she replies, leaning against the kitchen island and folding her arms. 'Talk, Ben.'

Right. Yes.

Here goes, then . . .

'He wasn't playing any kind of practical joke,' I say firmly. I've practised this line in my head a few thousand times in the last couple of days. 'Harry, I mean. I called a few of his old friends, and the man who ran the hospital back then. They told me what happened. My mother filled in some of the details as well.'

I have been *very* thorough. There was no way I was coming all the way here without knowing exactly what to tell Alice. I have to get through to that logical and sensible part of her brain that I know is there – when it's not being comprehensively controlled by all of the emotions still swirling around inside her about Joe.

Alice sniffs. 'Then what was he doing?'

My lip trembles. '*Dying*, Alice. My brother was dying.'

Her eyes widen slightly.

Yes, that's right. *Listen* to what I'm saying. *Hear* me. Because if nothing else, I'm leaving here today with you knowing the truth, and me having defended my poor brother properly.

That's a bloody good reason to fly halfway across the world, isn't it?

'It was the leukaemia,' I continue. 'The bloody leukaemia that up until then he'd kept hidden from everyone.' I'm not going to cry. This needs to be firm. This needs to be hard. This needs to be *strong*. 'My perfect brother, Harry, who I thought was the bravest and most rock-solid person I'd ever known, was terrified of admitting to anyone that he was sick – including himself.'

I pause to see if Alice wants to reply. She does not. She just stands there staring at me, obviously trying to process.

'He collapsed during an exam of someone with a nail through their foot. Leukaemia will do that. Weakness and persistent fatigue are a common early symptom, and Harry hid it from everyone to the extent that he pushed himself way too hard that day, and collapsed. He suffered what's called a grand mal seizure during the collapse, which meant he required the help of the nurses. He vomited as well, so his airway was obstructed, and—'

The sob that bursts from the deepest part of my soul feels like I'm holding on to pain itself.

I have had to relive my brother's death more in the past three weeks than at any other time in my life. All so I can come here and tell the one person who needs to know about it more than anyone.

'Oh Jesus, Ben,' Alice exclaims, and starts towards me, her arms opening.

I don't want her to hug me. I don't need her to hug me. I need her to *listen* and *understand*.

I hold up a trembling hand. 'He would never . . . He would never have wanted to risk anyone's life,' I tell her. 'He was scared, and not thinking straight, and I'm sorry it was the day Joe came in. I truly, truly am. But it wasn't Harry's fault Joe died. *Please* believe that. It was nobody's fault. The heart attack Joe suffered was huge, Alice. A myocardial infarction with full coronary blockage. Nobody could have done anything for him.' God, it's so hard saying this to her, but I *have to*. I just *have to*. '*Please* trust me on that too. I used . . . I used to be a doctor, just like Harry. Please *believe* me.'

I hope she bloody does, because I can't say anymore. I am exhausted and hungry, and I love my brother more than anything else.

I can't say anymore.

281

Alice does hug me then, because I really don't have the strength to push her away.

Alice

Stupid, stupid, stupid, stupid, *stupid*.

What an evil bitch I am.

What a bloody fool!

What a self-centred, idiotic *monster*.

I forced this man away from me, and then forced him to fly across the bloody *planet*, just so he could tell me something I should have known in the first place.

Harry didn't do it deliberately.

That's not the person Ben has spent the last decade telling me about.

I wail apologies over and over at Ben as I continue to hug him as fiercely as I possibly can. I can't believe he came all the way here. All those hours. All those miles. I'm well used to that hideous flight, so I know how hard it is – and I do it for far better reasons than just trying to convince an emotionally messed-up woman of her own irrationality.

'Can we sit down?' Ben says in a small voice.

'Of course!' I reply, and lead him to the couch. 'Can I make you a cup of tea?'

He nods at me through the haze of tears in his eyes. 'Yes, please.'

Thank God for that. If I'm making a cup of tea, it means things might not be that bad.

For the briefest of moments I'm thoroughly ashamed of such a Pommy way of thinking, but then the Australians insist on drinking the absolute worst tea imaginable. Nobody has ever felt better after a cup of sodding Bushells.

Luckily I have PG Tips, bought at vast expense from Coles, which is just as well, as both Ben and I need good British tea right about now.

Once it's brewed I bring the cup over to Ben, who takes it gratefully.

I sit down in the armchair to the side of the couch and start to apologise again.

He holds up a hand. 'It's okay, Alice. I never came here looking for apologies. I just needed you to understand what actually went on that day.'

'I do, Ben. I really do. *Now.*'

'And I am sorry Harry was there that day.'

I shake my head vociferously. 'No, no! You shouldn't apologise for that!'

'But I will, because Harry really *shouldn't* have been there. He should have told people how sick he felt long before then. He shouldn't have kept it to himself. If he'd have been stronger . . .' There's a tired resignation in Ben's voice now. I hate it. 'He should never have kept it to himself, but he didn't want to worry anyone. He didn't want to look *weak.*'

'He wasn't weak,' I chide gently.

The look in Ben's eyes grows fierce. 'Yes, he *was.* He should have talked to someone. He should have been stronger.' His eyes become dull. 'Still, at least me and Harry finally have one thing in common, eh?'

'Don't say that, Ben!'

Oh *God.* All that good work from a few weeks ago feels like it's coming undone in front of my eyes . . . and it's all my bloody fault!

Ben holds up a hand. 'No, no. It's fine. Don't worry, I'm not backsliding. If anything, it makes me feel *better.* I feel like I understand my brother properly for the first time in my life. We both had our failings, our inadequacies. Born most likely from the way we were brought up. Our mother and father were never good at the emotional stuff, as you know. I always thought it affected just me . . . but I was evidently wrong.' He smiles now, and my heart starts to beat a little slower because of it. 'I feel closer to Harry, knowing what I know now. Does that sound strange?'

I lean across and put a hand over his. 'Not at all. It makes perfect sense.'

'Do you understand what actually went on and why now?' he asks, and he's pleading for me to say yes. Every fibre of his being screams it.

I won't disappoint him.

'Yeah. Yeah, I do understand.' I look out of the window at the darkening skies and the drizzle. 'I've been . . . I've been looking for someone to blame for so long for what happened to Joe that I think I've lost my mind a little bit.'

'We've both lost our minds a little bit over the past ten years,' Ben points out. And I struggle to disagree with him.

I wipe my cheek. 'Nobody was to blame, were they?' I say in a dead voice.

Ben breathes slowly and deeply through his nose for a few moments, looking down at the floor. He's lost in thought – and *memory*, I'll bet. He was a doctor for quite a while, after all.

'No. They rarely are,' he says. 'It was all just a gross and unfair series of circumstances, mistakes and human frailty that . . . that meant Joe couldn't be saved. And I'm so sorry to have to say that, Alice. Even all these years later.'

I hold out a hand and absently wipe the tear away from his cheek as well. I leave the hand against his face when I'm done. 'Harry couldn't be saved, either, Ben,' I tell him. 'We both lost the people we love because of all of those things. Because of the unfairness of it all. Nobody is to blame.'

Something slides off my back.

It's so tangible a feeling that it gives me a shiver that runs down my spine.

Years.

Years and years of one overriding emotion.

All because I wanted and needed someone to blame.

All the nightmares, all the days lost in my own head, all the times I closed the door on the world. All the times I kept people away. Kept up a front.

I've spent so long bemoaning the waste of Joe's life that I've wasted mine away as well.

A numbness overtakes me, which I guess is probably my brain's way of stopping me from spiralling into an inescapable depression right here and now in this living room.

Still, I think that's better than being angry.

Certainly easier on the heart, anyway.

'Do you think . . . Do you think you could find me a hotel to stay in?' Ben asks. His face has gone very grey and his eyes are suddenly hooded and heavy.

'You're not going anywhere, my lad,' I tell him. 'I have a perfectly good spare room, with a bed that's never been slept in.'

He smiles at me gratefully. Though I think there's a fair degree of relief in that smile too. I wouldn't offer my spare room to someone I no longer wanted to be friends with, would I?

I help Ben into the spare room, and leave him with his head face down in the pillow. He's snoring before I even get a chance to close the door behind me.

Sleep does not come for me, though. Not least because it's only six thirty in the evening, and I haven't just flown across the world.

Instead, I spend the rest of that day lost in thought, and looking out over Sydney harbour at night. The lights from passing pleasure boats mesmerise me a little, and time passes almost as slowly as they cross my field of vision.

I can't fully explain the process I go through, but the nearest I can get to it is 'unclenching'.

I know this sounds like a word you'd apply more to a description of something happening to your bottom . . . but I can't think of a better word, so you'll have to forgive me for that.

With the unclenching comes a fair degree of regret.

And again, I'm aware of the unpleasant imagery that's probably conjuring up.

It's certainly unpleasant for me, as I think back on all the mornings I've woken up with a sore jaw from night-time bruxism, or the times I've stared out of these same bifold doors, with my fists tight and my brow furrowed.

And of course, I think of Joe. In his red plaid boxer shorts, or shouting at that squirrel – and all those other little occasions that have imprinted permanently on my conscious mind. His death lending them far more significance than they ever would have had otherwise.

And I think of Grant.

Poor, kind-eyed Grant, who I never called back, and never spoke to again, because I was so angry at the world – and shied away from anything the world put in front of me to try and distract me from that anger.

The same anger that pushed my best friend, Ben, on to his brother's grave, and forced him to fly all the way out here to tell me how wrong I've been. How *silly*. How *unfair*.

I can't exactly stay angry at Harry Fielding for not being open with anyone around him, when I've been doing exactly the same thing for a decade, now can I?

I look up at the clock. It's just gone midnight.

I make a pact with myself at that moment.

This will be the last night I do this. The last night I waste staring out of the bifold doors, and at the past, with my fists clenched.

Because nobody was to blame.

Including me.

Ben

Sydney is a rather lovely city, all things considered.

In the four days I spend with Alice, recovering both my strength and my relationship with her, I wander all over the lower north shore of the harbour. Sometimes I do this alone while Alice is at work, and sometimes I do it with her. The walks with her are better, partly because she knows where to get the best coffee, and partly because it gives us a chance to repair something that very nearly broke beyond our ability to fix.

Alice's anger has certainly lifted, and I thank God for that. I wish I could say the same about her melancholy, though.

Most of our conversations inevitably steer back around to talking about how much time she thinks she's lost to an emotion that did her no good whatsoever. I absolutely agree with that sentiment, but she talks like her life is almost over. As if there is no chance now for it to change. That all her opportunities have passed her by, thanks to being so wrapped up in the grief over Joe's death.

I try to point out to her that she's a woman in her forties, not *eighties*, but she's having none of it. The die is cast in her mind.

She also seems to forget that she has one hell of a successful career in the hair industry, no matter how many times I try to remind her.

That is the nature of a proper melancholy, though. It doesn't particularly appreciate anything that attempts to lift it. Including me.

Thus, I am not much more than a sounding board for Alice's depression on those walks, and by the fourth day, I am deathly afraid I have no idea how to break her out of it.

Okay, I do have *one* idea, but Sydney really is a big city . . . and trying to find one man in the morass of city folk would be like looking for a needle in a stack of suntanned, flat white-drinking needles.

But it would be *perfect*, wouldn't it?

And she kept the serviette with his number on before, didn't she? Because it *meant* something to her. It was *symbolic*, wasn't it? That's what she said. Symbolic of another life . . .

What's the betting she never got around to throwing it away, even after that date went so wrong?

If she did keep it, and I could find it, and then find Grant . . .

If I could at least get them talking to one another again.

Then I could hopefully do for Alice what she did for me at that rugby match.

Yes.

That would be . . . *just right*, wouldn't it?

Alice

'Alice?'

You need to stop.

That's what Joe told me in the dream last night.

For the first time ever.

I didn't even get as far as the doors to the A&E department. He stops me in front of them with a raised hand. He's wearing nothing but his red plaid boxer shorts.

You have to stop, he tells me again.

I can't!

Yes, you can. You know why.

But if I keep trying, sooner or later I can get there in time, can't I?

No, you can't.

Don't say that!

I have to, he says and immediately collapses on to the ground, forcing a scream from my mouth that echoes around the building.

'Alice?' I feel the hand shaking me on my arm and snap out of the daze as best I can. I didn't get back to sleep after that strange twist to my least favourite dream in the whole wide world, and I'm suffering for it today.

'What?' I reply to Madeline in an absent tone, forcing my eyes away from the road outside, and the memory of my nightmare.

'Kelsey's foils need to come out, and you said you'd cover it?'

Did I?

Did I really?

Yes, of course I did. We're short-staffed today because Orna's out with Covid and Marie is still on honeymoon in Bali. So I'm mucking in with things I haven't done in a good long while. Running a hair salon is a guaranteed way to make sure you never actually do any hairdressing.

'Sorry, Mads, I'll get it done.'

Madeline gives me a rather doubtful smile and turns to walk back to her current customer.

I *have* to shake myself out of this malaise – at least enough to get on with my work. I can daydream about horrible things on my own time.

Kelsey looks up at me and smiles as I go back over to where she's sat in the chair at the back of the salon. I'll probably have to continue to hear all about her Pomeranian as I take her foils out. Kelsey loves her Pomeranian. And she loves to talk about her Pomeranian. And show you TikToks of it. Repeatedly.

The Pomeranian in question often looks like it wants to be anywhere other than on TikTok – but it is small and weak of jaw, so it has no real choice in the matter. I think its name is Floof.

As Kelsey starts to regale me with the story of how the colour she's having put in her hair today will match the dye job she got Floof last week, I drift off again to a place I do not wish to visit, but I have no choice in the matter.

I imagine my feelings about it are similar to Floof's every time Kelsey produces her iPhone and points it at him. Neither of us wants these things in our lives, but neither of us has a choice. I am also small and weak of jaw – when it comes to pushing away my past anyway.

I don't really hear the door chime as it goes behind me. Mindy at the reception desk will deal with whoever it is, leaving me to concentrate on Kelsey's foils – and Floof's utter despair at his continued employment as TikTok flavour of the month.

As I'm concentrating on removing a foil – which is something that has to be done with some care and consideration for a dye this strong – I hear my name called.

'Alice?'

'Give me a second, Ben. I just have to do this and I'll be with you.'

He's turned up early for lunch again.

Ben's been with me a week now, and I think he's starting to come to the end of his honeymoon period with the Sydney lower north shore. He doesn't fly back to the UK for another three days, and is clearly running out of things to keep him occupied on his own. Hence the fact we've had lunch together three days in a row. Which is fine – it makes a change from being on my own, but Kelsey's foils must come first, so he'll just have to wait.

'Er, I kind of need you now,' he says, in an unsteady voice.

'Well, you'll just have to—'

The words die in my throat as I look up at the reflection of the room behind me.

Grant is standing next to Ben.

I spin around in horror.

'Sorry to do this here,' Ben then says, 'but I wanted it to happen somewhere where you wouldn't be able to . . . you know . . . punch me.'

I may punch him anyway, even if it is in front of my staff and all these customers.

Grant holds up a hand. 'Hi Alice,' he says rather sheepishly. I get the impression he's not sure about being here at all. I get the further impression that he most certainly *wouldn't be*, were it not for the machinations of the man standing next to him.

'Hi Grant,' I say to the man I haven't seen in three years, in a faraway voice. 'What's going on?'

'Your friend persuaded me to come over,' Grant tells me. 'Told me that you've missed me?'

My eyes inexorably cross to Ben's now slightly pallid expression.

My soon to be very punched in the face best friend holds out his hands. 'Now, don't be angry. I had to get you two in a room together – preferably one with witnesses, for my own safety.'

Grant also looks at him daggers. 'She *hasn't* missed me? Why did you tell me that she had on the phone, mate?'

'No, no,' Ben insists, 'she absolutely *has* missed you.' His face crumples a bit. 'She just hasn't admitted it to herself yet.'

'Alice? You'd better let me take over,' Madeline says from beside me. She's noticed that I've pulled poor old Kelsey around in her chair by her half-attached foil. Kelsey doesn't seem to mind all that much, though. She looks rapt by the drama unfolding in front of her. As does everybody else in the salon.

Ben Fielding has turned DiMarco's into a particularly bad episode of *Home and Away*, and I'm going to kill him for it.

'Thanks, Mads,' I say to my assistant, and move away from Kelsey – who, rather inevitably, has pulled out her iPhone. I am too small and weak of jaw to protest.

'What have you done?' I say to Ben, walking over to where both men are stood in the middle of my salon.

How long it remains my salon after this, I do not know. Not sure how happy Paul is going to be about it being turned into a soap opera.

'I wanted you and Grant to see each other again,' Ben says. 'And I wanted to . . . repay you for what you did for me.' He points at Grant. 'This was the best way I thought of doing it.'

I stare at him open-mouthed for a moment. 'Buy me a bunch of bloody *flowers*, Ben,' I say, absolutely incredulous that he thought bringing the man I ruined a relationship with to my place of work was a better idea.

Grant actually chuckles at this. It's a warm, very pleasant sound that does things to my insides.

Doesn't matter! We called him Joe. *This is so embarrassing!*

'How did you find him?' I say to Ben, somewhat aware that we're both talking about Grant like he's not stood in the room with us.

Ben looks extremely guilty all of a sudden. 'Well . . . I had a little hunt around your apartment while you were at work . . . and I found the serviette.'

'You found the serviette,' I repeat. 'The serviette that was *where*, Ben?'

His face flames red. 'In your bedroom,' he says in a tiny voice.

'*Where* in my bedroom, Ben?' I demand, arms crossing very slowly.

'In your bedside cabinet,' he mumbles.

'In my bedside cabinet,' I snap back at him.

A bedside cabinet that contains many things.

Many things that I *do not want my male best friend to know about.*

'You kept my phone number in your bedside cabinet?' Grant says, looking at me in amazement.

Oh *God* . . .

Now I'm the one looking red-faced. 'Yeah. I did. I don't know why, after what . . . happened, but I just . . . felt like it was right. Like . . . it was symbolic of the way things . . . could have been, if I hadn't . . . you know . . . I'm so sorry.' It sounds strange to apologise for keeping someone's phone number in your bedside cabinet, but that's not really what I'm apologising for, is it?

'You see!' Ben exclaims, pointing a finger at me. 'I was *right* to ring Grant and bring him here!'

The look I give Ben suggests that he could not be more wrong if he had a ten-thousand-dollar grant from the government and a long run-up.

'It's nice to see you,' Grant then says. He looks around at all the people who are staring at us in rapt silence. 'Though, yeah . . . maybe not *here.*'

'No! It *had* to be here!' Ben insists.

'Why?' I say, horrified.

'Because you have to *see*,' Ben says. 'The same way I had to. You have to . . . stop hiding. Stop keeping away from everyone. The same way I did. You knew I wouldn't get what you were trying to tell me without that crowd of people, and all the clients I used to work with. The same goes for you, Alice.'

'Does it?'

'Yes, of course.' He smiles. 'We're very similar in that respect. So that's why I brought Grant here.'

'To embarrass me?'

He shakes his head. 'No! To show you what you can *have*, if you let yourself. To show you who you can *be*, if you just let go of the past. If you just let your barriers down.'

I look at Grant. 'I messed it up!'

His turn to shake his head. 'You didn't. Not at all. You may have thought you did, but I totally understood. I told you that in the final phone call we had. We could have . . . carried on, you know. If you'd wanted it. I really did like spending time with you, Alice.'

'No, you wouldn't have . . . I wouldn't have . . .' I can't think of the right words to say. What the hell are the right words to say? 'I can't . . .'

'Yes, you bloody can,' Ben says.

'No, Ben. It's not that easy!'

He steps a little closer to me. 'Yes, it is.'

God! Why is he being like this? In front of all these people! I can't do this in front of *all these people*! I can't let them see the state I'm in! I can't let them *see*!

'If you want to, you can move on,' Ben now says in a soft voice. 'It's okay.'

I shake my head. 'No. It's not okay. It's not okay for you to bring poor Grant here, and try to force me back into seeing him!'

Ben ignores this. He's known me for ten years and knows when to ignore me. 'You can let go.' He gathers up my limp hand in his. 'You can let *him* go.'

I snatch my hand back. 'No! You don't get to tell me what I can and cannot do, Ben!'

Part of me is now a caged tiger.

'*He'd* want you to let go,' my best friend says, refusing to open the cage.

'No! You don't know that! You don't know what he'd think!'

'Yes, I do. Because you've told me all about Joe, haven't you? The same way I told you all about Harry.' He looks deep into my eyes. 'They're *gone*, Alice. But *we're* not. *You're* not.'

'Stop it,' I reply, voice lame. 'Not in front of all these people. Not in front of Grant.'

Ben wraps his arms around me. 'Let go,' he says gently into my ear. 'I love you, and you are my sister. Please . . . let go.'

Well, that really does it.

Ten years ago – hell, more than ten years now – I thoroughly embarrassed myself by bawling in front of Ben Fielding dressed as Kermit the Frog. That was at a time when even the idea of moving on from my poor Joe would have felt like a complete and utter impossibility.

Sad to say, I don't think much has really changed in the past decade.

Not until this moment.

And I don't *need* permission to move on . . . but it's very nice to have it anyway.

My arms crush Ben – my little brother – in an embrace that's fierce enough to take his breath away.

And of course I'm crying – but for the first time they feel like tears of *release*. Like I'm excising some part of myself, through the most thorough rinsing imaginable. The doors on the tiger's cage burst open, and he's free at last.

I know Joe would want me to move on.

He would have wanted it *years* ago.

He was a kind man, who was thoughtful and even-tempered. He'd probably be quite horrified at the idea of me hiding away from the world for a decade, and carrying around so much anger and pain about what happened to him.

That's not the woman I married, he would have told me. *The woman I married deserves to be happy . . . not sad because of me.*

For years I've thought I heard Joe's voice in my head, but I think this is the first time it's actually the truth.

From somewhere off to my left I hear someone start to clap.

I'm not sure what the reaction should be to a middle-aged woman and her best friend (brother) standing in the centre of an upmarket hair salon, crying into each other's arms – but I guess applause is one way to go?

I look up to see it's Madeline. She has a genuine look of surprise and relief on her face. I guess I haven't been able to hide away from people as much as I thought. The barriers we think are a foot thick are sometimes paper-thin to the people who know us.

The applause is taken up by the rest of my staff and the customers – because what the hell else can they do, eh?

Thankfully, Grant does not start to clap as well. I don't think I could take that. But he is smiling broadly. That's good enough for me.

Wiping the tears away, I part from Ben's embrace.

'Nicely done,' I tell him.

He bows his head. 'Thanks very much.'

'But what exactly do we do now?'

He thinks on this for a moment. 'I believe the best thing I can do is pop off back to the flat. I think the best thing *you* can do is have lunch with Grant.'

'I meant a little more long term than that,' I confess.

'Ah, well that's easy too,' Ben tells me. 'We *live*, Alice. We live . . . because they can't.'

And frankly, that's the best motivation I could ever think of.

To live.

To move on.

To remember.

I think I can do that.

What do you think, Joe?

I love you, Alice.

And I will always love you too, my heart.

Which is why I will go to lunch with Grant, like Ben suggests – and try to live a life that's as full in the future as it has been empty in the past. Because that's what you'd want me to do.

And you should always do what your heart wants, shouldn't you?

The Final Year

ENDINGS AND BEGINNINGS

Ben

'I'm done, Harry,' I say to the grave in front of me. 'It was good while it lasted . . . but I think I'm done.'

He doesn't answer. He rarely does these days.

'I know you wanted me to dress as RoboCop this year, but I think this outfit suits me a little better, if I'm being honest with you.'

He couldn't disagree. The three-piece suit I'm wearing cost more than I was comfortable spending, but Katie pushed me into buying it anyway – and she was right to do so. I look bloody *fabulous*. Dark-green tweed is my thing, it appears. It was my father's too, so I guess that makes some sort of sense.

'I'm done with the fancy dress, Harry,' I continue, 'which may upset you a little bit . . . but then I don't think it'll upset you *that much*, will it? Because I'm pretty sure part of the reason you did all this was to see how long it would take me to say *no*. To see how long it would take me to stop doing what you told me.' I smile. 'Over ten years, if you're keeping count. And every one was worth it.'

I look down at my watch. It's midday. 'That day on the podium . . . that used to be the proudest day of my life, you know?' I wave a hand. 'Of course you know, that's why you made me stand here for two minutes and fifty-nine seconds for the past decade. But I have to apologise to you . . . because it's not the proudest moment of my life anymore, I'm afraid. Sorry about that, bro. That's now something that happened five weeks ago.' I look at the watch again. Every other year, I'd be halfway through Freddie Mercury's first chorus. 'So, I can't do that anymore, either. You'll see why in a minute, and I don't think you'll mind in the slightest.'

I hear the sound of people approaching from behind me.

'I love you, Harry,' I tell him. 'And I will miss you until the day I die. But that's a long way off yet. And I promise to make the most of the time I have.' My eyes narrow a little. '*Not* dressed as bloody RoboCop.'

With that, I turn and see just what I expected.

Alice Everley walking towards me in a very fetching summer dress and hat. Nice to see she's dressed up for the occasion as well, just like I asked.

And she's not alone.

Probably for the first time in ten years.

Alice

I thought I might feel a pang of regret or shame as I walked through the cemetery gates with Grant next to me.

I thought there was still a part of me – very deep down – that would take offence at it.

But instead, I felt nothing more than his hand in mine.

Which, if you've ever been in love, you'll know is actually the biggest thing in the entire universe. It's very far away from being *nothing*.

And am I actually in love?

I don't know. I'm still untangling emotions a full year on from everything that happened, and that doesn't feel like anywhere near enough time to know how I feel. I spent a decade loving, and clinging on to, a man who was no longer alive – so you'll forgive me if it takes me a little more time to decide how I feel about this one.

But I don't dream about the hospital anymore.

And the feel of Grant's hand in mine makes me feel safe.

You can deduce what you want from those two things.

I'm not going to bother trying, because it's far too time-consuming, and I don't intend to spend the rest of my life caught up inside my own head.

However, I think we can take Grant's presence here as a good sign that I've moved on from Joe's death more than ever before, don't you?

I spot Ben standing in front of Harry's grave and my heart leaps. Because he's dressed like a normal human being. In a very nice dark-green suit that fits him just as well as Grant's blue suit fits him. No silly fancy dress costume this time around.

If ever you needed evidence that his brother's shadow doesn't loom as large in his life anymore, it is surely this.

Ben turns and smiles radiantly as he sees me and Grant coming towards him.

'Hey little brother,' I say as we draw close.

It's a silly affectation, maybe.

But it's a small lie wrapped in a big truth, and that suits us both very well.

'Good morning, sis,' he replies, and we hug.

Ben then shakes Grant's hand. 'How you going?' my boyfriend asks.

'I am very well, thank you, Grant,' Ben replies, and for probably the first time since I met him, I believe what he's saying 100 per cent.

'Have you . . . done your bit?' I ask Ben, nodding down at Harry.

He shakes his head. 'Nope. Done with that, just as much as I'm done with the costumes. Harry would understand, I'm sure.'

'Yes, I'm sure he would,' I reply, my eyes moving across to Joe's grave.

I squeeze Grant's hand in mine.

Harry isn't the only one who'd understand.

If Joe was here right now he'd be *beaming*, I am sure of it. Because look at me, would you? I look like a million bucks, and feel pretty damned good too. Despite the jet lag.

'So, are you going to tell me why you wanted us dressed up to the nines for this?' I ask Ben. The phone call last week was extremely cryptic about why he wanted me to make such an effort.

He shrugs. 'Well, apart from anything, I thought it'd be nice for once if I wasn't the only one dressed up just to stand in a graveyard,' he chuckles. Then his expression turns softer. 'But there is another reason.'

I roll my eyes. 'Come on, then, out with it!'

'I'd like you to meet someone.'

My eyes go wide. 'Who?'

Ben looks past me, over my shoulder, indicating with his head. I turn . . . and see Katie walking towards me. She must have been in the church.

Katie is pushing a pram.

I have cried many times in this graveyard, but never for this reason. Never for something so *wonderful*.

301

'Oh, my God!' I exclaim, whipping my head back to Ben. 'How did you keep this a secret?! I demand. '*Why* did you keep this a secret?'

'I didn't just want to tell you over the phone, like a normal, boring person,' he replies. 'And come on . . . this is the place where we met. It felt like the perfect place for you to meet my son for the first time.'

I guess I can't argue with that logic, and I do live ten thousand miles away. It wasn't exactly hard for Katie and Ben to keep me in the dark.

'Hi Alice, hi Grant,' Katie says as she parks the pram in front of us.

'Hey Katie!' I say, and give her a hug, before turning my gaze down to the little ball of loveliness in the pram.

The little boy is tiny, and swaddled in white.

'How old is he?' I ask.

'Five weeks,' Ben replies. 'This is pretty much his first proper trip out of the house.' He yawns. 'Ours too, for that matter.'

I look at Ben through the veil of tears – something I'm well used to doing. 'He's beautiful,' I tell him.

Ben nods. 'He is, indeed – although I think Katie is responsible for that more than me.'

For the first time in my life, I don't feel the need to correct him for his outrageous self-deprecation.

'Would you like to hold him?' Ben asks.

'Yes, please, if that's alright?' I say, looking to Katie for confirmation.

She smiles, and gathers the bundle up – who, while probably not all that delighted to be pulled away from his nice warm pram, does not complain too much, other than emitting a soft gurgle and shaking his tiny balled-up fists for a moment.

Katie passes the baby to me, and I have to be careful not to let the tears hit him on the forehead.

Ben was absolutely right to leave it until today to tell me about his son.

It means that whenever I come here – which I surely will for the rest of my life – I will do it with a very happy memory in my head.

It'll be my protection against the dark.

'What's his name?' I ask, looking up at Ben.

Ben leans forward, and a tiny hand wraps itself around his index finger.

'Alice Everley,' he says in a voice bursting with pride, 'I'd like you to meet Joseph Harry Fielding.'

Ben

'We call him Joe, though . . . obviously,' I add.

Don't worry, she doesn't drop him.

I make sure to be as close as possible when I tell her his name, though – just in case.

'Oh Ben!' Alice says with a sob that I knew was coming.

It takes quite a lot for me to hold back the tears, if I'm honest.

But it's *perfect*, isn't it?

How could I name my firstborn child anything else? How could I bring a close to such a difficult period of my life – of *our* lives – without such an appropriate gesture?

From death, comes life.

I'm sure that's a proverb I heard somewhere – probably in that church over there, when I was a small boy, and couldn't wait to get out to go play somewhere more fun with my big brother.

Harry would probably be a bit put out that he gets the middle name slot, but I don't think I could look down at a little Harry for the next ten years of my life.

Partly out of fear he was going to start hanging bits of my bicycle from the nearest tree.

Besides, he *looks* like a Joe.

My Joe.

But he also needs to be Alice's *Harry*, so there's one more thing I need to tell her.

Good job she's handed Joe back to Katie, really.

'I have to ask you to do something for me,' I say to Alice as she wipes away her tears with some tissue that has appeared, as if by magic, from Grant's pocket.

Good man.

'What's that?' she asks, dabbing at one eye.

Right.

Hold it together, Fielding.

You're fine, bro. Just relax and say it.

'You are my family,' I begin, lip already quivering. 'And you are Joe's family as well. So Katie and I would like you to be Joe's godmother, if you'd be happy to do it.'

'Oh Ben!' Alice cries and wraps her arms around me.

'I'll take that as a yes?' I say, my voice thick with emotion.

Joe, who has woken up properly for the first time since I put him in his brand-new baby seat in the car, giggles at that moment – which I guess tells me that he approves of our decision. Though it could just be wind, of course.

He is at the very beginning of his life – and in some ways, so am I.

Alice too.

. . . our new lives, anyway.

Lives that will never be devoid of the grief and loss we feel for those that are gone, but always balanced with the love and support of those still with us.

The people we love die.

But the people we love *live* too.

And so should we.

ACKNOWLEDGEMENTS

As ever, books are never the work of one person, even though they get to hog all the limelight on the cover. So I'd like to thank those involved in *Grave Talk*'s production. These include my agent, Ariella, and my editors, Sammia and Sophie. Also, as always, my wife Gemma, for letting me bounce ideas off her, and for putting up with me in general. I'd also like to thank anyone I've spoken to about losing someone they love. Their insight has been invaluable. And finally, I'd like to thank you for buying and reading *Grave Talk*. This book has been something of a departure for me in terms of tone and content, but I hope it's one that you have enjoyed. My very best wishes.

ABOUT THE AUTHOR

Nick Spalding is the bestselling author of eighteen novels, two novellas and two memoirs. Nick worked in media and marketing for most of his life before turning his energy to his genre-spanning humorous writing. He lives in the south of England with his wife. Find out more about Nick and his books at www.nickspalding.com.

Follow the Author on Amazon

If you enjoyed this book, follow Nick Spalding on Amazon to be notified when the author releases a new book!

To do this, please follow these instructions:

Desktop:

1) Search for the author's name on Amazon or in the Amazon App.
2) Click on the author's name to arrive on their Amazon page.
3) Click the 'Follow' button.

Mobile and Tablet:

1) Search for the author's name on Amazon or in the Amazon App.
2) Click on one of the author's books.
3) Click on the author's name to arrive on their Amazon page.
4) Click the 'Follow' button.

Kindle eReader and Kindle App:

If you enjoyed this book on a Kindle eReader or in the Kindle App, you will find the author 'Follow' button after the last page.